HOLES IN THE GROUND

Monsters exist.

Linguist Andy Dennison-Jones knows this all too well. He and his veterinarian wife, Sun, have been chased by them before, and barely escaped from a secret underground government facility with their lives.

Now they once again find themselves trapped alongside a collection of creatures straight out of hell. Fighting with them is an unlikely group of misfits, including a misplaced British kid, a former spec-ops soldier, and a strange Irishman who might be the oldest living thing on earth—if he's even alive at all.

Filled with the kind of slam-bang action, wicked scares, and sly humor that have earned J.A. Konrath and Iain Rob Wright millions of fans, HOLES IN THE GROUND is both a collaboration and a continuation of both authors' previous work (ORIGIN by Konrath and FINAL WINTER by Wright) but also serves as a perfect introduction to their worlds.

The devil you know is just as bad as the devil you don't...

HOLES IN THE GROUND by J.A. Konrath and Iain Rob Wright

Some secrets have teeth

HOLES IN THE GROUND

Edition: June 2014

HOLES IN THE GROUND

J.A. KONRATH & IAIN ROB WRIGHT

FOREWORD
BY J.A. KONRATH

I became aware of Iain Rob Wright when I saw several of his books on Amazon.com in the *Customers Also Bought* section of my technothriller novel, ORIGIN.

I liked what I saw. I liked it a lot. Scary, science-based thrillers laced with black humor and a lot of suspense. Sign me up.

We collaborated on the Jack Daniels/Sarah Stone mystery STRAIGHT UP, and it was a pleasure working with Iain. When he told me he had a cool idea to continue the storyline of ORIGIN, I encouraged him to go for it.

It's a fun experience, as a writer, to have another writer re-envision your characters. Especially since, in this novel, they interact with some of Iain's characters from his horror novel THE FINAL WINTER. That said, as I was working on the second draft of this book, I wondered if I should change things to make it read more like ORIGIN. Iain is British. I'm a Yank. Our tones and styles vary. Our sense of humor is different. Hell, we even spell "humour" differently.

I spent a long time thinking about this.

Certainly, fans of ORIGIN will expect a sequel to be very similar. But then, Iain Rob Wright fans will also expect something similar to what they've grown to love, and I count myself among his fans. Ridley Scott's ALIEN and James Cameron's ALIENS were very different approaches to the same story, and they're both worth seeing.

So I followed Iain's approach. I admire his work, and enjoy his take on my work. During my rewrite, I tried my best to match his tone and style, and expand upon what he had envisioned for the storyline.

The end result was the novel you're about to read. But if you're curious about Iain's original version, we've included that as a bonus.

That's right. You can also read HOLES IN THE GROUND before I added anything, and there are many scenes that significantly differ.

Fans of my writing, and fans of Iain's writing, and fans of ORIGIN and THE FINAL WINTER, should all find something to like here. And if you've never read either of us before, I think this is a fun introduction to both of us.

I hope you enjoy this as much as I did.

HOLES IN THE GROUND

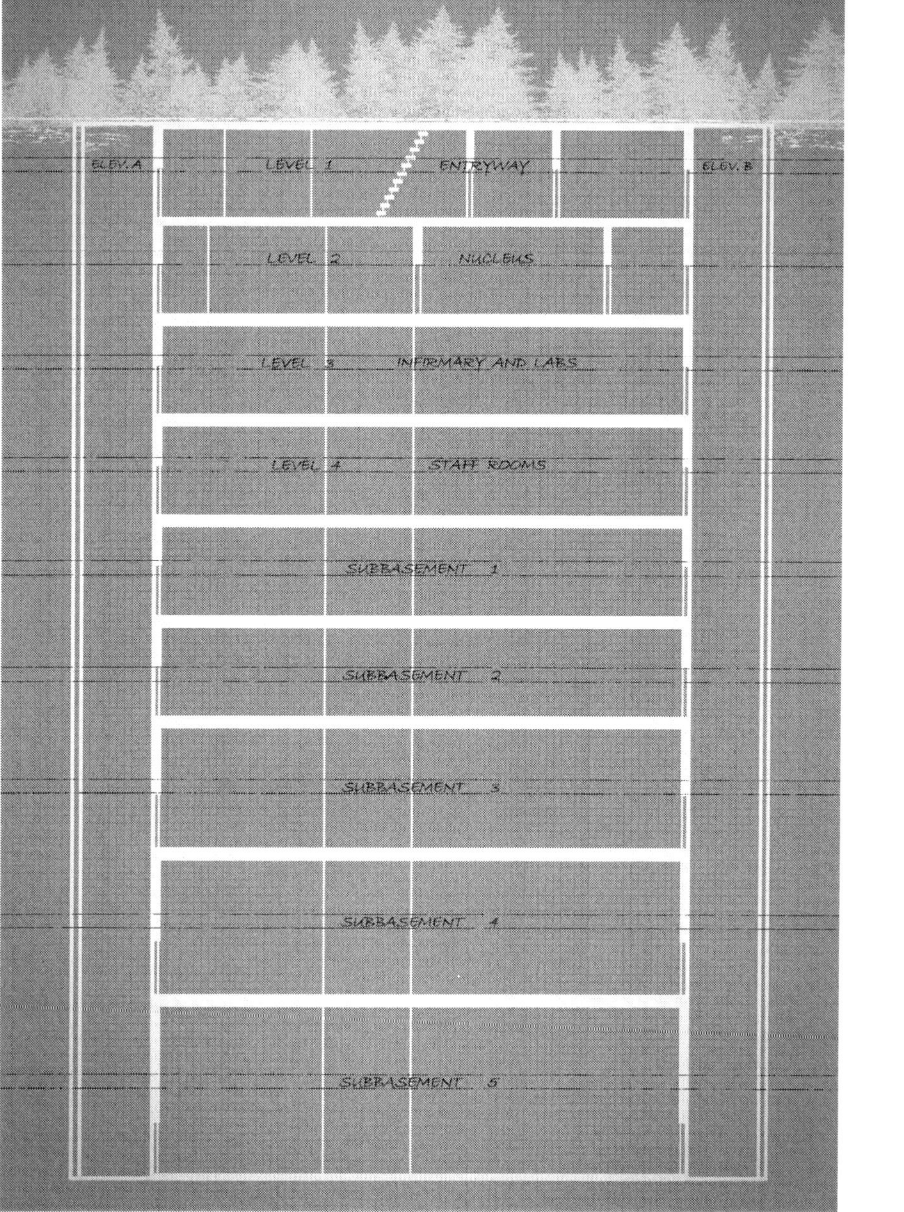
NEW MEXICO MONSTRUM FACILITY
THE SPIRAL
ELEV. A
LEVEL 1
ENTRYWAY
ELEV. B
LEVEL 2
NUCLEUS
LEVEL 3
INFIRMARY AND LABS
LEVEL 4
STAFF ROOMS
SUBBASEMENT 1
SUBBASEMENT 2
SUBBASEMENT 3
SUBBASEMENT 4
SUBBASEMENT 5

PROLOGUE

Jack Cullum had heard about cattle mutilations, but he never expected to see one. Not one this horrible. Not on his own ranch.

The bull was in the north east corner of the pasture, mostly. Much of it was spread out over several yards, entwined in the barbed wire fence, strewn throughout the grass. Almost as if someone had dropped a twelve hundred pound tray of lasagna from a great height.

Jack crouched down next to the severed cow head and wiped some blood off the ear tag with his thumb. Thunder 112, a two year old Black Angus. Son of the legendary Mr. Toro—a bull rated #6 in marbling and #8 in calving ease in the Spring Sire Evaluation Report. A straw of Mr. Toro's semen had cost Jack fifteen hundred dollars. Money that had been hard to come by.

The rancher pushed back his hat and wiped a sleeve across his forehead. The midday Texas sun made the breeze feel like an electric hair dryer. This would have to be cleaned up before it began to rot. Or cook. He'd have to borrow Charley's trailer, shovel the remains onto that. Burying something as large as a bull was impossible.

Except for the carcass and the growing legion of flies, the pasture was empty. The rest of the herd was badly spooked. They'd gathered around the pens, refusing to graze. He had to get them back into their routine quickly.

Jack looked over the remains again, wondering how this could have happened. Bobcats weren't dumb enough to attack a full grown bull, and even a pack of coyotes couldn't have caused this much damage. There were no tracks or spoor, other than cattle.

That only left one possibility.

Jack searched his mind for anyone with a grudge against him. His ranch was small and relatively new. He posed no economic threat to anyone locally. The cattle market had been on an upswing, and everyone was doing better than expected. Jack liked his neighbors, and they him, often trading equipment and offering labor. But it had to be a man. Or a team of men, armed with axes and saws. Nothing else could have done this much damage. Thunder 112 was barely recognizable as an animal—there wasn't a piece of him left that couldn't fit into a garbage bag. Jack also noted parts were missing. There should have been more of the skeletal remains. And more innards. Even spread out, there was less than half a bull left.

There was movement to the right, at ground level. Jack turned, expecting a bird or some other small scavenger. At first glance it appeared to be a snake, long and black, slithering in the grass. But the rancher realized with a jolt that it wasn't a snake at all. It wasn't even an animal.

It was Thunder 112's tail. Detached from the body and slowly undulating.

Jack blinked, figuring the heat was playing tricks with him. He stared hard, willing the tail to stop moving.

It didn't.

Holding his fear in check, he approached the tail. Jack was expecting to see a gopher, perhaps, pulling on it. Or even a string, tied to one end while the other went off into the plains, being yanked by some practical joker. Silly ideas, to explain the unexplainable. But all he saw was a severed bull's tail, lying in the gore-soaked grass, wiggling like a dropped garden hose.

Reflex, the rancher assured himself. Had to be. Muscles could twitch for a while after death. Lop off a chicken's head, it could still run around for a few minutes. This had to be some bizarre reflex.

Jack was reaching out to touch the tail when something large hit him from behind.

The rancher sprawled face-first onto the grass. The sensation was similar to being thrown off a horse. His chest and back ached, and he could feel the tail squirming under his belly.

Jack rolled over to face his attacker, and his mind refused to accept what he saw.

This couldn't be. He was a God-fearing man. He went to church. How in the name of Christ could this be happening?

"Where issssss Monnnnnnstruuuuum," the thing said as it squatted beside him.

Jack was so terrified he couldn't speak.

"Answer meeeeeeeeee."

"I… I… I don't know what you want."

The creature tilted its head to the side, apparently thinking. Then, with a quick swipe of its talon, it ripped out Jack Cullum's windpipe.

Jack was still alive, praying to God for mercy, when the thing began to feed on him.

CHAPTER ONE

The hotel room's phone rang so loud that the receiver rattled on its cradle. While there were many things that Andrew Dennison-Jones was thankful for—his business was doing well, his debts had evaporated, and his beautiful new bride slept naked beside him—an early morning phone call still irritated the hell out of him. Especially since he slept so poorly, waking from bad dreams several times each night.

RING.

RING.

RING.

Andy shot an irritated glance at the clock next to the bed. Coming up on 7am San Diego time. Any chance of regaining sleep now was ruined. Once Andy was awake, he stayed awake.

He rolled over and fumbled for the receiver. "H-hello?"

"Mr. Dennison?"

Andy rubbed sleep from his eyes. "Yes. And it's Dennison-Jones."

"This is the hotel manager. I've been receiving reports of a disturbance on your floor. Is everything okay?"

Andy cleared his throat. "Huh? Yeah, everything is fine. We're sleeping. Or *were* until you woke us up."

"My apologies, sir. I have been trying to call the rooms adjacent to you, but they are not answering. I'm unsure what exactly is going on, but other guests have been complaining of shouting and...someone speaking in a strange language."

"I'm American."

"Of course, sir. It's just that the credit card details you provided us are registered to Worldwide Translation Services. I thought—"

Andy blew out a breath of exasperation and blinked his crusty eyelids. "You thought it was me. But it wasn't. It's our honeymoon."

"Of course, sir. I am sorry to have woken you."

Andy considered calling the man an asshole in a dozen different languages, but let it pass. The manager was still speaking when Andy hung up the phone. He slid back down beneath the covers and turned to face his bride.

Sun was awake. Her eyes were open. A smirk adorned her face as she spoke in a dozy whisper. "I hope you're not making clandestine calls to other women, Mr. Dennison-Jones. I only married you yesterday."

Andy smiled, recalling the previous day and how wonderful everything had been. A small, private ceremony, just the two of them and a judge. Luck had brought them to San Diego—they'd won a contest and been given free plane tickets. They decided to make it a honeymoon, and hopped on a jet after tying the knot. It had been Sun's idea for Andy to enter the 21st century and hyphenate their last names as a married couple.

When Andy told his buddies he was now Andrew Dennison-Jones they would call him whipped. And he wouldn't mind a bit.

He kissed her forehead. "It was the hotel manager. Apparently someone has been speaking in tongues and he thought it was me. Obviously he thinks I'm some kind of hell raiser."

Sun laughed. "If only they knew the truth."

Andy chuckled and ran his fingers along Sun's naked hips. Her skin was hot and inviting. Her perfume mingled with her natural musk.

It was time to do what honeymooners did.

Just as he began kissing Sun's neck, there was a pounding at the door, loud enough to startle them both.

"Did you order room service?" Andy asked.

Sun shook her head.

Another loud pound.

"Maybe it's the *real* hell raiser," Sun whispered.

Andy stared at the door. There was a chance that whomever was at the door was the aforementioned troublemaker, the person causing all the complaints. It might be a bad idea opening up.

Or perhaps Sun was talking about another type of hell raiser. One who, quite literally, raised hell on earth. The cause of Andy's nightmares.

Could that be who is at the door?

"Would Bub knock?" Andy asked. He was naked, but suddenly felt even more exposed. Vulnerable and unprotected.

Afraid.

"That's not knocking. That's pounding. But I don't think he would knock. He'd just bust in and kill us both."

Not a pleasant thought, but a true one.

Andy swung his legs out of bed and reached for the bathrobe on the nearby chair.

"*TlhIngan maH!*"

What the hell? It didn't sound like a hellspawn, but it didn't sound exactly human, either.

He glanced back at Sun. She was on her feet, a knife in her hand.

"Where did you get that?"

"I brought it on the plane."

"How'd you get a knife through TSA?"

"It's ceramic. Metal detectors won't catch it."

Another smack on the door, and Andy flinched.

"Want me to check?" Sun asked.

She was strong. Stronger than he was, Andy knew. But he saw the tension on her face, saw her hand trembling.

Sun had the same nightmares Andy did.

"I'll check," he said. He slowly padded over to the door, cautiously, in case it suddenly burst inward. When that didn't happen, Andy leaned forward enough to check the peephole.

A bleary-eyed teenager stood in the hallway, wearing a Wrath of Khan shirt.

Andy let out the breath he'd been holding. "Some kid," he told Sun. Then, to the door, he said "What do you want?"

The boy wobbled in place, part human being, part strawberry jelly. Then he repeated the strange expression. "*TlhIngan maH!*"

Andy rubbed a hand across his chin. "Is that… Is that *Klingon?*"

"*Qapla!*" the kid yelled.

"There's some Star Wars geek in the hall?" Sun asked.

"No. Some teen who obviously got into the mini bar. And it's Star Trek, not Star Wars."

"What does he want?"

"Maybe he's out of mixers."

"nIteb Qob qaD jup 'e' chaw'be' SuvwI'!"

"What did he say?" Sun asked.

"Why do you think I speak Klingon?"

"You speak everything."

Andy sighed. "He said a warrior doesn't let his friend go into battle alone."

"He could be trying to warn us," Sun said.

"Sun, no one knows we're here."

Sun rolled her eyes as if to say, *of course they know we're here.*

The teen knocked again.

"Go away," Andy told him.

"Is he hurt or something?" Sun asked.

"No. He looks drunk. Or high."

"Should we help him?"

Andy made a face. "Why?"

"Because we're good people who help others."

"You can call down to the front desk, let the hotel manager deal with him."

Sun got out of bed. "We should see what he wants."

"You want me to let him in?"

"He could be trying to warn us about something."

"He could be a random idiot."

"If he tries anything, I got your back." Sun held out the knife.

Andy wasn't going to fight her on this. Not when they'd been married for less than twelve hours. He grunted and opened the door.

The boy staggered forward, and Andy had to put a hand out to hold him up.

"W-what are you doing in my room, dude?" the kid asked in a British accent.

Andy shoved the boy back a step. He did so firmly, but not so hard as to provoke a fight. "This is *my* room, *dude.*"

"Really?"

"Really."

"You gotta help me. I… I smoked something. I don't know what it was."

"Why would you do that?"

"Peer pressure." His face broke, then he began to giggle. "I'm kidding. No one forced me. I just like drugs."

"Go like them somewhere else," Andy said, starting to close the door.

The boy pushed back but smiled merrily, as if Andy's resistance was an amusing challenge to contend with. "I thought this was my room. It looks like my room."

"It's a hotel. All the rooms look alike. Are you here with your parents?"

The boy sneered but couldn't seem to control his facial muscles enough to keep the expression on his face. "Parents? Don't talk to me about… about parents. Bloody parents."

"We should help him."

"He's not a puppy, Sun."

Sun Dennison-Jones was a veterinarian by trade, which was a side of her at odds with the side that had snuck a ceramic knife onto a plane. But she had a thing for strays.

Which, Andy supposed, was why she had fallen in love with him.

Andy sighed again. "What's your room number, kid?"

The boy's eyes rolled back in his head for a moment, then a brief flash of sobriety seized him. "204."

"This is the fourth floor. You're not even on the right level."

"Let's get him cleaned up." Sun had moved behind Andy, surprising him. She rubbed a hand over his rump and squeezed. She'd put on a robe.

Andy shook his head at her. "You want to let this moron inside our room?"

Sun shrugged her shoulders. "Today is our first day as man and wife. What type of couple do you want to be? One who closes the door in people's faces, or one that helps people when they need it?"

Andy wanted to be the type of couple who had sex, so he complied. He pulled the boy in by his shirt before closing the door with his foot.

"Hey!" he said, shaking free. "Shatner signed this shirt!"

"Maybe you should ask Shatner to help you find your room."

"Is he here? Awesome!"

Sun took the boy by the arm and sat him down on one of the room's plush armchairs. "What's your name?"

"Jerry."

"Okay, Jerry. My name is Sun, and this is my husband, Andy."

"Sun? Funny name."

"I'm Vietnamese," Sun added.

Jerry nodded and smiled. "I like Italians."

"Of course you do," Sun said, as if his reply made sense. She squatted down and put a hand on his forehead. "Temp slightly elevated, skin clammy, sclera pink."

"Sclera?" Andy asked.

"The whites of the eye."

"So he's just stoned?"

"Hell yeah!" Jerry hooted.

"Could be something more than pot," Sun said.

"So we call 911."

Jerry shook his head. "No cops, dude. I'm straight."

"Do you like coffee, Jerry?"

"Are tribbles born pregnant?"

Sun looked at Andy. He gave her a nod, then shrugged.

Sun figured out the K-cup coffee machine while Andy sat with the boy in silence. His best guess was that the lad was late teens to early twenties. He was wearing jeans and Nikes and his faded Star Trek T-shirt did indeed have a signature on it, done in black marker. A button pinned to his chest read: "PROBE ME HARDER". The boy's greasy shoulder-length brown hair looked like it hadn't been washed in weeks.

Sun handed the boy a steaming mug.

Andy asked, "So, Jerry, where did you get the drugs? Friends?"

He shook his head. "I'm here alone."

Sun looked sad. "Alone? You came all the way from England on your own?"

"Nobody else would come. I only have one good friend and he... well, things are messed up between us right now. It's a total arse ache."

"What a sweet expression."

"I got the gear from Batman."

"You got your drugs from Batman?" Andy asked. "Does Commissioner Gordon know?"

"Some guy dressed as Batman. Cosplay, dude. The Bats was hanging with some Gundum manga otaku—real anoraks—and we stoked up the Graffix. But the gear was minging, man. I'm tripping my bollocks off."

"I'm fluent in two dozen languages and have no idea what you just said."

Jerry made a face. "Cosplay. Otaku. It's the CCC this week."

"CCC?" Andy and Sun said simultaneously.

"The Comic and Conspiracy Convention. Media geeks get together with all the conspiracy theory nuts. A lot of people are dressed up like comics and movies and shit. Isn't that why you're here?"

"We're here on our honeymoon," Sun said.

"Oh. That's cool. You guys into anime?"

"No," Andy answered.

"How about conspiracy theories? John Lennon being shot by the IRA in cahoots with the MI5? Project Cumulus in Gibraltar, British government trying to control the weather? It's a real mindscrew when you see guys in tinfoil hats talking to guys dressed like X-Men."

"I bet." Andy looked at his wife, giving her an imploring *can we get him out of here now* expression.

"And the aliens crashing at Roswell, New Mexico? All the secret shit going on at Area 51? You know those were all a cover-up, right? America is even worse than Britain for covering shit up. You guys are the kings of burying secrets. Area 51 is the least of it."

Andy felt his jaw clench. Sun's demeanor changed from cordial to dangerous.

"What do you mean, Jerry?" Sun asked, her tone low and even.

"People think the US is hiding aliens. That's bollocks. They're hiding the devil. Had him in a secret underground lab." He sipped from his mug. "This coffee is good. What flavor is it?"

"Coffee flavor." Andy leaned in close to Jerry, measuring his words. "What do you know about this secret underground lab?"

"Just what I read on the Internet. Compound was called Samhain. Bunch of people died. It was tied to that nuclear explosion, the one they called a power plant accident. Any idiot knows nuclear reactors don't explode, they melt down. Get this—they say they called the devil Bub. Like Beelzebub."

Sun was on him before Andy could stop her, the ceramic knife at the boy's neck.

"Who are you and who sent you? Tell us, now!"

Then there was another knock at the door.

CHAPTER TWO

Sun turned in the direction of the knock. She looked panicked, and Andy knew he shared the expression.

Their past together was... complicated. They had lived through something they could never share with others. Something involving the very things Jerry was talking about.

Something terrifying.

Andy moved quickly to the door and peeked out through the peep hole.

Two men in black suits and sunglasses.

The *Men in Black* from the movies, geeks dressing up as Will Smith and Tommy Lee Jones?

Or the *real* men in black, from the Secret Service?

"Are you going to cut my throat?" Jerry asked curiously.

Sun ignored him, focusing on her husband. "Is it...?"

Andy nodded.

The phone rang, startling them both. Andy had a sick feeling he knew who it was.

Sun left Jerry, who looked bewildered, and picked up the phone. She spoke in a monotone voice. "We already did our part." Pause. "We're on our honeymoon." Pause. "Believe me, I understand national security, but I don't see why he'd be needed. We were told we could get on with our lives, Mr. President."

"Whoa," Jerry said. "Is that the man?"

Sun hung up. Andy felt his stomach clench. "Let them in," she said. "We don't have a choice."

She was correct. Among the many things Sun and Andy had signed in order to return to civilian life after their tenure at Samhain—oaths and pledges and vows and confidentiality agreements and NDAs swearing to never reveal what they knew—there was a price for being left alone. At any time, they could be called back into service.

Fighting the US government was like fighting the tide.

Besides, Andy did feel a smidgeon of responsibility for what happened at Samhain, and he knew Sun did as well.

Good people had died.

Worse, something very bad had escaped.

His hand shaking, he let the Secret Service in. They closed the door behind themselves.

The one on the right said, "Good morning, Mr. Dennison. Mrs. Dennison."

"It's Dennison-Jones," Andy said, feeling deflated. "We just got married."

"We know. I'm Agent Johnson. This is Agent Williams. Who's that?"

"He's not with you?" Sun asked.

"I'm Jerry." He stood up, and suddenly didn't look stoned anymore. "I run the Stop Government Secrets website. Is this about Samhain?"

The agents exchanged a glance. Then Agent Williams said, "Get out of here, kid, before you get hurt."

"The people have a right to know! It's all true, isn't it? All the rumors! All the guesses! You really do have Satan locked up! I knew I could prove this! My site is going viral, bitches!"

Agent Williams calmly reached into his pocket and removed a taser.

"Is that a taser?" Jerry asked.

Agent Williams shot Jerry in the chest. The boy jerked and began to convulse.

For a few seconds, Andy dispassionately watched Jerry flop about like a fish on a jetty. When the volts were cut, Jerry lay still with a faint smell of ozone hanging in the room. Andy turned to agent Johnson. "We're not going. We're on our honeymoon."

"We're not giving you a choice. It's only for a few days, and you'll be well compensated for your time, Mr. Dennison."

"Dennison-Jones. Does Sun have to go?"

"That's up to her."

Andy said, "You're not going" at the same time she said "I'm going."

They had a stare down, and Andy blinked first. He always did.

Could this honeymoon get any worse?

"What about the kid?" Sun asked.

"I want to go, too!" he said, half-whine and half-croak.

"Who is he?" Agent Williams asked.

"We have no idea," Andy answered. "He knocked on our door a few minutes before you did."

Agent Johnson squatted down next to Jerry, grabbed his hand, and pressed it against a small, electronic device that looked like a smart phone.

"Are you reading my fingerprint?" Jerry rasped. "I heard about these things. We're just one step away from a one world government planting ID chips in our arms to track our movements."

Agent Johnson eyed the screen of his device. "Jeremy Preston. UK citizen. Wanted for major theft. NSA has a file on him as well."

"They do?" Jerry sat up, eyes wide. "Cool! I didn't think anyone was paying attention to me. Hey, how do I get these little electric barbs out of my chest?"

"Pull, really hard," said Agent Williams.

He did that and yelped. "Getting tazed sucks."

"That's the point. What are you doing here, Jerry?"

"I'm here to interview Andy and Sun. I'm the one who flew them to San Diego."

The free plane tickets. Andy winced. He'd known it was too good to be true. After Samhain they couldn't count on anything being a coincidence.

"So you're not some stoner kid who knocked on our doors accidentally," Sun said. "You're a con artist who lied to us."

Jerry yanked out the taser probes and yelped. "I *did* send you plane fare. That cost me almost all the money I had. Look, all I want is your story. On video, of course, for my ClipShare channel. I'm going to get some sick hits."

"We would be shot for treason for talking to you, you moron," Andy said.

"I'll pixelate your faces. No one will know it's you."

Andy rubbed his eyes, feeling a headache coming on. "Except for the Secret Service and the President of the United States."

Jerry turned sheepish. "Well, I wasn't expecting that."

Sun looked at the agents. "What happens to him?"

Agent Williams shrugged. "He's a foreigner. We could detain him without due process under the Homeland Security Act."

"Like in Guantanamo or Abu Ghraib?" Jerry's voice went up an octave. "And then what? I'm in jail forever without a trial?"

"That, or you're executed," Agent Johnson said.

"Or you accidentally die during enhanced interrogation." Agent Williams shrugged. "It happens."

Jerry shook his head and clasped his hands together. "Please let me come with. I'm begging you. Please. I don't want to be killed or imprisoned or subjected to torture."

"*Advanced interrogation*," Agent Williams corrected.

Andy wanted to be angry this was happening, and angry at Jerry, though the boy wasn't actually responsible. Instead, all he felt was fear, and pity.

"Can't you just erase his memory and dump him somewhere?" Andy asked.

Agent Johnson said, "We don't have that technology perfected. *Yet.*"

"So our choice is to bring him, or he disappears?" Andy said.

"Your choice," Agent Williams said. "The President is allowing you to bring whomever you'd like."

"How generous of him," Andy said, his frown deepening.

Sun squatted down next to Jerry. "If you come with us, Jerry, you can't put this on your website. No videos. No blogging. No telling anyone, ever. Do you understand that?"

The kid just nodded.

"And you're not really stoned right now?"

"I was acting. I poked myself in the eyes so they were bloodshot. I just want to know the truth, Mrs. Dennison-Jones. Finding it is all I have."

Sun gave her husband a look. Andy frowned.

"Bring him along," he said.

A few minutes later they were hauling their bags and being corralled into the obligatory black helicopter idling on the hotel's lawn. Several spectators, both hotel staff and guests, stood around gawping at the spectacle.

The Government obviously doesn't do clandestine *anymore.*

Andy, Sun, and Jerry strapped themselves into their seats. Sun looked determined. Jerry looked excited. Andy felt like throwing up.

The rotor blades started spinning. A feeling of weightlessness heralded the beginning of the flight and before long the chopper was a hundred feet above the ground, zipping away at eighty miles an hour. Andy watched the ground whiz by beneath them, and his gut told him this was a really, really bad idea.

"Don't worry," Sun said over the roar of the chopper's twin engines. "We never really were the relaxing type anyway. This is far more *us*."

"You think?"

Sun leaned up against him and rubbed his thigh. "I'm still going to find some time to get you alone, my sexy man."

Andy felt himself brighten at the suggestion, but not enough to chase away all the worry. "Sun, I love you more than anything, but we know what happened last time."

"Nuclear explosion," Jerry said, grinning.

"This is a private conversation. But, yes, it ended in a nuclear explosion." Andy looked into his wife's deep brown eyes. "Do you really see this ending well?"

"Maybe things will be different this time. Safer. More secure. There's always the chance the government learned from their mistakes."

Jerry laughed. "Yeah. Right. They do that all the time."

Sun reached for Andy's hand, held it tight. "Well, whatever happens, we're married, we're together. How bad can it be?"

Andy stared out of the window as the city of San Diego gave way to lonely countryside. Sagebrush and tumbleweeds dotted the landscape and the Laguna Mountains loomed in the distance.

"It could be as bad as last time," Andy said. "That's how bad it could be."

"Nothing can be as bad as last time."

Andy pressed his forehead against the window and closed his eyes. "We'll see."

CHAPTER THREE

The chopper followed along the coastline but headed inland after about two hours. Andy didn't know this part of the country too well, but he considered that they might be heading over palm valley towards Constitution 1857 National Park in Baja, Mexico.

Last time it was the desert, this time it's the wilderness.

The chopper began its descent and Agent Williams, sitting up front with the pilot, muttered something into the mic attached to his headset. Obviously somebody down below was expecting them.

Sun's hand tightened around Andy's. He squeezed back.

Andy stared out the window at the approaching treetops and thought about the events of the last few years. It was likely that they would soon be adding more unwanted experiences to their mental résumés. Andy had known this time would eventually come. He and Sun being summoned like this had been inevitable from the moment they'd walked away from Samhain. They were involved in something that was not yet over.

Perhaps it never would be.

The helicopter touched down in a clearing between a circle of Jeffrey pines. The steel skids struck rocky ground and the cockpit bounced briefly before settling down and coming to rest.

Agent Williams twisted in his chair and nodded at Sun and Andy. "Get out and somebody will meet you."

"This is *so* cool," Jerry said.

Andy glanced at him. "Trust us, it's not cool. It's probably going to end with all of us running for our lives."

"That is *so* cool," Jerry said.

Andy shoved Jerry out of the door and then turned around to help his wife make the three foot drop to the rocky landing pad.

The clearing was baked, the ground hard and parched. Shadows covered one side of the area while the sun beat down ferociously on the other. There was no wildlife nearby; no birds, no squirrels. Andy craned his neck and looked around. Three hundred and sixty degrees of woodland, not a building nor soul in sight.

One of the agents dropped their bags, then the chopper quickly jumped back up into the air. It tilted left and then headed right, clearing the treetops by mere inches. Within seconds it was out of sight, the distant humming of its propellers the only evidence that it had ever been there.

"Whoa!" said Jerry, looking up at the sky. "Did they just leave us here?"

"Just wait," said Andy. "We're not alone. Someone is going to pop out of somewhere."

"Mr. and Mrs. Dennison-Jones, I presume?"

Andy spun around. Behind them stood an older gentleman in military uniform. From the amount of ribbons on the man's chest, both his rank and experience were distinguished.

Andy walked to meet the figure, aware of the drill after having been through a similar situation before. He held out a hand to shake the man's hand. "It's Dennison-Jones."

"Isn't that what I said?"

Andy realized it was. He'd been so used to correcting people that he hadn't caught it.

"I suppose you did. I take it you're the head honcho?"

"I'm General Austin Kane. Welcome to Project Monstrum, facility 26. Or, as we here call it, the Spiral."

Monstrum. Great.

Kane offered a bony hand, which Andy shook firmly. It felt like clutching a wispy tree branch.

"And this must be Mrs. Dennison-Jones."

"Ms." Sun said, taking his hand.

Andy explained, "We're married, so we combined our last names, but we don't feel the English honorific should change just because of how many X chromosomes you have."

"Whipped!" Jerry said. "If I ever get married—"

"Don't bet on it," Sun said, staring him down.

Jerry shut up.

"And this must be the extra baggage I was informed about. Jerry Preston. Tell me, son, what compelled you to steal from—"

"Nice to meet you, General," Jerry offered his hand. "I'm happy to help out in any way I can."

"Yes, well, if you don't, you'll be sent to a black site, and then we'll go after everyone you care about."

"Wha?"

"Kidding, of course." The General raised his eyebrows. "Or am I? Now let's get everyone inside for a quick briefing. I'll send someone up for your bags."

Sun and Andy looked at one another. Then Andy nodded to the General. "Lead the way."

Andy, Sun, and Jerry followed Kane over to a large pile of logs between two leaning pine trees. Close inspection revealed that they were fake, made of thick, painted plastic and secured to a large metal plate. The plate slid aside automatically as they approached, revealing a murky stairwell leading into the earth. It was Samhain all over again.

"The Spiral has recently been upgraded," Kane told them. "But I'm afraid the entrance has seen better days. Mind your step on the way down as some of the steps have decayed after so long underground."

Everybody headed down the staircase. The large metal plate slid closed above them and a line of naked bulbs on the ceiling switched on. Many of the bulbs had blown-out or were flickering.

After a few hundred harsh, concrete steps, the staircase ended at a set of modern aluminium doors. The doors slid apart as the group got closer, revealing the shiny interior of a burnished steel elevator vestibule big enough to hold an SUV.

"The refurbishments start here," said Kane. "After the Samhain incident, a majority of our facilities were revamped and retrofitted with new security protocols. Each room and hallway has an alarm." He pointed to the wall, at a red square with a lever on it. "Pull it, and the entire complex goes on lockdown. We also have a small contingent of armed security staff, so please don't be alarmed by the sight of weaponry."

Andy felt simultaneously better and worse. It was good that the facility was more protected than Samhain had been, but bad that it was yet another facility that needed to be guarded in the first place.

"Needless to say," Kane said, "but everything you are about to see must be kept in absolute secrecy. You all know what will happen if you don't. Now, please, step into the elevator."

The group stepped inside the vaulted cabin. There were no controls on the wall. Kane simply said, 'Spiral, Level 2'.

The elevator began to descend.

"It automatically detects my security card." Kane produced a credit card sized piece of plastic from his pocket and showed it to them. "Without one of these cards or a visitor's access fob the elevators will not work. Only a few key people have full access, and even if they have the card they also need specific codes to do certain things, like open cell doors. Just one of our many security features."

"I feel like I'm on an episode of *Fringe*," said Jerry.

"Believe me," Andy said. "The awe wears off quickly."

"Let's try to stay positive, honey." Sun took his hand. "We don't know anything yet."

"I *am* positive," Andy said. "I'm positive it's going to be awful."

"Don't be overly concerned, Mr. Dennison-Jones," Kane said. "We've got a good team here, and a good facility. There hasn't been an accident at the Spiral for eight years."

"Let me guess why I'm here. Did you get some new addition? Something that looks like a demon from hell?" Andy folded his arms. "If so, your eight year safety streak is about to end."

"We have a lot more here than demons, Mr. Dennison-Jones. You'll find it is nothing like Samhain."

The elevator shuddered to a stop and the doors immediately opened. What greeted them was like nothing they had ever seen before.

It was not at all like what Andy had been expecting. General Kane had been right.

It was nothing like Samhain.

CHAPTER FOUR

Sun was concerned about her husband. She knew that beneath his veneer of calm, Andy was terrified. How could he not be? After what had happened the last time they'd been underground courtesy of the US government, it was a wonder he'd managed to remain sane. The same was true of her, of course. Despite the contentment she had found in Andy's arms, and the outright joy that her engagement and recent marriage had brought, she was still deeply damaged. She often lay awake in bed, knowing that Andy, too, was probably feigning sleep beside her. She would think about the terrors they had seen together and knew that if sleep eventually did find her it would be draped in a shroud of nightmares.

And now it seemed as though her nightmares were about to receive a follow-up booster shot.

When the elevator doors opened, Sun's apprehension was alleviated somewhat. Samhain had been a technological kluge beneath the desert, much of it older than anyone working there. But what she was looking at now was an entirely different ball game.

"Welcome to Spiral level 2," said General Kane. He stepped out in front of them and gestured like a magician revealing some great illusion. "Or as we like to call this area, the Nucleus. We're fifty meters down. But there's far more than just this."

Sun stepped out of the elevator and glanced around, tilting her head in all directions. The vaulted ceilings were a hundred-feet high above an area the size of a football field. Glass partitions separated numerous banks of blinking computers and expensive modern desks. There were so many people milling about the area that it could have passed for the call center of some mundane corporation.

"This is where 80% of the facility's staff operates," said Kane. "From here we can control security, communication, and all other aspects of the day-to-day running of the site. Our entire network is powered by one of the world's most powerful super computers and protected by the most sophisticated firewalls in existence."

"I bet you get some killer frame rates on *Call of Duty*," Jerry said.

"With a computer like that, why do you need a translator?" Andy asked. "With all this power you could translate the Voynich manuscript."

"We did that already," Kane said. "Interesting stuff." Apparently they'd deciphered one of history's most perplexing riddles. But before Andy could follow-up, Kane added, "Tell me, Mr. Dennison-Jones, do you know Manx?"

Andy nodded. "A Goidelic language, a dead branch of Celtic that was once popular on the Isle of Man."

"In the Irish Sea?" Jerry asked.

Sun frowned. "Please tell me you're just holding a leprechaun, and need my husband to learn where he buried his pot of gold."

"Unfortunately, no, Ms. Dennison-Jones. But we've got some things that make leprechauns seem positively normal. Follow me."

The group re-entered the elevator and this time Kane gave a different command: "Subbasement 1."

The elevator began to descend.

"We're heading another hundred meters down," said Kane. "It will take a few minutes. In the meantime let me explain why this facility is not like one you may have seen before. Samhain was built in 1906 by President Roosevelt and was designed to contain a single subject. This facility is far older and grander in its purposes."

"How much older?" Sun asked.

"The site's footprint has changed dozens of times since its initial construction. It has expanded, been dug down deeper, reinforced. The very first facility here was above ground and much smaller. To answer your question, this site has been in operation in some form or another since 1812."

"Bullshit!" Jerry said.

"Not at all. The facility was commissioned by the founding fathers themselves, including Thomas Jefferson, John Jay, and James Madison, along with Joseph-Napoleon Bonaparte, who was king of Spain at the time. This area was New Spain back then, and the facility was built by the Masons and the Catholic Church."

"Okay," Sun held up a hand. "You're starting to get Dan Brown on us now. You expect us to believe that there's some sort of conspiracy dating back almost all the way to the birth of our nation?"

Kane laughed. "A conspiracy? I don't know if I'd describe it like that. But it was for the greater good, most certainly. As for it dating back to the birth of our nation, things go back much further than that."

Sun frowned. She rubbed at her arms and felt goose bumps. The air in the elevator chilled as they cut deeper into the earth. "How much further back?" she asked.

The elevator stopped. The doors opened.

"We're here," said Kane, stepping out into the corridor and gesturing to a huge painting on the wall in front of them. The focus of the picture was a saintly figure in wonderful, golden robes.

Kane smiled at them like a monkey who'd been taught how to smoke. He told them, "Our project was created by St. Clement the first. In the year 94."

Sun shook her head. *It couldn't be.* She scanned through her brain's knowledge banks, fact checking her own thoughts. The man in the painting, St. Clement, was the third Pope in history, consecrated by St. Peter himself. Sun had taken a great interest in religious history since Samhain. Things she had once thought ancient and unimportant had become pressing concerns.

"What you are about to see," Kane said, "was started by a group of devoted individuals coming together under the collective name of Deus Manus."

Sun looked at her husband for an explanation.

He quickly gave one. "It means 'God's hand'."

Kane nodded and smiled. "It does indeed. The reason this facility stands is to protect humanity from the worst evil to ever walk the earth. And with that cryptic introduction, allow me to introduce you to some of our guests."

CHAPTER FIVE

The corridor in which they were standing had clean magnolia walls. They curved slightly, as if the hallway was circular and joined back on itself like a snake consuming its own tail. Spaced apart every ten feet or so was a collection of doors. They were thick steel, maybe titanium, and had viewing hatches like you would find in a prison. There were no locks, nor any handles on the doors. Instead, each door had a small LED touchscreen built into the wall beside it.

"There are four main levels to the upper facility," Kane explained, "such as the Nucleus on level 2 and the staff dormitories on level 4. Below those four levels are five subbasements; with this being the first: subbasement 1. Each subbasement is a curved hallway with elevators on either end. The deeper you go, the more, well, *colorful,* the guests become. Of all the places to begin your tour, this level is probably the wisest place to begin. The lower levels may be a tad too much to take in without being properly acclimatised beforehand."

Sun breathed in, and her olfactory senses were assaulted by smells of strange animals. It brought back, unbidden, memories of the last time she'd seen Bub. She saw him all the time in her nightmares. She didn't relish the prospect of seeing him again. Or anything equally evil.

Kane stopped and turned around. Sun almost bumped into the back of him, and Andy almost into the back of her. Jerry was dawdling several feet behind with an anxious look on his face.

"Okay, let's start with cell number 9. As good a place as any." Kane went up to the nearest door and pressed his thumb against the LED screen. It flashed green and let out a friendly beep. Kane then prodded at the panel several times with his index finger, navigating various menus.

The hatch at the top of the door slid open.

"Take a look," said Kane.

Sun looked over at her husband. Andy had grown pale. He was staring at the hatch but making no move towards it. She knew the memories of Samhain were flooding back to him, just as they were to her.

Sun touched Andy's hand with hers. "I'll go," she said.

She took a step towards the door. And then another.

Then she was standing in front of the hatch. Taking a deep breath, Sun leaned forward. Her eyes went wide.

"What the hell is that?"

"That, Ms. Dennison-Jones, is an imp. Quite harmless in most instances, but they can still give a nasty bite. Real nasty."

Sun stared into the cell. The interior was almost like a habitat at a zoo. It was a vast rectangle, stretching fifty feet backwards in a widening arc. Sun spotted a rock cave and a small pond amongst artificial reeds and rubbery plant life.

The creature inside was almost human, childlike in its stature and no bigger than thirty centimeters tall. What made it decidedly *inhuman* was its green, glistening skin, sticky as an earthworm's. A ropey tail swished behind the creature and a pair of cranial bumps rose behind its ears like stunted horns.

The imp realised that it was being watched through the hatch and returned Sun's gaze. She couldn't be sure, but she thought she saw its ears prick up and its tail begin to wag faster.

Is it happy to see me?

Sun stood aside so that Andy could take a look. His reaction was equally as shocked. As soon as he had seen enough, Jerry took his turn.

"You're winding me up," he said. "That's some kind of animatronic. Either that or you've been messing around with nature like that dickhead in *Jurassic Park*."

"I'm sorry, but I don't get the reference," said Kane.

Jerry's eyes widened. "You never saw *Jurassic Park*?"

"If you are referring to a movie then I'm afraid I have to admit to finding little time for such things. The recreation area of the Spiral has an extensive video library but I prefer books."

Jerry huffed. "*Jurassic Park* was a book first, man."

"The reference is still lost on me."

"It's about dinosaurs. Scientists clone dinosaurs so they're no longer extinct."

Kane chuckled. "Who says they're extinct? We have several of them down here."

"Cool!" Jerry said. "Which ones? Got any Velociraptors? Did you know Carcharodontosaurus was a bigger predator than T-Rex?"

"I don't know their names, but some we have are big."

"Excuse me," Sun interrupted the exchange. As fascinating as dinosaurs were, they weren't malevolently intelligent and plotting the destruction of the world. "Can you explain a little more about what you have in there? You said it's an imp? As in *a little demon*?"

Kane nodded his head slowly. His aging eyes had narrowed and the corners of his mouth turned downwards. "I'd have thought you'd be willing to believe in such things by now, Ms. Dennison-Jones. As for it being a demon, I don't know. All I can say is that the dirty little thing is an organic life form and that the first one was captured several centuries ago. It was housed in Sarajevo until the hostilities there led to the facility becoming compromised."

"A Sarajevo facility? What the hell was the US government doing there?"

"You misunderstand. The facility did not belong to the United States. It was under the control of the Bosnian government. The society of Deus Manus goes beyond boundaries. It is older than many of the nations which exist today and has influence exceeding them all. It is a collective of societies, organizations, individuals, and governments, all unified in the quest to capture and contain evil."

Sun raised an eyebrow. "Evil?"

Kane gestured to cell number 9. "I don't mean the notion of evil—some philosophical debate about the inner nature of man. I mean evil as a living, breathing being, like that thing in there. This facility—and many others like it—were built to contain the predators that have haunted men's nightmares since the dawn of time. We are the jailors of nightmares. The Spiral is a giant underground prison; the safest maximum-security prison ever built. And there are dozens of others just like it, all over the world. The cells are mostly automated. Food is released from shafts in the ceilings and water is piped in through several taps."

"Live food?" Sun asked.

"It depends on the particular needs of the guest. If they require something live, or fresh, we ship it in daily. Imps, for example, prefer chickens. They eat everything, including the feathers."

"Are they intelligent?" Andy asked.

"Maybe a bit dumber than chimpanzees."

"How about the other creatures you house here?"

"None as smart as we are, Mr. Dennison-Jones. That's why they're in the cells, and we're out here."

Jerry tapped on the hatch. "This is mad. My blog readers—"

Everyone turned to stare at him.

"—will never know, because I'm never telling anyone. Frak, silence sucks. Last night I had breakfast with two guys dressed as Borg and a dude who insisted the Book of Revelation was happening right now. They'd flip out if they knew this." He caught a look from Kane and quickly added, "But they never will."

"How many *guests* do you have here exactly?" Sun asked, dreading what the answer might be.

"Each subbasement has eighteen cells. They are all mostly full."

Sun did the math. "You have almost ninety creatures held here?"

Kane shook his head. "You're assuming that occupancy is one per cell." He pointed back at cell number 9. "Take a closer look."

Sun went back over to the hatch and peered inside. She waited a moment, but then she saw it.

"There's more of them in there."

Inside the habitat, several more imps appeared from amongst the foliage. They were of varying sizes, but all had the same green skin and swishing tails. They gathered in front of the rock cave and faced the hatch, four in total.

"We let the dirty little things breed," Kane said. "But we keep their numbers low. Once a year we cull any creatures that are over the thresholds we set. Either that or we use them for our research."

Sun looked in at the group of childlike creatures and suddenly felt a tug of guilt. "They're a family?"

Kane folded his bony arms. His demeanor had become much cooler. "You could call it that, I suppose. As much as you would call a pack of rats a family. Come on, I'll show you the next cell."

The group moved on like a tour group in the world's most surreal museum. They stopped in front of cell 10 and Kane once again operated the LED panel beside the door.

The hatch opened.

Sun was again the first person to look inside. This time the interior was a blank canvass of grey bedrock. In several places the ground was puckered, rising up into small craters. The whole habitat reminded Sun of the surface of the moon.

I don't see anything.

Then something caught her eye. It was about twenty feet inside. She adjusted her vision and focused on one of the craters. Something big was lurking inside. The only thing that distinguished it from the shadows was its brief fidgety movement.

"It's... a unicorn!" Sun said.

The creature had a magnificent, pointy horn jutting from its skull. It whinnied like a horse and pawed the ground.

"Why the hell would you keep those things?" Jerry said. "The imps I can understand. But those things aren't monsters."

"Everything here is some sort of monster," Kane answered. "Deus Manus keeps them separated from the world."

"If everything is a monster, why not kill them all?" Jerry asked.

"Our job is to guard, not to kill," Kane said. "The Deus Manus order believes all living things were created by God."

Jerry pulled a face. "So God created evil? What kind of God would do that?"

"The same God who created the bubonic plague, which wiped out two hundred million people in the 14th century, and the Spanish Flu, which wiped out over fifty million less than a hundred years ago. The God who destroyed Pompeii when Vesuvius erupted, the 1931 Chinese floods that killed millions, the 1960 Bhola cyclone that killed hundreds of thousands, the 2010 earthquake in Haiti that left two hundred and thirty thousand people dead. There have been hundreds of famines and natural disasters, countless diseases. The Lord moves in mysterious ways."

"You may not be able to control an earthquake," Andy said. "But you could certainly take care of the creatures in this facility."

"Andy!" Sun nudged him. "It's a unicorn!"

"It could be some sort of evil unicorn. Maybe it eats people."

"The unicorn eats hay, Mr. Dennison-Jones. It's not tame, but compared to many of our residents it's mostly harmless."

"So why keep them a secret?"

"We can't risk revealing them to the world. The founders of Deus Manus were devoted to God. They locked away anything they felt was intrinsically evil or came from hell. I'm not about to second-guess them. They lived during a time where creatures like this walked the earth. If our ancestors thought the imps and unicorns were dangerous, then so do I."

"But there's no records, no history."

Kane shrugged his shoulders. "Like I said, Deus Manus was created by the world's most powerful elite; people who not only wrote the history books, but dictated the very direction of civilization. Humanity matured knowing only what these men allowed it to."

Sun bristled. "No one has that right. No one has the right to take ownership of history."

"Yeah," said Jerry. "Those Deus Anus blokes were bang out of order."

Kane pursed his lips. "Like it or not, what we are tasked with here is more ancient and more important than anything else in existence. We are the keepers of humanity, and it is our calling to prevent the evil kept inside this hole in the ground from corrupting the modern world."

"Fine, whatever you say," Andy said. "It still doesn't explain why you brought us here. Unless the unicorn speaks Manx."

"This is just a prelude to prepare you for what you are about to see. The reason you are here is buried deep in subbasement 5. But first, we want you to meet our most recent guest. We think it's someone you might recognise."

Sun glanced anxiously at her husband, and saw he'd begun to sweat despite the cool temperature.

Kane motioned back towards the way they had come. Back towards the elevator. "Shall we head down?"

CHAPTER SIX

In the elevator, Kane reached into his pocket and brought out two navy blue disks. They looked like a pair of rubber bath plugs. "Take these," he said. "They will allow you limited access to the LED control panels and other parts of the facility. Just press them to the thumb scanners. Your temporary four-digit codes are 1-2-3-4. If you need me, just access the intercom function on any of the screens."

Andy and Sun took the rubber disks and pocketed them.

Jerry flapped his arms. "What, no love for the J-man?"

"Son, you shouldn't even be here. Just consider yourself lucky to be a spectator."

"I prefer the term 'watcher'," Jerry said. "Has a nice ring to it. Jeremy Preston is... *The Watcher.*"

"Call yourself whatever you wish, Mr. Preston. Just make sure that you stay out of trouble. Or you will be Jeremy Preston... *the departed.*"

Jerry rolled his eyes. "That was lame."

"We'll keep an eye on him," Sun said, clapping the boy on the shoulder.

Still picking up strays, Andy thought.

Kane sighed. "Yes, see that you do."

The elevator stopped and the doors opened. Subbasement 5 was darker than the floors above. Unlike the rest of the facility, this area had not been recently refurbished. The walls were bare and cracked, with seams of mud pushing through from the surrounding earth. There were armed guards standing at the entrance. The uniforms they wore were not military, but more like black-ops, with pouches and utility belts in abundance. The insignia on their upper arm was a golden sword with clouds above it.

Andy tried to control his encroaching panic, but with each step his feet seemed heavier and his nerves shakier. He gripped Sun's hand like she was dangling off the side of a cliff.

Kane glanced back over his shoulder. "What I want to show you is just down here. The cells up ahead are see-through. Six-inch bulletproof glass. It's imperative that we can see what the guests are doing at all times. These are the really nasty ones."

He marched ahead and stopped beside a pair of armed guards. He exchanged pleasantries with the two men while the rest of the group caught up. Andy peered into a cell as they passed it and stopped when he noticed movement. There were piles of hay on the floor, and one of them shifted as he stared.

Then something from the opposite side of the room scuttled towards the door and took Andy by surprise. He pulled back from the hatch and let out an involuntary yelp.

"You're perfectly safe," said Kane. "There are two females inside. The males fight when not kept alone. The main colony is in Moscow. These two were lent to us for scientific study. Their venom is quite toxic. It explodes living tissue."

Andy leaned back up against the hatch and peered inside again. Thc crcatures he saw inside were no different than harvestmen spiders—also known as daddy longlegs, except a hundred times as big. The two jet-black arachnids had oval bodies the size of an exercise ball, and their spindly legs spread out a span of three meters, each thick as a man's wrist.

The hair on the back of Andy's neck pricked up.

The two gigantic spiders moved toward the hatch, their mandibles chittering. Venom dripped from fangs the size of steak knives.

"Ugh, I hate spiders," Jerry said, grimacing. "I read about a dude in Australia who was bitten by a funnel web. The tissue rotted straight off the bone."

The partially desiccated corpse of a small pig was partially covered in webbing, and on the floor of the cell were bones.

"Sheep bones," Sun guessed.

She would know. Sun had had a lot of experience with sheep.

"What I mean to show you is over here," Kane said. "Please come and take a look."

Here goes, thought Andy.

He took a deep breath and peered through the glass. Cell 4 was nothing but a large white room with a stone bench, hay scattered around the floor.

"I don't see anything. Did you bring me here just to see a bench?"

Kane cleared his throat. "Look up, Mr. Dennison-Jones."

Andy craned his neck and glanced towards the room's ceiling.

Behind him, Sun gasped. "Oh God."

Jerry whistled in awe. "It's that demon! He's real!"

Andy glared at the batling in the cell. It was a mini version of the abomination he and Sun had faced off against years ago. The thing that had almost killed them both—and had succeeded in killing most of their colleagues. Its flesh was a muddy red color, matted with coarse fur. Its muscular arms bore talons, and its feet ended in goat-like hoofs.

Andy's eyes narrowed at the creature. "Bub..."

"I understand that you have met before," Kane said.

Andy nodded, not taking his eyes off the subject of his recurring nightmares. The demon hovered eight feet above the ground, the black, leathery wings sprouting from its back flapping as fast as Andy's heartbeat. It had the same malevolent, sideways-blinking eyes as its creator, and gave off the same barnyard smell, even through the thick glass.

Andy cleared his throat and ground his teeth. Then he turned to face Kane. "You have to destroy it."

"That's unacceptable."

"Why? This thing is pure evil. Keeping it alive is just inviting disaster."

Kane fiddled with his shirt cuffs momentarily and then folded his arms across his narrow chest. "As I understand it, there are many more of these things out there. Better that we learn what we can from this one so that we may have a better chance of destroying them all."

"How many others?" Andy asked.

"You're not cleared for that information."

"The President said I had full access."

"I'll ask him when I speak to him again."

Andy returned his gaze to the batling. The batling glared right back at him. "You're making a mistake."

"No. No, he's not." It was Sun speaking. Andy was surprised she didn't agree with him. "We need to be smart about this," she said. "Killing one would achieve nothing with so many more out there. What's more important is figuring out what these things are up to, and where to find the rest."

Andy closed his eyes and wished to be somewhere else, anyplace else but here. But it would be burying his head in the sand to not admit that his wife was right.

"So what's the plan?" he asked Kane. "What are you going to do with this thing?"

Kane shrugged. "Discover all we can. Ms. Dennison-Jones, you're welcome to pick up where you left off at Samhain. Tackle the situation from a biological standpoint; study the creature's physiology, et cetera. We also need you both to try and communicate with it. Use your knowledge of Bub to try and find out as much as possible about what these 'batlings' are planning."

"What about me?" Jerry asked.

Kane glared at him. "You stay out of the way and try not to give me any reason to shoot you."

Jerry swallowed. "I can do that."

"But this creature isn't the main reason you were brought here," Kane said. "There is something else we want you to see. Or, more specifically, something that wants to see *you*."

That raised goosebumps all over Andy's body.

"Those aren't air vents," Sun said, pointing to large, square holes in the walls in between cells. They looked like chutes, and were large enough for a man to crawl into. "I hope they don't lead outside."

"They do not. I'm afraid we learned some difficult lessons after Samhain, Ms. Dennison-Jones. In case of an uncontainable security breach, the entire Spiral is rigged to fill with a quick-mix concrete. Anything alive down here will be fossilised within minutes of the concrete setting, while the floors above would remain unaffected. The elevator shaft would also be filled in and sealed."

"Bub has been buried once before. It didn't hold him."

"The nearest Deus Manus facility is in Texas. They'd send a clean-up team to make sure nothing was left alive. But it is a moot point, because the cells are escape proof. Now follow me."

Kane led them further down the corridor. They passed by a whole host of monstrosities along the way.

There was a hairy, snarling beast that looked a lot like the classical description of a werewolf. Its black fur was matted. It growled at them with canine teeth ten centimeters long.

A large, regal-looking creature that was equal parts eagle and lion. The front of its body was like a bird of prey, its hindquarters like that of a jungle cat—a griffon, if Andy knew his mythological creatures.

A dinosaur, similar to the velociraptors Jerry had mentioned, but taller and thicker and covered with red and orange feathers. The LED screen next to it said it was an *Achillobator.* It was standing still, swaying left to right, its plumed, striped tail swishing.

There was also a humanoid creature that could have passed for a man if not for its dislocated lower jaw and dagger-like teeth sticking out through the torn flesh of its cheeks. Its eyes were jet-black, with pupils so large that the whites were not at all visible. Its fingertips were barbed like fish hooks, and it glared at them with malice and utter hatred as they walked by its cell.

Really don't want to be trapped in a room with that thing. Or any of these things.

Up ahead, the transparent cells were coming to an end. Another elevator punctuated the conclusion of the corridor. As Andy approached the final cell he glanced hesitantly inside, wondering what horror he would see next, but he was surprised to find a perfectly normal-looking, middle-aged man, sitting in a chair. The handsome male was dressed in tweed slacks, a fancy collared shirt, and a long grey overcoat. He watched Andy with bright eyes.

"And this is the reason we've called you here," Kane said.

The man stood, walking slowly to the glass partition. He said, "Ayr Ain, t'ayns Niau, Ca⊠herick dy rou dt'ennym, Di jig dty Reereeaght."

It was the language of the Isle of Man. Manx. It was also very familiar.

Andy answered in kind, "Dt'aigney dy rou jeant er y Talloo myr t'ayns Niau, Cur dooin nyn Arran jiu as gagh laa."

The man smiled, apparently pleased. In a thick Irish brogue he said, "Welcome to Project Monstrum, Andrew Dennison-Jones."

General Kane stepped forward, eyes wide. "You speak English."

"I speak many languages, General. Manx is an oldie but a goody, as they say. Did you know the last native speaker of

Manx died in 1974? Languages, just like species, can go extinct if the situation warrants it."

Andy studied the prisoner. The man had messy brown hair that fell down to his shoulders, and an umber carpet of stubble clung to his face.

"Quid est tibi nomen?" Andy asked. *What is your name?*

"Ah, Latin. Another dead language, unless you count those cheeky religious bucks trying to keep it around. My friends call me Lucas. Thrilled to make your acquaintance, so I am."

The way the man said 'thrilled' sounded like 'trilled'.

"A pleasure," said Andy. "So, what are you… in for?"

"We're not sure," Kane interrupted. "Lucas has the distinction of being unlike any of the other residents housed here."

"Why's that?" Sun asked.

"He's here voluntarily. We never captured him. Seven days ago he just appeared inside this cell and has been here ever since. He doesn't eat, he doesn't sleep. He's not even organic as far as our tests can find."

Lucas continued to smile pleasantly.

Sun cleared her throat and took a second look at the man inside the cell. "Not organic. What do you mean?"

"I mean his blood tests contain no DNA, and his tissue samples are inconclusive. It's almost like he isn't a living creature."

"Your definition of life is a tad limited, General." He glanced at Sun. "How does modern science define life, Dr. Dennison-Jones?"

"It's something structurally composed, which regulates its environment. It has a metabolism. It grows. It adapts. It reproduces. Responds to stimuli."

"Can't the same be true of fire? Or electro-magnetism? Or the earth itself? The bloody great stars in the sky, for that matter?"

"It has a consciousness," Sun said.

"Do algae have consciousness?"

"Maybe they do."

"And maybe the earth does as well. Perhaps you should be less concerned with defining life, and more concerned with what the world is trying to tell yee."

"What is the world trying to tell us?" Andy asked.

The man smiled sweetly. "That we're all buggered."

General Kane frowned. "Until now, he's only spoken in Manx. Except for three English words that he kept repeating."

"What were they?" Andy asked, but he realized he already knew.

"They were *Andrew Dennison-Jones*," Kane answered.

"Did anyone tell him about me?" Andy asked.

"Not that we know of."

"When did he start asking? I've only been Dennison-Jones for less than a day."

"Just after he arrived."

"Lucky guess," Lucas said, shrugging his shoulders and grinning.

"How is it you have no DNA?" Sun asked.

Lucas shrugged. "More luck, I suppose. DNA is a killer, you know. Everything with DNA dies."

"So how do your cells multiply?"

"If they multiplied, I'd be double me size! I'd have to get me some new clothes, I would."

Andy stared at Lucas. Lucas stared back with an amiable smile on his face. There was nothing to suggest the man was anything more than a forty-year old Irish rogue.

"Unafanya nini hapa?" Andrew asked. *What are you doing here*, in Swahili.

"Mimi kuzungumza na wewe." *I am talking to you.*

"Do you know my name?" Jerry asked, getting in on the exchange.

Lucas seemed to regard the youth for a moment. "Is it important for me to, Jerry-lad? You wouldn't remember, but we've met before."

"When?"

"At a pub in your home town."

"I don't believe you."

"I'm not asking you to. You don't need to listen to me, nor seek my approval. I'm not your father. You should go home and make up with Ben while there's still time."

Jerry backed away, his jaw going slack.

Andy asked in Croatian. "Zašto želiš ovdje?" *Why do you want me here?*

"You'll know in due time, Mr. Dennison-Jones. I'm sure Austin wants you to meet the rest of the team, and no doubt you're hungry. We'll have a chat later."

Lucas sat back in his chair. Further attempts to engage him were ignored with polite nods. Eventually, General Kane led the group down the hall.

"What was it you said to him at the start?" Kane asked.

"He was reciting the Lord's Prayer in Manx. I filled in the next few lines. Apparently he can also speak Latin, Swahili, and Croatian."

"He's an enigma, that one. We haven't had any idea what to do with him, which is why we had to call on you. He smiles all the time, and has been cooperative, but something about him is... wrong."

"You mean the fact that he seems to know everything, can come and go at will, and has no DNA?" Sun asked.

"It's more than that." Kane reached the elevator and folded his thin arms across his chest. "Of all the mysteries the Spiral contains, he's the biggest. He might also be the most dangerous."

CHAPTER SEVEN

While Sun and Andy went to meet their new colleagues, Jerry was escorted to his room by some dick with a gun, who practically frogmarched him inside. The whole experience left Jerry feeling abused and upset.

Story of my life.

At least the new digs were pretty sweet. The living quarters they'd provided him were almost as big as the two-bedroom flat he used to share with his mother back at home, back before she'd…

Got to stop thinking about the past, dude. Dwelling has got me in enough trouble already. I can't even go back home because of what I did.

Still, I landed on my feet with this place. I came to America to get a website interview and ended up in a real life episode of the X-Files. I'm like a cooler Fox Mulder.

And that vet chick would make a pretty good Scully.

Except that she's married. And way out of my league.

And old. She has to be in her mid-thirties.

Jerry decided to take a load off. He lay down on the room's plush double bed and stared up at the ceiling.

This is so messed up.

I'm alone in a strange country, and now I've ended up stumbling across something so top secret it blows away my wildest dreams. They're not going to let me leave; not after what I've seen. I don't even want to think about those giant spiders. Shite!

They have the entire freaking cast of Hammer Horror *down here in the flesh. I swear one of those things I saw was a goddamn werewolf.*

No, no way will they'll let me go after seeing all this.

Even if they do, all I have to look forward to is getting nicked by the Old Bill as soon as I set foot back home.

My life is over one way or another.

Be careful what you wish for…

Jerry reached into his back pocket and pulled out his iPhone. No signal, naturally, but there was WiFi. Password protected, though. He scrolled through his photos until he found a picture of his best friend, Ben. Somehow that weird guy, Lucas, had known about him. He also claimed to know Jerry. The strange thing was, Jerry sort of felt the same way. Sometimes he had weird nightmares of being trapped with a group of strangers in a pub because it wouldn't stop snowing outside, and he could almost—but not quite—recall someone like Lucas in those dreams. It was the feeling of having memories that were not his own that had first led him to trying to find out the truth behind conspiracies. It turned out that he was right to, because he had stumbled right into the middle of one now.

He flipped through a few more pics, found a selfie of him and Ben in Ben's Dad's video shop, standing in front of a wall of DVDs.

Wonder what you're up to, buddy. Hope you're okay.

But Jerry knew that his friend was not okay. Not after what had happened.

Wouldn't be surprised if you never speak to me again. I really wish you were here, though, 'cus this place would blow your mind. All of the times we spent discussing horror movies, and aliens, and government secrets, and I end up in a place like this.

Ben was a large part of the reason Jerry began the Stop Government Secrets website. He'd always told Jerry he was wasting his time, living without purpose, so Jerry had given himself a purpose. To uncover the truth behind all the weird rumors and stories and conspiracies he and Ben always joked about. That had led him to learning about Samhain. After hundreds of hours of research and training—and yes, computer hacking did require a lot of training—Ben had connected Samhain to Andy and Sun, and had hatched a plan to interview them in person. Get them to the Comics and Conspiracies Convention, pretend to be a fanboy, and then befriend them until they trusted him enough to spill the truth.

And then...

And then betray that earned trust by putting their secrets on his website.

Shit, I'm a total shit. No wonder no one likes me.

I don't even like myself.

Jerry felt a tear well up in the corner of his eye. He quickly sprang up off the bed to keep it from taking root. The key was to occupy himself. Sitting still or lying down would let in all of his regret, and there was way too much of it for a coward like him to bear.

Maybe I deserve whatever happens to me. If a bunch of gits-in-black knock on my door and make me 'disappear', maybe I'll finally find some peace again. Maybe I'll manage to get some sleep finally.

Even if it ends up being permanent.

Jerry located the suite's bathroom and stripped naked for a shower. He hoped the hot water would burn the bad thoughts right out of his head.

It didn't.

CHAPTER EIGHT

General Kane led Andy and Sun into a vast room. Like the 'Nucleus' upstairs it was full of desks, computers, and various hi-tech equipment that seemed to do nothing useful other than blink and beep. Andy found it mightily impressive.

Wonder if it all runs on Windows Illuminati.

Kane strolled over to a large conference desk taking up the center of the room and pulled up a seat for Sun. She sat. Andy found himself a chair beside her. He looked around, observing the room in closer detail.

There were several offices that led off from the central room. People in lab coats occupied some of them, but most were empty. At the far side of the room, chatting in a huddle, were three men wearing black-op suits and shouldering mean-looking assault rifles that didn't fit any design which Andy knew of. Behind them was a door, labelled: LABS 1-4.

"This is the conference room," Kane said. "This is where you and the team will share notes and make use of the more basic research equipment. Each member of the inner staff also has their own private office, but the efforts here are mostly communal. In other words, everyone shares what they know with each other rather than sitting on information to further their own agenda. There is no individual glory here—it's all about the mission."

Andy wondered how that was working out. In Andy's experience, personal growth and reward were driving forces. When those were removed, people became lazy.

Kane continued.

"There are four fully-equipped labs down here, to which everyone has access, under the supervision of Dr. Gornman. I am in charge here, but beyond that everybody has their own autonomy within their own specific area of research. You take orders from me and no one else. That needs to be very clear."

Andy and Sun said nothing, but both nodded.

Kane leaned forward to reach an intercom unit set into the middle of the desk. He pressed a button and said, "Can I have everyone in the conference room, please, to meet our newest additions?"

They sat in silence for a few moments while people started to funnel out of the adjacent offices. Each of the newcomers pulled up a chair at the large desk. It began to resemble a meeting of the joint-chiefs.

"Okay," Kane said. "We have over fifty people in this facility, but this is the main team. Allow me to start the introductions. Everyone, this is Andrew and Sun Dennison-Jones. Andrew knows several dozen languages, and was summoned by the President himself to communicate with the Manx man. Sun is a veterinarian. They were both assigned to Project Samhain, and were there when it... *ended*."

Andy stared at the blank faces regarding him, and decided smiling and waving was the wrong way to go. Instead he nodded curtly.

Kane indicated a large man in one of the black ops suit. The guard had a long raggedy Rasputin beard and biceps the size of melons. On his belt was a huge sidearm, a pager, a knife, a leather pouch, and a police baton. Two equally-large black men flanked him on either side.

"This is Sergeant Steve Rimmer, head of Spiral security. Either side of him are his team leaders, Mike Handler and Tyler West. Any security breaches, or personnel conflicts, will be dealt with by Rimmer and his team.

Rimmer nodded but didn't speak. Handler and West both said hello and smiled.

"Next we have Dr. Larry Chandelling, who is our lead scientist and head of information technology. Any tissue samples you need analysing will go through him and his team of assistants. Likewise, any questions about our computer systems here should be directed his way."

"Glad to be working with you," the doctor warmly said. He was a skinny, middle-aged, weasel-featured man, but wore a friendly smile. "I'd be very interested in hearing about Samhain, and sharing notes."

Kane waved a hand. "We can get to that later, Dr. Chandelling." He moved on. "Our Head of Medicine is Dr. Thandi Gornman. She holds doctorates in Medicine and Psychiatry and has overall control of the labs. Dr. Gornman will dispense any drugs that you may need for personal use or for the care of the various guests we contain. She is also quite the expert with our IT systems here, but try not to bother her unless absolutely necessary. She runs a tight ship."

Dr. Gornman had short, straight black hair and sharp features. She appraised them from behind horn-rim spectacles and seemed to frown at what she saw. "Do any of you have any medical conditions I need to know about? Diabetes, for instance. Or depression. Speak now or forever hold your peace."

Sun shook her head. Andy considered his hemorrhoids, and decided to stay quiet.

"Then I don't expect to see very much of you, except for mandatory weekly sessions. We can schedule them soon."

"What is that?" Sun asked.

Kane answered. "The stress of working in a secret underground facility, surrounded by monsters, tends to accumulate.

The powers that be deemed it wise to have a full-time psychiatrist available to the staff. Everyone meets with Dr. Gornman once a week to chat."

"Does that chat include a psych eval?" Sun asked.

Gornman smiled placidly, like the head shrink she was. "No one judges, here. But if I feel someone is unfit for duty, they are removed from the facility."

Kane clasped his hands in front of him. "Thank you, Dr. Gornman. Finally, let me introduce Gwen Nester. She works in the library which is located to the east side of this room."

A young redhead directly opposite Andy gave a warm smile. "Call me Nessie. I'm the facility's expert on ancient theology and belief structures. The boring stuff."

"If you don't mind me saying, you look young," Andy noted.

Nessie shrugged her shoulders but didn't seem to take offence at the comment. "I'm afraid there's very little interest in cultures from three thousand years ago. There's a limited talent pool to pick from. My predecessor sadly passed away this year. But I have devoted my entire adult life to studying the ancient world, so I promise you I know more than enough to be of use. Plus I used to watch *The History Channel* obsessively, back when it used to, you know, actually air history programs." Nessie cleared her throat. "That was a joke, by the way."

Andy smiled politely, but he wondered if Nessie might be a liability. She was mid-twenties and brimming with positivity, but neither of those things tended to help when you were fighting for your life against hellspawn.

"Pleased to meet you all," Sun said.

"Me, too," Andy concurred. "Has work already begun on analysing the batling?"

There was a collection of frowns and grunts around the table. Kane addressed the confusion. "Mr. and Ms. Dennison-Jones refer to our new arrival as a 'batling'."

Dr. Chandelling nodded and looked amused. "As good a name as any. I was calling it flying goat thingy. The official channels have been referring to it as a 'faustling"'

"Have you discovered anything about it yet?" Sun asked.

"Not much." Nessie frowned. "It was captured in the woods above the entry hatch a few days ago."

The Head of Security, Rimmer, pulled at his scraggly beard and sniffed. "The weekly perimeter sweep discovered a pile of bodies in the clearing above. Dead mule deer, bobcats, big horn sheep. It was as if an alpha-predator had started wiping out all of the local fauna. When one of our security teams went out to investigate they found your batling feasting on the carcass of a cougar. They opened fire and tore the thing to pieces before bringing the remains underground. Within the hour it had completely healed and come back to life. Our subsequent attempts to harm it have resulted in temporary injuries at best."

"Bub could regenerate by manipulating his DNA, and the DNA of other organic matter," Sun explained. "He's got these—stingers—in his palms. They're like syringes. He uses them to inject some sort of DNA mutator serum into tissue. He created the batlings, and looked exactly like them, only larger. Stands to reason they have the same ability to heal as he did."

Dr. Gornman nodded. There was a hint of disdain on her face, a slight narrowing of her eyes and downturn of her pointed nose. "That much is quite obvious. We need to discover the source of the ability, though. If we can harness the ability to heal instantly we can transform mankind. Just think of a world without injury, without disability. We would be the saviors of the human race."

Sun leaned in closer. "You don't think people tried figuring that out at Samhain? They had Bub locked up for over a century and gained nothing from him. It's tempting fate to even try. Stopping him should be our only priority."

"The Samhain facility was a relic, improperly administrated," Gornman said. "Human error, and faulty protocol led to the security breaches there. Bub should have been brought here when he was discovered."

"Why wasn't he?"

"President Roosevelt didn't trust anyone but the US to keep an eye on him," Gornman answered. "Which turned out to be a huge mistake. They should have brought the creature to us, or to another Deus Manus facility. We have the very best security, the best technology, and the very best minds."

"Okay," Sun said. "Then I'll ask again, what have you learned so far?"

Gornman made a face. "Nothing conclusive yet, but tests are ongoing. It's just a matter of time until—"

"So you have nothing."

Gornman folded her arms.

"We know that the thing does not sleep," Dr. Chandelling said, scratching at his pockmarked chin. "We know that it feels pain, but not always. It can't be killed. It doesn't seem to get sick. We bombarded it with a few simple strains of flu and chickenpox. It contracted neither."

"You can try every virus you have," Sun told them. "Nothing will have any effect. The only thing we found that hurt Bub was radiation—and even that didn't finish the job."

Dr. Chandelling nodded rapidly. "Yes, yes. I read your debriefing after Samhain. I heard that you hit Bub with a huge dose of rads. I would be very excited to hear your experiences first-hand."

"It's not something we're particularly comfortable talking about," Sun said, "but we'll share what we know. That batling you have locked up is part of something bigger. It can't be a coincidence you caught it nearby. We need to figure out what Bub's game is."

Gornman shook her head slightly. "You're over-reacting. Deus Manus has kept watch over thousands of dangerous creatures for thousands of years. We are more than equipped to handle a single batling."

"Bub isn't a giant spider or an imp," Andy said. "He wanted to enslave mankind. And he had the means to do it. If that batling knows what Bub knew, and has his abilities, you all better put on some long rubber boots because we're in some seriously deep shit."

Gornman frowned. "The mistakes at Samhain were a combination of human and technical error. That can't happen here. We're much more technologically advanced than you were, and our staff is more experienced. It takes years to be inducted into the Order. Many, such as Dr. Nester here, are groomed since college to be inducted. The batling will be contained. The only threat to this operation is newcomers who don't understand the protocol."

Andy leaned forward on the table like an angry cop doing an interrogation, except he was the one being scrutinised. "I couldn't care less about your *Order*. But if you treat that demon like it's just another attraction in your crazy little zoo, it's going to kill you, me, everyone here, and the whole goddamn world."

"At ease," Kane ordered. Then he addressed Gornman. "Andrew and Sun Dennison-Jones are here at the insistence of the President. They have full access to anything they need, and you'll listen to what they're saying. That's an order."

Gornman didn't seem to like it. "What about that straggler you brought in with you? The English boy?"

"How do you even know about him?" Kane asked.

"It's my job to know what's going on around here, Austin."

"No, Dr. Gornman, it is not. That is *my* job, and you may address me as 'Sir' or 'General'. Now go and wait in my office."

Gornman popped up from her seat, spun around and marched away with her heels clicking on the tiled floor.

Andy winced. *For a psychiatrist she seems to have some serious emotional issues.*

"What's with the Manx man?" Sun asked around. "What do you know about him?"

Dr. Chandelling sat up in his seat and grinned. "He's very interesting, very fascinating. He's like nothing we've ever seen before. Every test we run on him comes up implausible. He has cells, but no DNA, either in the nucleus or mitochondria. He has blood, but we can't type it. No antibodies, no antigens, no leucocytes, no platelets—just plasma and red cells. He doesn't eat, sleep, or...you know, go to the toilet. He's just *there,* chatting away happily in that strange language."

Andy rubbed a fingertip against the bridge of his nose and had a quick think. "Don't you find it a bit weird?"

"It's extremely weird," Nessie said. "He's kinda cute, though. I mean, in a devilish rogue sort of way." When no one answered, Nessie looked at her shoes and said, "Nevermind."

"I meant the timing," Sun said. "Right before you catch the batling, you also have a mysterious, non-human stranger turn up and ask for Andy?"

"The timing could be entirely coincidental," Dr. Chandelling said. "We can't find any correlation between the two. The batling has terrestrial relatives. Lucas, as you call him, is something else entirely. They don't seem to be related, at least, not organically."

"Maybe spiritually?" Nessie said. She'd apparently recovered from her embarrassment. "Many ancient texts delve into the war between light and darkness, good and evil. It's woven throughout history, regardless of culture or time. When the evil spirit shows up, a savior appears."

"You think the Manx man is the savior?" Andy asked.

Nessie shook her head. "He could be. But he also fits into the mold of a prophet. Someone who foretells of a savior. Remember... he gave us your name, Mr. Dennison-Jones."

Andy frowned.

If I'm the savior, then we're all doomed.

CHAPTER NINE

Who do they think they are?

Dr. Gornman paced the floor of Kane's office on level 2. The carpet beneath her feet was a deep pile and her heels caught every few steps, adding to her frustration.

I've dedicated the best part of ten years of my life to this facility. Is this any way to repay me? Letting outsiders come in and undermine me? Who does Kane think he is, chastising me in front of them? Without me his precious facility would grind to a halt. It's not like that incompetent, misogynist fool, Chandelling, could take charge if I decided to leave.

That's exactly what I should have done years ago. Left. With my experience I could work in any lab in the world. I only came here because I mistakenly thought I was doing some good in the world. But that was nothing but a fantasy. This isn't God's work. The Spiral is nothing but a prison—and like any prison it is ineffectual and does nothing to change the inmates. All we're doing is warehousing a bunch of creatures that could be of real benefit if we actually did something with them other than keep them in cages.

This whole place is a paean to old-fashioned thinking. A bunch of flashy new computers doesn't change that.

I could have gone somewhere else, where my skills would be appreciated, instead of deep down in this cesspool where nothing worthwhile ever happens.

But then, I would have missed out on these recent events...

"Dr. Gornman?" Kane entered the office and moved over to his desk. "Please, take a seat." He gestured to the chair opposite.

Gornman dumped herself down, folded her arms.

Kane leaned forward on his desk and sighed. "Look, Doctor. You are a valued member of this team and undoubtedly the brightest person here."

Gornman blinked. She wasn't about to be swayed by flattery. She knew she was smarter than anyone at the Spiral—she didn't need an antique General to tell her that.

"But when we have guests at this facility, it is our obligation to welcome them and to accommodate their needs."

Gornman stayed completely neutral.

A twinge of frustration—perhaps even anger—flashed across Kane's face. "The Dennison-Joneses are here at the request of the President via the Director of Homeland Security, who may I remind you is the Grand Registrar of the Order, like his father, and grandfather before him. We are sworn to follow his instructions to the letter. That is the oath you made, Dr. Gornman. Am I correct?"

"Yes."

"So you will work alongside the Dennison-Joneses and avoid acrimony. But most of all, you will never again question my authority or circumvent my command of this facility. Is that clear, Dr. Gornman?"

Gornman gave no answer.

"Is. That. Clear?"

Gornman said softly, "Yes, it's clear, General. I understand. I understand that my time here has amounted to absolutely nothing at all."

Kane remained sitting. He kept his tone calm. "You are an ordained knight of the most secretive organization in existence, with access to secrets beyond most people's imagination. But, as always, you are free to give that up. You can retire your membership and leave any time you want."

You wish I would. But I have other plans.

"I advise against that, however," Kane continued, "because your commitment here has not gone un-noted. I'm an old man, Dr. Gornman, and there are not as many Generals to replace me as there once were. The time of personnel-laden wars is over. Drones and computers have replaced flesh and courage. The Order does not have access to the human resources it once did."

Gornman stayed silent, letting the man talk. It was one of her strengths.

"You heard about Oklahoma? Their new Head of Facility?"

Gornman nodded. "Dr. Gary?"

Kane blinked slowly. "Yes, *Doctor* Gary. The order is changing its policies. It is no longer a given that a facility head position is only available to those who have served in the military. Before Dr. Gary was promoted, he was doing your job."

"Are you saying that I could be in charge here?"

Kane nodded. "I am saying that you most likely *will* be in charge when I'm gone. But only if you show that you can follow orders and respect the chain of command. The Senior Wardens won't accept someone questioning them."

Gornman took it in, made it fit into her head. Then she nodded. "I understand. I wasn't thinking about the bigger picture. I allowed my ego to take over. I felt like I wasn't being given the credit I was due."

"The thing about credit, Dr. Gornman, is that it takes a long time to accrue but can be lost in a heartbeat."

"I won't question you again."

"Good. You can go now."

Gornman stood up and hurried for the door.

"And Dr. Gornman," Kane said before she exited.

Gornman turned around. "Yes?"

"One more thing. I was reviewing some security footage, and saw you at Cell 4 with the faustling. You were holding pieces of paper up to the glass but not speaking."

That's because I didn't want you hearing me, you voyeuristic fossil. I knew you had nothing better to do than spy on your personnel.

"I was showing it some pictures, trying to gauge its intellect."

"What pictures?"

"A variety. Animals, landmarks, famous people. Just trying to provoke a response. Obviously it didn't work. Its first communication was with the Dennison-Joneses."

General Kane tapped his fingers together. "I see. Dismissed."

Gornman left the office, hiding her smile as she did.

CHAPTER TEN

Breakfast was as over-the-top as everything else in the Spiral, and Andy's stomach had been overwhelmed by the selection offered by the cafeteria buffet on level 4. Through the kind of anomaly only possible at breakfast buffets, he had somehow ended up with a bowl of muesli, a plate of eggs, several slices of bacon, some yogurt, and a banana. It was a strange selection, but he wasted no time in digging into it all.

Sun had opted for a lighter breakfast of an apple and two slices of toast.

Both of them had slept well; the bed in their suite being even softer than the one they had been given in the Coronado the night before. Now that a new day had begun, they were both ready to get to work.

"I can't believe how different this place is from Samhain." Andy said as Sun bit into her Granny Smith. "The produce alone is a revelation."

Samhain had fed its staff from two large freezers, with deliveries being sparse.

"I guess things have changed," she said. "Now the government hides its secrets in plain sight. They probably bring supplies in here every day and gag any attempts to bring attention to it.

The Press may as well have their paychecks signed directly by the US treasury these days."

Andy bit a strip of bacon in half. "I wouldn't doubt it. This place is pretty amazing, though. It must have cost billions."

"Let's just hope they spent it wisely."

Jerry came over with a plateful of sausages and a tall glass of orange juice. He was wearing a white T-shirt with STOPGOVERNMENTSECRETS.COM emblazoned across the chest, obviously an iron-on made with a desktop printer. He took a seat at their table and noticed Sun appraising his large stack of pork-links. He shrugged. "I'm cutting out carbs," he said, before tucking in like a starving caveman.

"There are carbs in the OJ," Andy said.

"I know. But those are liquid carbs, not food carbs."

Andy considered telling him there wasn't a difference, but decided there wasn't any point.

After devouring several of the dozen sausages, Jerry wiped his mouth with the back of his hand and sipped his juice. Then he pulled a face. "These sausages are tiny. The ones in England are big and fat, much nicer."

"Maybe they have a suggestion box," Sun offered.

Jerry took a big gulp of orange juice. "So all the rumors about Project Samhain, keeping ol' Scratch under lock and key, those are true?"

Andy put down his knife and fork and laced his fingers together in front of him, elbows on the table. "You know you're sworn to secrecy, right?"

Jerry nodded. "Big bloke named Rimmer came to see me last night, made me sign a stack of papers while he flexed his biceps, trying to look mean. Said if I ever said anything about this place to anyone, he'd make sure I ended up having an uncomfortable experience with that unicorn on subbasement 1."

Andy and Sun exchanged a glance. It felt strange to be talking about it, since they hadn't in so long, but Andy eventually said, "It's true."

"Was it actually the devil?"

Sun nodded. "It was like the batling in the cell on Level 5. Only a lot bigger."

"But was it Satan?"

"Let me put it this way," Andy said, pushing away his plate. "If Satan does exist, Bub was a prime candidate."

Concern crossed Jerry's face. "If it was, *is*, Satan, that means there's a heaven and hell, don't it?"

Sun said, "I don't know, Jerry. It could be."

"So we could actually be punished for eternity for things we've done in the past?"

"It depends on the religion and the dogma," Sun answered. "Is it true that you're wanted by the police back in the UK?"

Jerry's expression became even bleaker. "I robbed some money from a tosser. He had it coming."

"But you're wanted," Sun said. "Aren't your parents worried about you?"

Jerry started shovelling more sausages into his mouth, swallowing them down in loud gulps. When he was done he let out a long sigh. "I don't have any parents. My mom died last year of lung cancer and my dad… my dad is the 'tosser' I stole from."

"I'm sorry about your mother," said Sun. "You must really miss her."

Jerry nodded. "She was the only person that ever really cared about me—well, *her* and my best friend, Ben. But now he won't even talk to me after what I did."

"Why not? What did you do?" asked Sun.

"Never mind. I don't want to get into it. What are you guys up to today?"

Sun smiled, seemingly content not to push the subject. "We're heading back down to level 5," she said. "Did you want to tag along?"

Andy shot his wife a stare, but she ignored it.

Jerry's face lit up. "Yeah, I would really like to. Even if I can't tell anyone."

"Knowledge for the sake of knowledge," Sun said. "A noble pursuit."

Andy cleared his throat to gain the floor. "What we're doing is going to be very dangerous, Jerry. You need—"

"I won't be any trouble. I'll do whatever you tell me to. Just let me come." He stared at Andy for what seemed like ages and then said, "Please, man. I need this."

Andy sighed. "Okay, fine, but don't get in the way. And follow every direction we give you."

Jerry smiled and nodded.

"Okay," Sun said. "Looks like our new research team is ready to go. Let's head downstairs."

They left the cafeteria and headed down to level 5 via the large, buttonless elevator, calling out the level in order to do so. As they walked, they met General Kane in the corridor. He was standing outside one of the cells and glaring at whatever was inside. At one point he even stabbed his finger against the glass and raised his voice.

Kane saw them coming and stood to attention. "Ah, Mr. and Ms. Dennison-Jones. Good to see you up and about so early. Shows a good work ethic. And Mr. Preston, am I to understand that you will be accompanying them?"

"If that's okay," said Jerry. "I promise not to get in the way."

"Just remember what I said and behave yourself. Anything you do, I will hold the Dennison-Joneses accountable for. Bear that in mind."

Jerry nodded.

Andy glanced inside the nearby cell—cell number 5. It belonged to the werewolf creature. The animal seemed to be glaring intently at Kane, snarling as he did so.

"You two know each other?" Andy asked.

Kane turned and glared into the cell again. He prodded his finger at the glass and the werewolf snarled louder. "Me and Fido here have a history. When I first started at the Spiral, I made the mistake of going inside his enclosure to take some samples." He rolled up his left shirt cuff to reveal a gnarled streak of scar-tissue from his elbow to his wrist. "Not a mistake I'll make again."

"Can you change into a werewolf?" Jerry asked.

"What? No, of course not."

"Then it isn't a werewolf. It's just a big wolf."

"It doesn't really matter what he is. He's the last of his kind, so it won't be long until werewolves really are just a figment of people's imagination."

Jerry moved up closer against the glass. He looked inside at the snarling beast. "He's the last one?"

"Yes. There used to be more, but they grow old and die eventually. This one just turned eighty last month. Another thirty, forty years and he'll be dead and buried."

"Extinction shouldn't be allowed," Sun said, her veterinary background obviously speaking up. "Why haven't you tried to breed them?"

"There aren't any left to breed with." Kane moved up closer to the glass and knelt down so that his eyes were level with the creature's. "You hear that, Fido? Once you're gone, your entire species will be finished. No more mongrels like you."

The beast rumbled deep in its chest.

Jerry said, "Maybe he bit you because he doesn't like being locked up. Or being called *Fido*."

Kane shot him a stern glance, and the boy cowered.

Andy cleared his throat. "Where can we find you if we need you, General?"

Kane straightened up and adjusted his shirt. "My office is on level 2." He strode off down the hall without another word.

Andy looked into the cell. The werewolf had stopped snarling and had padded away towards the back of the cell. There was a bundle of blankets and what looked like some rubber chew toys there.

"Dude doesn't like Wolfie," said Jerry. "Not surprised he chomped on that old fart. Don't blame him for being grouchy when they lock him up like Hannibal Lector and tell him that his whole race is about to become extinct. That shit was cold."

Sun nodded. "I understand that these creatures are considered dangerous, but if General Kane escaped with just a bite on the arm, he got off lucky. A wolf this big could have bitten him in half."

Andy shrugged his shoulders. "The guy's been here for years. Who knows what these animals have been responsible for in that time? Maybe everything in the Spiral really is evil. We only just got here. Let's keep an open mind."

Sun gave him a sideways glance. "Evil? Like that family of tiny imps upstairs? I would be surprised if they were any more evil or dangerous than foxes or badgers. They're just animals. Animals that the church once decided it didn't like the look of and shoved underground. Wouldn't be the first time the Catholic Church buried something."

"Sun," Andy said. "We know evil exists, right?"

"If you want to get into a philosophical discussion of evil, Andy, we can leave out animals."

"Bub wasn't evil?"

"He was selfish. A murderer. He understood the misery he caused because he was self-aware. But you can't apply that line of thinking to a wolf or a spider looking for a meal or defending itself."

"You'd think differently if you were trapped in its web," Andy said.

"What are you saying?"

"I'm saying it's too soon to go all Greenpeace when we haven't seen what any of these animals are capable of. Maybe Wolfie here is really a cuddly Corgi in his heart, but let's give the two thousand year old secret society a little bit of credit before we start petting him, okay?"

Andy thought he'd angered his wife, but after a small hesitation she nodded.

Dr. Chandelling appeared at the end of the hallway. He waved a hand at them excitedly as he jogged towards them. "Ah, you're all here. Wonderful. Eager to get started, I'll bet."

Sun waved back. "Good morning, doctor."

"Good morning. Do you have your access fobs yet?"

Andy pulled the blue rubber disk from his pocket and examined it. "If you mean this thing, then, yeah."

"Good. It will give you access to the cells if you punch in your code, but don't do anything without informing General Kane and getting armed security guard assistance. That's how we do things since the General's, um, accident." Chandelling gave a sideways glance into the werewolf cell.

"I think that guy is more of a cat person," Jerry said.

"Yes, General Kane has a somewhat troubled relationship with our resident *Canini*. Working in the Spiral can place a strain on the strongest of people, but that's a discussion for another day. Were you still intending to speak with the Manx man first, before the batling?"

Andy nodded. "We're heading there now. He's still in the cell at the end of the corridor?"

"He certainly is. Come on, I'll take you folks over."

They headed down the corridor towards the door where Dr. Chandelling had entered. Inside the final cell, Lucas was standing up against the glass, waiting as if he knew they were coming.

"Good morning, Dr. Chandelling. Andy. Jerry. Sun. How was your morning fry-up? Just toast for you, Sun-lass?"

Sun's eyes widened. "Can you read my mind, Lucas?"

The man laughed. "Do I need to, when there are bread crumbs on your shirt?"

Sun looked down, then brushed herself off.

"Why are you here, Lucas?" Andy said. "Do you like being locked up?"

Lucas smiled. "Who says I'm locked up?"

"You can leave any time you want?"

Lucas nodded. "I could be anywhere. I chose to be here."

"Why?" asked Andy. "Why are you here?"

Lucas grinned ear to ear. "I'm here to watch what you do, Andy. It all depends on you."

Andy felt himself get goosebumpy again. "What does?"

"Armageddon," Lucas said. "And I got meself a front row seat."

CHAPTER ELEVEN

Kane sat down in his office and poured himself a whiskey. He always enjoyed having guests at the Spiral, it broke up the monotony of seeing the same old faces day in day out. But usually the guests were members of Deus Manus from other facilities. Andy and Sun Dennison-Jones were ordered to be here. It was obvious they'd rather be somewhere else, and Kane agreed they should be. It was hard enough maintaining control with eager volunteers, let alone begrudging ones.

The employees at the Spiral were allowed to come and go freely, but they were sworn to secrecy and were usually given some grand fiction to tell their families about why they worked away from home so much. It was really up to them what cover they used when leaving the base, so long as it stood up and was never questioned. Since the base itself was in the middle of a Mexican national park, commuting required a helicopter, but anyone who needed a weekend off or a vacation could easily put in a request.

Kane had not left the facility in years.

His work had long ago consumed him. The world had moved on and modernized to a point that he no longer recognized it. The last time he had ventured outside he'd visited his niece in Anaheim. It had been incredibly awkward.

People had changed. Everyone from children to grandparents now walked around with chirping phones attached to their heads. Computers had invaded the home of every family and nobody spoke to one another anymore. Even the roads had gone bad; clogged up with insane drivers honking their horns and barging in front of one another. No. No, thank you. Kane didn't want to be a part of *that* world. He was meant for higher things, positions of quiet honor. He was meant to be right where he was, in the Spiral, doing God's work.

Kane was also concerned by the presence of the English boy. Not only was he a foreign national, but he had a checkered history and seemed of no use to anyone. They couldn't induct him into the Order, or trust him in any way. Kane had no idea what to do with young Jeremy Preston. But he would have to be dealt with, sooner or later.

Everything had to be dealt with, sooner or later.

Kane grabbed the phone on his desk and dialled an outside line. The call went through to his counterpart at the Texas facility.

"Kane, good to hear from you, old friend. How are things your end?"

"Good to hear from you, too, Robson. Things are clockwork over here. You know the saying: I'd rather be bored than fighting for my life."

"What about your unexpected guest? The Manx guy. Any news?"

"He's speaking English now, but not saying much. But the Manx man is not why I'm calling. I wanted to check in with you about the faustling—or the 'batling' as my people have taken to calling it. Not the one we have here; the one you have at your site."

"It's still here. Level 5. Safe and sound."

"Any new developments?"

"No. It killed that cattle rancher downstate, but since it arrived here it's been downright tame. Almost as if..."

"Yes?"

"I dunno. It's almost as if it *wants* to be here. I know you shot yours to pieces before bringing it in, but this one didn't even try to put up a fight. It just sat there, by the entrance, and let itself get caught."

Kane slouched back in his chair, switched the phone from one side to the other. "You hear from Tulsa and Vancouver?"

"Yeah. They still have their faustlings safe and secure, too. I hear that England's got one now as well."

Kane lurched forwards. "The Kent facility?" That made more than a dozen sites now after Chile finding one in the hills of Santiago. "What are these things up to?"

"I don't know, old buddy. I hear you have the survivors of Samhain with you. To tell you the truth the rest of us are all relying on you for answers. I've been trying to track down that other survivor of Samhain, Dr. Frank Belgium. Guy seems to have fallen off the grid. You're the only one with any kind of information on these things, thanks to your guests."

Kane sighed. "I'm not sure I'll get anything useful from them. Samhain was a disaster and they were partly responsible. I don't have much faith in their abilities."

"Still, you have a better chance than the rest of us. It's clear that these things are converging on our facilities. There has to be a reason."

Kane rubbed at his chin and suddenly felt very tired and ancient. "I agree. I guess we're just going to have to wait and see what happens. Stay safe, Robson."

"You, too."

But when General Kane hung up the phone, he didn't feel safe. For the first time since he'd been attacked by that damned wolf years ago, Kane was afraid.

CHAPTER TWELVE

"Why do you want to talk to me?" Andy asked the Manx man. "How do you even know who I am?"

Lucas was still grinning. "Oh, I know you well enough, lad. I know the very core of you. The brokenness and fear that you've carried with you ever since you went down that wretched hole in the desert."

"You know about Samhain?"

"I know about lots of things. Everything from where to find the world's best pint of bitter—that would be a little place in Scotland called the Clachaig Inn by the way—to what color underpants the Pope wears." Lucas chuckled. "Purple, if you can believe it."

"Fascinating," Dr. Chandelling mumbled as he scribbled on a notepad.

Andy put his hands on the glass. "So are you going to be forthcoming and tell us the secrets of the universe?"

Lucas placed his palms against Andy's. "I'm afraid I have to let you work things out for yourself, lad. I'm here to witness, and occasionally advise. But I'm not here to interfere."

"Why not?"

"What is it those bouncy black fellas say in their delightful rap songs? Don't hate the playa, hate the game. The rules have already been defined, the wheels already in motion. They see me rollin, they hatin."

Jerry moved up beside Andy and folded his skinny arms across his chest. "Are you like a ghost or something? Why can't they run any tests on you?"

Lucas turned his attention to Jerry and raised a fuzzy eyebrow. "Ah, young Jeremy Preston. Did you get hold of Ben, like I said?"

Jerry took a step backwards. "How the hell do you even know...?"

"Don't worry, lad. Ben forgives you. Deep down, he forgives you. The two of you have been through a lot. Even more than you know or remember."

Jerry frowned and turned away.

"It's a valid question," Sun told Lucas. "What exactly are you? You're *not* human."

"Few things in this place are, lass."

"So what are you?"

"I am what I am. One of God's creations, same as you, same as him."

Dr. Chandelling mumbled something to himself, his tongue peeking out the corner of his mouth as he took notes.

"You know for sure that God exists?" Andy asked.

"We can discuss the nature of God, but I'm not sure you'd be able to grasp it." He glanced at Sun. "Any more than you would the nature of evil. Our perceptions become our realities, our reality clouds our perceptions, and our ideas and fears all get blended into the mixture, so by the end of the discussion you'd be more confused than when you started. But do you really want to talk about God, or about the fella a few doors down?"

Lucas glanced sideways as if he could see through the cement walls of his cell to where the batling was.

"Bub?" Andy asked.

"I know all about that cheeky little monkey, Bub. He had you believe he was a little grander than he really is."

"You're saying Bub isn't dangerous?"

Lucas huffed. "Oh, no, that egotistical feck will quite happily wipe humanity off the face of the earth. And he's strong and sly enough to do it. I'm just telling you not to give him more credit than he's due. There is indeed a God, even though he's mightily misrepresented and misunderstood. But there are other things, too. Things you have within these very walls that were nothing to do with God's plan. God isn't the only creator in this world."

Andy's eyes narrowed. "Bub."

"Aye, Bub has his thumbprint on a few of the world's more unpleasant surprises. People ask why God lets bad things happen to good people. The answer is because this world does not belong entirely to Him. There's a power struggle. A battle between black, white, and every other color in between." Lucas lowered his voice, and his bright expression soured. "This earth is a warzone—and the enemy is about to make a big move. You could think of this as D-Day, only this time it's the Germans who are storming the beaches."

"And which side are you on?" Sun asked.

"I'm in the stands, watching with a pint and a bag of crisps. But if it matters, I'm rooting for you folks. I've grown fond of you over the years. Sweet little things that you are."

"Why not help us?" asked Andy.

"This isn't my fight, lad. Tis not my place."

Sun folded her arms. "Fine, but you still haven't said what you want with my husband. You called him here."

"Aye, I did. Whatever happens deep down in this hole in the ground is going to be on him. I'm just here to see the game play out. It should be very entertaining."

"What about your history?" Andy said. "Are you from the Isle of Man?"

"I was. Once upon a time. Among other places."

"Where have you lived?"

"Everywhere."

"How many languages do you speak?"

Lucas beamed. "A few more than you."

"How old are you?" Andy asked in Turkic.

"Very old. But don't I look good?"

"Are you human?" in Russian.

"No. But close enough to get through airport security."

"What are you?" in Cherokee.

"I came before man. Some say with the dawn."

"What is your real name?" in Portuguese.

"I've gone by many names. *Lucas* has suited me for a while now."

"Is this really Armageddon?" in Korean.

"That depends on how well you handle yourself."

"Can you die?" in Sanskrit.

"That depends on the definition of death. Mr. Dennison-Jones, might I suggest that you pay less attention to me, and more to the little bugger plotting to destroy humanity?" Lucas made a head gesture toward the batling's cell. "To use a sports analogy, you're wasting time talking to the spectators when you should be out on the field, playing ball."

Andy tried more questions, but Lucas sat down and smiled politely, staying silent, as he had yesterday. It was disappointing, not only because Lucas obviously knew more than he was letting on, but because Andy had many questions about ancient languages that he guessed this man—or whatever he was—could answer. Lucas was, quite frankly, astonishing.

The quartet eventually quit trying with the enigma in front of them, and went to visit the Spiral's newest occupant. The one Andy had dreaded seeing again.

They headed twenty feet down the corridor until they were face-to-face with the batling. It hovered before them like a hummingbird, leathery wings flapping with tremendous speed. Like Bub, its metabolism was obviously extremely efficient.

"Dennnissson."

It spoke in a deep voice, with a harsh rasp to it, a sound not dissimilar to raking autumn leaves. Andy heard that voice often in his nightmares. It wasn't any more pleasant hearing it again for real.

Andy cleared his throat and said, "It's Dennison-Jones now. Are you Bub?"

"Yeeeessssssssssss."

Though it was much smaller than the demon they'd encountered at Samhain, it was a perfect replica. Same hooves, same horns, same teeth. It also instilled the same fear. Andy had a powerful urge to run away, as fast and as far as possible.

"You remember us?" Sun asked. She looked just as skittish as Andy felt.

Bub's eyes widened. Its pupils were horizontal, like that of a goat. *"Weeeeee reeeemeeeember."*

"How is that possible?" Andy asked. "How can it retain Bub's memories?"

"Epigenetics," Sun answered after a moment. "It is possible to inherit learned behaviors, including memory. Experiments have been done on mice and goldfish to prove it."

Bub's tongue, scaled like a snake, slithered out and licked its open eyes.

"Why are you here?" Andy asked.

"Finis enim prope est," the demon answered.

Andy couldn't help but wince a little. He translated for the others. "Latin. *The end is near.* How many of you are there?"

"Weeee are many. Weeeeee are leeegion."

"*We* are getting seriously creeped out," Jerry said, taking a step back.

"What are you feeding it?" Sun asked Dr. Chandelling.

"Raw meat."

"Has it tried to reanimate the meat?"

"No. So far we've only given it frozen hamburger."

"Smart," Sun said.

"Why is that smart?" Jerry asked.

"Freezing bursts the cell walls in meat. That would be difficult to bring back to life. Plus, the grinding would make it even harder for Bub to restructure the tissue."

"If I saw a hamburger jumping around, I'd freak out," Jerry said. "In fact, I think I'm already freaking out."

"Tell us your plan, Bub," Andy said to the demon.

"Humanityyyyyyy is over. Bellum internecinum."

"What does that mean?" Sun asked. "Bellum..."

"Bellum internecium. *War of extermination.*"

"How?" Sun asked.

The demon hovered, saying nothing.

"Maybe he needs a little radiation therapy," Andy said. "And a plutonium enema."

"Your deaths will beeeeeeee painful, Dennisonssssssss. We will eeeeeeeat you allliiiive."

Dr. Chandelling looked up from his notes. "The faustling hadn't spoken until you arrived. But if it retains the memories and intellect of the demon from Samhain, it's incredibly intelligent."

"It's smarter than we are," Andy said.

"And uglier," Jerry said.

The batling bashed itself into the glass. Everyone jumped back.

"Bite your tongue, boy. Or weeeeee shall bite it for yoooooooou."

"Go wank yourself," Jerry said, the false bravado obvious, but admirable. "You're in there, I'm out here, so bite me."

Bub smashed into the glass again, so hard its pig snout burst open in a bloody mess.

Jerry screamed falsetto.

Bub grinned, rows of jagged teeth stretching wide, and began to lick its blood off the window.

"I say we irradiate it until it talks, then kill it," Andy said.

"Seconded," said Sun.

"Yoooooooou can't kill meeeeeeee, Dennisons."

"Denison-Jones."

"It bleeds," Jerry said. "If it bleeds, we can kill it." Everyone looked at him. "You guys didn't see *Predator*, I take it?" No one answered. Jerry grimaced. "Christ, doesn't anyone watch movies anymore? We're right in the middle of *Cabin in the Woods* right now and I keep expecting to see Joss Whedon pissing about behind a camera."

The batling descended slightly, hovered at head height beside Dr. Chandelling. *"Hellooooooo doctoooooor. Caaaaan you heeeeeear usssssssss?"*

Chandelling dropped his notepad on the floor. His pockmarked jaw dropped open. "W-what did you say?"

"Hoooooooow isssssss your heeeeeeearing? Think it will laaaaaaaaast?"

"Doctor, are you okay?" Sun asked.

"Yes, I'm... I'm fine. If you'll excuse me I have to go and compile this data." Dr. Chandelling picked his notepad off the floor and hurried away.

Bub began to make a croaking sound, like a sick bullfrog.

"Is it choking on something?" Jerry said.

Andy shook his head. "It's laughing."

"I hate this thing. How big was the other one?"

"About ten feet tall."

"Jesus. It's a wonder you got out of there alive."

Bub banged into the glass again, hard enough to make everyone jump.

"Yoooooou won't thissssssss time," the demon said.

Chapter Thirteen

Dr. Chandelling holed up in his office and closed the door. The first thing he did was open up his prized StereoMatic 564 record player and put on the soothing tones of Bing Crosby. Chandelling had been born in the 70s but had grown up to the backdrop of his father's records. The music of his own generation had lacked the sophistication and class of the decades before. Russ Columbo. Peggy Lee. Frank Sinatra. Ethel Merman. Perry Como. Matt Monro. Ella Fitzgerald. Rudy Vallee.

Music that eased the mind and healed the soul. *Ear Valium*, he called it.

And Chandelling knew how lucky he was to be able to enjoy it.

As a youth, he was plagued with ear problems. Chandelling had had constant ear infections—otitis media with effusion—aka *glue ear*. During his first seven years of life, he barely heard half of it. A combination of never-ending antibiotics, and two tympanostomy tubes, finally restored his hearing, but he'd missed so much school he was behind in his studies until he caught up at age twelve. Other children continued to make fun of him through high school—glue ear would discharge fluid, which was smelly and gross and not the fast track to popularity.

Chandelling had taken solace in his old-fashioned music, and finally came into his own in college He'd grown enough that his Eustachian tubes no longer clogged constantly, which not only brought his hearing back to within normal ranges, but alleviated the social stigma. Though Chandelling continued to be shy and wary of people, he'd done well at the university, eventually earning his doctorate. The days of pain and humiliation were long gone.

So how did that creature know about his biggest fear?

Chandelling sat down at his desk and flopped into the soft Italian leather of his office chair, watching his goldfish, Satchmo, swim around in his aquarium. As the music played, Chandelling thought about the batling. Bub. Very few of the other occupants of the Spiral talked. That suited Chandelling just fine. He didn't like to talk, either. He maintained professional, if aloof, relationships with his co-workers, and hadn't discussed his personal life with any of them, with the exception of Dr. Gornman's required weekly therapy sessions. And those were supposed to be confidential, like speaking to a lawyer or a priest.

Perhaps Bub could read minds. Or was somehow supernatural.

The track changed to *Don't Fence Me In*, but it failed to sooth Chandelling like it usually did because of the last thing Bub had said to him.

"Hoooooooow isssssss your heeeeeeearing? Think it will laaaaaaaaast?"

Chandelling touched his ear, and couldn't help but believe he'd just been threatened. And the threat was not only serious, it was legitimate.

CHAPTER FOURTEEN

While Andy and Sun verbally jousted with the hellspawn, Jerry decided to walk up and down the corridor and check out the various other creatures imprisoned behind the glass walls. It was scary, for sure, but it seemed to be the 'okay' kind of scary, like a horror film or a rollercoaster. They were locked up. He was safe.

Supposedly.

He passed by a misshapen bear-like creature with long arms and ropey white body hair. It looked like what Jerry imagined a yeti to be like, but the text on the LED screen read: *Grendaline Historicum.* Long yellow claws. Long yellow teeth. Tiny curled horns, like a ram. It watched Jerry, its bright blue eyes following him as he passed

Another cell gave off a stench worse than rotting meat. *Homo Romero.* It was humanoid, green with decay, and lumbering around like the living dead. Which, Jerry guessed, was exactly what it was.

"So are you a slow zombie, like in all the 80s Lucio Fulci movies, or a quick one like *28 Days Lat*er and the *Dawn of the Dead* remake?"

No reply.

"Do you eat whole people or just brains?"

No reply.

"Can you even hear me?"

The zombie leapt at the glass, much faster than Jerry would have guessed, and grunted out, *"Braaaaains!"*

"Okay, questions answered. Cheers. You can go back to your lumbering now."

The next one actually made Jerry laugh. It was nothing more than a banana, lying in the middle of the cell. According to the LED, it was called Mu.

"What do you do?"

The banana didn't reply.

"Why are you on subbasement 5? How are you dangerous? In case someone walks on you and slips?"

"Nobody likes you," the banana said. "You're a loser and you're ugly and stupid. It's no wonder you're a virgin."

"Hey! That's mean!"

"Ugly. Small cock, too."

"Stop it."

"Ugly virgin with a baby dick. And such a disappointment to your family. Whoops, no family."

Jerry's eyebrows furrowed and his hands involuntarily clenched into fists. "Enough!"

"Nobody likes you, and if you ever want to have sex you'll need to pay for it. Double the asking price."

"You fucking dick!"

"Sticks and stones, ugly," the banana answered. "You can try some beauty sleep, but it won't help."

Jerry quickly moved on, feeling pretty bad about himself. No wonder Mu was on the bottom level. That banana could really say some terrible things.

The most frightening creature on subbasement 5 was the thing in cell 6 named Nosferatus Hominic. The monster looked mostly like a man, but its jaws were more like a shark's with rows upon rows of lethal dagger-like teeth, so many they tore through its lips and cheeks. When it saw Jerry it threw itself at the glass, clawing and snapping, its black eyes crazed with bloodlust. Jerry was glad for the six-inch barrier separating them.

In the next cell was Wolfie, or *Lycanus Canini* as the LED display noted. When the hairy, dog-like creature saw Jerry, it too came closer to the glass, but it wasn't in a threatening manner like the occupant of cell 6. Its breath fogged the window.

"Hey, there." Jerry placed a hand against it, as if petting the beast's snout. "Do you want to eat me? Or are you just bored?"

Wolfie sat down, its ears pricking up like a border collie's.

"Yeah, I think you're just bored. How long they have you caged-up down here? Years, I bet."

The creature let out a soft whine. It was somewhere between a begging sound and one of barely-contained excitement.

"I used to have an old dog named Betsie." Part of Jerry knew it was silly talking to a giant wolf, but he didn't care. "My mom was always working and I was at school, so Betsie would get left alone a lot. Whenever I walked through the door she would go completely barmy. She would run around the flat back and forth between the rooms, whining and yelping. When she finally calmed down she would sit on my lap with her legs in the air and I would tickle her belly. I can't imagine how miserable she would have been if we'd locked her up and just never came home."

Wolfie sat down, wagging his tail.

"I don't think it's right that they have you down here. You don't look dangerous to me. You may have bitten that General dude, but he's an asshole."

To Jerry's surprise, Wolfie let out a bark. It was the friendly, yippy bark that Betsie had used to make when he would come home from school.

Jerry grinned. "Dude, I would so adopt you if I could. Ben would shit his pants if he saw me walking you around the block. Oh yeah, right. You don't know about Ben."

Wolfie began to wag its enormous tail.

"Ben's been my best friend since, like, forever. We grew up together, were in the same class in first school. I think I used to get on his nerves sometimes. He was smart, had his shit together, you know? I've always been a bit of a disaster zone. He always stuck by me, though, through thick and thin. Thing is, he wasn't just my best friend, he was my half-brother. Only he didn't know about it. My mom had an affair with his dad when they were both really young. Mom got pregnant but he didn't want anything to do with it—the *prick*. He was getting married to another woman who was pregnant with Ben at the time. So I grew up without a dad. Through some crazy coincidence, I ended up making friends with Ben on our first day of school. Of course, I didn't know then that we were brothers. It wasn't until I was older that my mother came clean—although it took a bottle of vodka to make her tell me. I was shocked at the time; upset, you know? But in the end I decided to keep it to myself. Ben and I were so close anyway. What difference would telling him have made?"

Wolfie whined again. Ben stroked the glass.

"Ben's dad used to treat me like shit whenever he caught me hanging around with Ben. Used to warn him that I would bring him down. Who he was really slagging off, though, was my mom. He had money, a business, a nice little family. My mom had me and a crummy council flat. Ben's dad—huh, *my* dad—looked down on me and my mom like shit on his shoe from the moment I was born." Jerry took a moment to catch his breath. He was breathing hard and felt anger in his veins. "When my mom died he didn't even come to the fucking funeral. I was so mad." Jerry took a breath and let it out in a bitter chuckle. "I showed *him*, though."

Someone stepped out of the elevator at the end of the corridor and startled Jerry. It was a young bird with auburn hair and pale skin. Her red lips pursed when she smiled at him.

"Oh, hi. Sorry," he said. "I know I'm not supposed to be walking around here on my own, but the Dennison-Joneses are just down the hall."

"It's okay. Don't see what harm you could do anyway. General Kane is just being overly cautious. Being a hardass is kind of his job."

"Yeah, I suppose so. Doesn't mean I have to like him."

The girl giggled. "I'm Nessie. Pleased to meet you. You must be Jerry."

Jerry took her hand. It was soft and small, like holding a rosebud. "Pleased to meet you too. Take it you've been warned about me?"

"Nope. Dr. Chandelling just told me that we had a young Englishman on site. Love your accent by the way. Reminds me of my daddy a little. He was from Belfast. Not the same, I know, but it's still a nice change from all the American accents I'm used to hearing."

Jerry smiled. He wanted to say something funny, or at least interesting, but nothing came out.

"So, what are you up to?" Nessie asked him.

Jerry shrugged his shoulders. He wondered if she'd heard him talking to the creature in the cell. If she had, he was embarrassed about it. No point hiding it, though. Last thing to do in a secret underground government facility was act suspiciously. "I was just chatting with Wolfie here."

Nessie raised an eyebrow and gave him a lopsided grin that was extremely cute. "Wolfie?"

"Yeah, better than calling him *Lycanus Canini*."

"I suppose you're right. Don't know who came up with all the names, but they do lack personality. Wolfie here can be quite playful. I smuggled a few chew toys in and he seems to like them. Don't tell the General, though. They don't get along."

Jerry smiled. He was glad there was at least one person looking out for Wolfie. "So, erm, is there anything I can help you with? I'd like to make myself useful around here."

Nessie chewed the side of her mouth and seemed to think. "You can help me do some research in the library, but I'm only going to be in there for an hour or so. *Fatal Autonomy* is on later and I never miss it."

Jerry laughed. He was surprised that someone so bookish could be a diehard fan of a flaky TV cop drama. "You actually like that show?"

Ness nodded enthusiastically. "I love it." She put her hands up in front of her. "I know I know, it's kind of lame, but I just find it fascinating. I hear they base the killers on real life psychopaths."

"I think that fat lady cop is annoying, but the private eye hero is pretty cool, I guess."

"I know. He's so... dark. I wonder if he's like that in real life."

"Do you do that, too?" Jerry asked. "Whenever I see a show I like, I wonder how they'd act in person. I mean, I know Bruce Willis doesn't kill terrorists for real, but I wonder if he really is tough and funny."

"I love Bruce Willis. I've seen the *Die Hard* movies a billion times."

"Or Sigourney Weaver."

"Aliens!" Nessie squealed. "That scene where she has Newt and they walk into the queen alien's nest, surrounded by hatching eggs. I could never be that brave."

"But here you are, surrounded by monsters. That's pretty brave."

Nessie blushed. "It's not the same."

"It's not the same because that was a movie, and you're really here. Seriously, how would your friends freak out if they knew you were giving chew toys to a giant wolf?"

Nessie's smile fell away, and she looked at her clipboard. "I, uh, am going to go watch my show now."

"Maybe I'll give the show another chance," said Jerry, feeling his mouth go dry but not knowing why. He also needed to go to the toilet real bad all of a sudden.

Nessie didn't say anything.

Tell her you want to come with.

Come on, chicken. Tell her!

"Mind if I, um, tag along, watch it with you?"

"Uh, yeah. Sure. There's a TV in the library. It's at the end of this floor. It's pretty cool, if you're into that kind of thing. Lots and lots of old, rare books."

"Sounds neat."

Neat? Lame! What am I, eight years old?

Nessie smiled. "Yeah, it's actually super neat. Come on. I'll lead the way."

CHAPTER FIFTEEN

"What about co-existing peacefully?" Andy asked the demon.

For more than twenty minutes, he and Sun had been trying to get through Bub's surface malevolence, only to realize how deep the evil actually was.

"*Nooooooo peeeeeace.*"

"You have the ability to heal, to resurrect. You could save millions."

"*Humans are vermin. Doooooo you invite roaches to dine at yooooour taaaaable? Or doooo yoooooooooooou squaaaaaash them?*"

Perturbed, Andy said, "Our species could learn from each other."

"*Your speeeeeeecies will be myyyyyyy slaves.*"

"So you say. But I can't help but notice that you're the one locked up."

"*Foooooooor noooooooowwwww.*"

"You're really hung up on this evil trip, aren't you, Bub?" Sun asked.

"*Eeeevil isssss subjective. There are twoooo opposing forcessssss. Order and disorder. Both require enerrrrrgy.*"

"So you're disorder?"

"I am become death, the destroyer of wooorrrrrrlds."

Andy recognized the odd-sounding quote. It was last said famously by Robert Oppenheimer, after creating the atomic bomb, quoting the Bhagavad Gita.

"But you can also create," Sun said, "and give life. They say a cheetah can't change its spots, but you literally can. Why the fatalism?"

Bub's body began to twist and contort, and he abruptly turned himself inside out in a spectacle of splitting skin and cracking bone and churning organs, blood and tissue exploding out in all directions. Then his body began to reassemble itself into something human.

Something human, and recognizable.

Bub had transformed himself into their friend, Dr. Frank Belgium.

"Frank?" Sun asked.

Frank blinked. He was nude, a thin sheen of blood covering him. "Andy?" he said. "Sun? Is is is that really you?"

"It's not Frank," Andy said, backing away. "It's a trick. Bub can change into things, remember?"

Frank put a bloody palm on the glass. "Sun, you know it's me? Right? We we we worked together a long time."

It looked and sounded exactly like Frank. It even copied his strange speech patterns. Andy's heart rate doubled, and he felt as if he'd been slapped.

"Why am I I I locked up?" Frank said. "And and and naked?"

Frank began to move his hands over his body, rubbing in the blood like moisturizing cream.

"You look so so so pretty, Sun."

Andy stepped away from the glass as the Frank thing began to stroke itself. Sun cleaved onto Andy's side.

"Let's get away from it," Sun whispered.

"NO!" Frank bellowed. He stretched out his arm, and then it bent backwards at the elbow with a sharp *CRACK!*

Both Sun and Andy gasped, and as Frank screamed in pain he held up his hand, fingers splayed out, and each digit bent back, as if an invisible hand was breaking them one by one.

Then his leg snapped at the femur, a ninety degree angle that made the bone burst through the skin.

Frank continued to masturbate as his left foot began to twist, crackling like a bag of chips, rotating a full three hundred and sixty degrees until the skin split. His screaming became interspersed with bits of hysterical laughter.

Then his eyes popped out and hung on his cheeks by the stringy optic nerves.

That was their cue to leave.

"You won't essssscape me, Dennisonsssssss," the demon was back to using its normal voice. *"You won't essssccccccaaaaaaape."*

"That wasn't Frank," Andy told his bride as they hurried down the hall.

"I know."

"It's just Bub messing with our heads."

"I know."

"I still feel sick."

"Me, too."

Then they both bent over and puked breakfast onto the floor.

"What? Is married life *that* bad? There's still time for a quickie annulment."

Andy looked in the direction of the voice, and saw a cell occupied by a banana.

"Let's get out of here," Andy said.

"Don't leave," the banana replied. "We'll have a bunch of fun. Get it? *Bunch*? That is, until everyone here dies. Want to hear my maniacal laugh? Bwahahahahaha! EVERYONE IS GOING TO DIE!!!!"

They took the elevator to level four, and ended up in the conference room.

Sergeant Rimmer was sitting at a long table, watching his computer monitor while texting on his pager. Andy glanced at the screen and saw it showed live security camera feeds from several cells in the Spiral, including Bub's.

"I saw what that demon just did," Rimmer said. "You two okay?"

"Yeah," Andy said, still feeling sick.

"Did you learn anything new?"

"A banana insulted our marriage," Sun said. "Then told us we're all going to die."

"Oh. Mu." Rimmer shook his head. "He's some sort of multidimensional being. Supposedly can be everywhere at once, throughout all of spacetime and the multiverse. At least, that's what he says. He came in with a shipment of fresh produce and started insulting everybody. Teased Nessie to tears. We put him on subbasement 5 because no one likes him. I guess you could say he's fruit gone bad."

"Is he dangerous?"

"I don't think he's harmed anyone, physically. But some of his jabs are pretty pointed. He'd be really good doing one of those celebrity roasts."

Andy changed the subject. "Other than General Kane being bitten by the wolf, have there been any other problems at the facility?"

"No. Hasn't been a serious security breach on my watch for almost five years."

"How long have you been here?" Andy asked.

"Almost five years."

"So what did you do before that?"

"I was a Sergeant in the Army Rangers. On the ground during the invasion of Iraq."

"How did you end up here?"

"Stumbled upon something I shouldn't have."

Andy leaned forwards. "Really? Care to share?" He was less interested in the story and more interesting in getting the image of Frank Belgium out of his head.

Rimmer put down his pen and looked up at them. "I suppose I can tell you. Not that I particularly enjoy telling it."

Sun and Andy said nothing.

So Rimmer continued. "My unit was in the south-western Iraqi desert near Rutba. We were looking for a chemical weapons processing plant that Intel told us was in the area. We had managed to flip a guy in the Republican Guard. He'd explained that Saddam had several WMDs ready to launch the very moment he was declared dead or captured—kind of like a dead man's switch. One of the Army's primary objectives was ensuring that this was not true, or neutralising the devices in the case that it was. The plant south of Rutba was our first and only lead. We didn't want Saddam to know that we were on to his plan, so command sent in three Ranger units. My unit was in the area directly south of Rutba. So far we'd found nothing but desert, but we had an itinerary and we weren't going to bug-out until we hit every point on our map. But when a sandstorm came in, it ruined our radio equipment and left us all turned around on ourselves. I could have gone north towards the road and called the mission in as a bust, but I made the decision to keep heading south instead. We were in the middle of the desert, a perfect place to hide a facility. Turns out I was right."

"You found the chemical plant?" Sun asked.

"I thought so at the time. My unit came upon a group of single-story buildings surrounded by a half dozen 3-tonners—big trucks. There was no natural cover so we dropped down low and approached from two sides. We were sure we were about to strike a mighty blow for America." Rimmer blinked slowly as the story seemed to play out in his mind. "They opened fire on us before we even got halfway. I didn't realise at the time, but the area was covered by thermal imaging and radar. They saw us coming a mile away. By the time I even knew what was happening, my entire unit had been slaughtered and I'd taken a bullet in the neck. I thought I was done for, even started to pray. Bleeding out into the sand, I thought about all the wives and families of the men I'd just led to their deaths. I was angry, ashamed, and a whole bunch of other screwed-up emotions beginning with A. Even though I was dying, I wanted to get up and scream, to fight for my men. But every time I tried, my body would not move. Last thing I saw before I lost consciousness was two men running towards me. Neither of them were Iraqi soldiers."

"So what happened?" Andy asked. "Who were they?"

"Deus Manus. I'd stumbled upon the Iraqi chapter of the Order. They called their facility *Jahannam.*"

Andy translated the word in his head. "*Jahannam?* The Islamic concept of Hell?"

Rimmer nodded. "They brought me underground and locked me in a cell, vetted me for almost six months. Ran psych tests on me, background checks, the works. Checked up on every person I knew. After enough time had passed, the US government listed me as KIA—as well as all of the men in my unit, whose bodies they had relocated a hundred-miles north of where they actually died. That's when Deus Manus inducted me. I trained for a few years at the Iraqi facility and eventually transferred here, back home. This was my first major gig and I've been here ever since."

"You ever regret being here?"

Rimmer sniffed. "I regret *how* I got here, on the backs of my dead squad mates, but I don't regret being here now. It's important work. The things we keep down here are dangerous. After what happened in Samhain you both obviously understand that."

Andy and Sun said nothing. Rimmer's pager on his belt beeped, and he checked it.

"A pager?" Andy said, trying to alleviate some of the tension. "With all of this tech, isn't that old school?"

"Radio waves don't travel far in the Spiral. We're not sure why. Being underground is part of it, and there's a lot of interference from all the equipment, but the prevailing idea is that some of these creatures produce radio waves themselves, and block our transmissions. Standard AM and FM bands don't work. Cell phones don't work. The pagers work via an ad-hoc WLAN. We can text each other, small amounts of data at a time, and even then the texts can get delayed."

"Sounds... inconvenient."

"Do you really mean inconvenient? Or dangerous?"

"Dangerous," Andy admitted.

"Each floor has an intercom phone, so I can stay in touch with my men that way in case of an emergency. So far that's been all we've needed."

So far, Andy thought.

General Kane appeared from one of the side offices. He quickly took a seat at the table with them. "Any issues, Sergeant?"

"None at all, sir. All systems optimal. Outside perimeters clear. We're all alone out here as usual, sir."

"Very good."

Rimmer took his bundle of papers and left.

"Now then." Kane turned to face the Dennison-Joneses. "Did you find anything out about our guests?"

"No specifics." Sun crossed her arms. "But it's obvious that the batling is part of some kind of larger plan. If we're to believe the things it was saying to us, mankind should be preparing for some kind of war."

Kane huffed. "Against a handful of flying goat men? I've faced off against far worse."

"How many batlings are being held in Deus Manus facilities, General?" Sun asked. "Assuming you talked to the President."

"I did, and he gave you clearance. By last count, we have eighteen batlings. The one here is the largest."

"And were they all caught in close proximity to the facilities?"

"Yes."

"So they were trying to get caught."

"That is certainly one interpretation. But they're all locked up. This isn't Samhain. Samhain's main purpose was research. Here our main goal is containment. Nothing has ever escaped a Deus Manus facility."

"You know Bub can alter his own DNA and shapeshift?"

"I read the Samhain file, Ms. Dennison-Jones. What happened to you both at Samhain has frightened you. General Race's incompetence has rattled your faith in the ability of the human race to defend itself. We are top of the food chain for a reason, and nothing will knock us off that pedestal."

Andy rolled his chin against his chest and sighed as his neck cracked. He took a deep breath and tried to keep his arguments rational rather than idealist like Kane's.

"First off," Andy said. "There was nothing incompetent about General Race. Second, Bub, and that batling in particular, are like nothing else in this facility. He might just hold the secret to life itself. We had a theory that..." Andy sighed. He didn't want to waste his breath getting into theories which held no proof. He suddenly wished he hadn't spoken.

Kane folded his arms. "A theory that *what?*"

"That Bub created life on this earth."

Kane stared at them. He didn't blink, he didn't react. After several uncomfortable seconds had passed, he simply got up and walked away, shaking his head the whole time.

Sun and Andy looked at each other.

"Guess he must be a creationist," said Sun.

"I get the impression that having faith in God is a prerequisite to be inducted into Deus Manus. Even Rimmer mentioned something about praying."

"What about Dr. Chandelling, Dr. Gornman? Surely as people of science, what they have seen here must have made them question the existence of God."

Andy shrugged. "Maybe. Or perhaps it made them believe in Him even more."

Sun huffed and reached across the table to hold Andy's hand. "So what's the plan, hubby?"

"I don't know. But I have an idea."

Sun raised an eyebrow. "Torture Bub with radiation until he talks?"

"Even if we got permission, I don't think I could stomach that. And we both know the only reliable information extracted via torture exists in the realms of TV show like *24;* and I'm no Jack Bauer. But Bub isn't the only one here who knows something."

"The Manx man."

"I say it's time that Lucas and Bub Jr. meet face to face."

CHAPTER FIFTEEN

Fatal Autonomy had been a rerun, the one where they chased a serial killer known as the Gingerbread Man and the annoying fat female cop kept bursting into tears. Instead of watching it, Jerry and Nessie hit the library for research.

"So what are we looking for?" Jerry asked.

"Anything to do with the batling. Especially anything to do with the origin of its creator."

"Bub?"

"Yes, although that's just the name they gave him at the Samhain project. No one knows his real name."

The library on subbasement 5 was huge, not as big as a public library but vastly larger than a private library had any right to be. The ceilings were high, stacked with books of all sizes. Jerry picked up a dusty tome the size of a monopoly board and wiped his hand across the surface revealing the title: *Infernas Animas.*

"So this 'Bub'? He was like, what, a demon or something?"

Nessie leafed through the pages of the book she'd set down in front of her. "To tell you the truth, no one knows exactly what he is. They dug him up in Panama over a hundred years ago and he slept pretty much the whole time they had him at Samhain. Then, five, six years ago or so, he wakes up and wreaks havoc. The Dennison-Joneses and one other member of the Samhain team were the only survivors. Up until Bub awoke, the scientists at the facility thought he was the devil himself—Satan."

Jerry's eyes went wide. "No shit? You mean the devil and angels exist for real? Man, I would love to see an angel. Bet they're all badass with flaming swords and stuff."

"I don't think he actually *is* Satan, Jerry. The reports made it seem more like Bub is some kind of evolutionary origin for all things on earth. I don't know if I believe it myself, but they suggest Bub shared DNA on a basic level with all other species on earth. So either all life in the entire universe is carbon based, uses the same five nucleobases, and requires liquid water to survive, or Bub is terrestrial."

"Meaning Bub came from earth?"

"Or life on earth came from Bub. Some samples taken from Bub predate life on earth."

Jerry opened the book in front of him and turned to a random page. On it was an image of a woman being burned in front of a crowd of people. The text was all in a foreign language, but Jerry could figure out that it was a witch. "But Bub is gone now, he turned into lots of the smaller batlings, right?"

"As far as I know. That batling is pretty much a miniature replica of Bub himself. It would be interesting to know if Bub could reform again if all of the batlings came back together."

Jerry laughed. "Like some sort of Lego demon or one of those robots in the *Power Rangers*?"

Nessie giggled. "You're such a nerd."

Jerry frowned and looked down at his book, turning the pages one after the other without reading any of them. "Yeah, I get that a lot."

"No," said Nessie. "I like it. I think you're funny."

Jerry looked up at her. "What, funny in a good way?"

"Is there any other kind?"

"There's funny in an odd way."

"But odd is good, isn't it? Who wants to be normal?"

"I guess."

Nessie motioned for him to take the seat beside her. Jerry did so, his hands starting to sweat as he pulled back the chair.

"This book is all about the Nordic bronze-age. It has a chapter that indexes all the different cave paintings and rock carvings from that time."

"What time?"

"1700BC to about 500BC. That's really old, but not as old as you'd think. The earliest forms of civilizations may have started as early as 12,000BC."

Jerry whistled. "Crikey! So why are you not starting back there, at the beginning?"

"Well, with so much time to cover, I feel it's best to start with this period and work backwards and forwards based on what I find. If I find mention of Bub, then I'll go backwards a few centuries and search for something else. If I find nothing then I'll try something a little more recent. I'm trying to pin-point Bub's place in time."

Jerry nodded. It seemed like finding a needle in a haystack to him, but if it took an age to come up with something useful, then he would be quite happy to sit next to Nessie the whole time. Her reddish hair seemed to sparkle beneath the soft lights of the library and her rosy cheeks radiated warmth. She had a way of making Jerry feel comfortable; probably the first woman that had ever managed to do that, since he wasn't exactly the smoothest around members of the opposite sex.

"So, what makes you think there's anything about Bub in the history books? Wouldn't we all know about him if there was?"

Nessie smiled. "One of the first things you learn when inducted into Deus Manus is that there are certain history books written only to be read by a few people. Most of the books in this library were written by hand and reproduced perhaps only a dozen times. Deus Manus probably owns all of the reproductions as well as the originals. What we have in this library is the complete and concise history of the world. What everyone else has is just the Cliff Notes."

Jerry looked around at all the dusty tomes that lined the many shelves. "I think you just blew my mind."

Nessie chuckled. "Well, it's been a long time since I blew a man's anything." As soon as the words left Nessie's mouth there was a look of horror in her eyes. She placed a hand over her lips and shook her head. "I can't believe I just said that. My god, I've been in this hole too long."

Jerry felt himself turn red. "Hey, erm, don't worry about it. It was just a joke; a pretty funny one actually."

Nessie moved her hand away from her mouth and sighed. "Wow, I'm sorry. Still can't believe I just said that. Anyway, look at this."

Jerry stared at the pages in front of Nessie. On the page was a photograph of a cliff wall. Splashed on it in faded red paint was the image of a winged man with horns and the lower body of a goat. It looked just like the batling, only bigger. All around the winged figure were people on their knees, bowing before it.

"What is this?" Jerry asked.

"This," said Nessie, "is proof that people once worshipped Bub as a god."

"What people?"

"The Nordic tribes. We don't know a lot about them, as written sources are lacking, but we do know that they worshipped two gods—one good and one bad. It could be said that these two gods were actually a duality of one being—a good and bad side of one god. But it could also be that they worshipped the same god we do, a caring god in the heavens, and a second god, an evil god down here on earth."

"Bub?"

Nessie looked at Jerry and nodded. "Could be. If they really did worship Bub, then we know that he is at least three-thousand years old. Let's go back further."

Jerry stood up and went over to one of the bookcases. "What can I get you? Remember that I am here to serve."

"Ooh, I always wanted my own assistant. Can you get me that big blue book just over there?" She pointed. "It should say *Hadzabe* on the spine. It's a book on a Stone Age tribe from Tanzania. I want to see if I can find Bub in a different time and location."

Jerry located the book and brought it over. "You want to find out if Bub got about a bit?"

Nessie laughed. "Yes. It would be good to see just how far his influence stretched, just how many civilizations were touched by him."

Jerry sat back down at the table and opened the book. "Okay," he said. "Let's Google this bitch, old school."

Jerry saw out the corner of his eye that Nessie was smiling at him, and that made him smile too.

Chapter Sixteen

"So how are we going to do this?"

Andy looked at his wife and wished he had a clear-cut answer to give to her. They were still sitting at the conference table and had been discussing the plan of getting Lucas and the batling together for the past hour. "I'm not sure," he said. "I think the best man to ask would be Rimmer."

Sun nodded. "Let's get him in here, then."

Andy leant forward and examined the intercom in the center of the table. There was a small LCD display and some buttons. After a couple of seconds, Andy worked out how to use the device and put a call through to the security office.

"Rimmer. Who's this?"

"Andy and Sun. We're still in the conference room. Would you be able to come meet with us?"

A sigh came from the speakers, but Rimmer said, "I'll be there in five."

Andy leant back in his chair and folded his hands on his lap. He spent a couple minute's thought on the logistics of what he wanted to achieve.

"Maybe if we can divide one of the cells in two, it would work."

"How will we move one of them to the other's cell? We know the batling is dangerous, but Lucas could be too."

"There has to be some way of moving the occupants. I mean, how do they get them in here in the first place? You heard it yourself that they move specimens between facilities from time to time."

"We blitz the cell with sleeping gas," Rimmer said, entering the room. "Then we head in as quickly as we can and secure the prisoner inside a titanium cargo crate. In this case we may be able to use simple handcuffs and drag the inmate down the corridor."

Andy frowned at Rimmer. "You heard what we were talking about?"

Rimmer pointed to the intercom. "I was listening on the intercom. I can access it remotely."

"You should be working for the NSA," Andy said. "You're wasted here."

Rimmer deadpanned. "The NSA can't afford me."

"So," Sun said. "You think it can be done? Moving Lucas and the batling together?"

Rimmer pulled at his raggedy beard. "Seems like a stupid idea to me, but you're the eggheads. I'm obliged to facilitate whatever you think is best—within reason."

"Is there a way to divide one of the cells?" Andy asked.

"Maybe. They aren't very big on this level, but we may be able to rig something up. Give me a few hours and I'll work something out. One thing I've learned, being down here, is that these creatures will take any chance they can to escape. You better clear things with Dr. Gornman. She'll make a fuss if you don't."

Andy rolled his eyes. "Great. I've been looking forward to working with her. She seems like such a charmer."

Rimmer deadpanned again, but the corners of his mouth twitched as if fighting a smile. "Dr. Gornman is a brilliant scientist. I imagine having her level of intellect can be a burden at times."

Andy nodded. He was aware that being a genius could be at the detriment to other mental functions—most notably, social skills. He himself had struggled to maintain relationships in his formative years due to his intelligence, and had seen first-hand, with the likes of his former colleague, Dr. Belgium, that the smartest people were usually the most awkward.

"I'll meet up with you folks later," Rimmer said, and then left the room.

Andy looked at Sun and gave her a forlorn smile. "Shall we go deal with Gornman now or later?"

"Let's get it over with."

They headed away from the conference table towards the back of the room, over to the door that read: LABS 1-4. Andy pushed open the door and held it for his wife. Sun stepped through and looked around.

"Sure puts Samhain to shame," she said.

Andy stepped inside and took it all in. They were standing in a clinical white corridor that had several glass cubicles on either side: small examination rooms and offices mostly. Up ahead was a vast laboratory. All four of its walls were glass and the equipment inside was cutting-edge. Andy could not even imagine what most of it was for. Standing inside the lab, wearing her lab coat was Dr. Gornman. When she saw them approaching, the aggravation was clear on her face.

But then she smiled and waved at them.

Andy and Sun exchanged confused glances. "Perhaps she's accepted us being here," Sun suggested.

Gornman gave them a hand signal that suggested she would be 'two minutes' and then started to pull off her latex gloves, depositing them in a waste-disposal tub. Thirty seconds later she was opening the door to the lab and stepping out.

"Mr. and Ms, Dennison-Jones. Welcome to the labs. This is our level-1 lab. You can perform the more benign experiments here such as cultures and DNA sequencing. The other labs are more secure. That's where we do our more sensitive experiments."

"I'd be lost in any of them," Andy said. "I'm not science-savvy."

Gornman smiled. "I could say the same about myself and foreign languages, Mr. Dennison-Jones."

"So what are you doing?" Sun asked.

Gornman frowned. "As you no doubt found with Bub, the batling seems to share DNA with just about every other species on earth. I performed an x-ray on a tissue sample we got from the batling and observed degradation under even the mildest doses of radiation, so that seems to be a weakness. In other words, I haven't yet discovered anything that you didn't already know when you got here."

"Well, I'm sure you'll find something," Sun said. "Let us know if we can help."

Dr. Gornman looked down at her shoes like a scolded child. "I'm afraid I was a little brusque before. You must understand that, working down here, so far from civilization, one tends to become stuck in their ways."

"It's okay," Sun said. "I was once in the same environment. I understand cabin fever all too well."

"Well, I apologize sincerely. Anything you need, just let me know."

"Now that you mention it," Andy said. "We were hoping to get your help with something."

"Yes?"

"We want to move Lucas and the batling into the same cell."

Gornman's eyes went unnaturally wide. "You want to place two different creatures in the same space? Are you insane?"

Andy sighed. *Didn't take long for the brusque to return.*

"We think it's the best way to find out if Lucas is here because of the batling or vice-versa. We need to know if they are here for related reasons."

Gornman rubbed at her forehead and let out a long breath. When she looked at them again, she was calmer, but it seemed forced. "Okay, okay. I hope you can excuse my surprise. It's just that we've never attempted such a thing down here before—least of all with the guests of subbasement 5. But if that's what you want to do, then it is my duty to accommodate you. Now, when were you hoping to achieve this feat of insane peril?"

"We were hoping to get it done this afternoon," said Andy. "Sooner the better."

"Of course, why wait and plan when you can rush right in. Let us get started then."

"So you approve?" Andy asked, somewhat suspiciously.

Gornman stared at him and raised both her eyebrows. "Of course. I'm happy to help, Mr. Dennison-Jones."

Dr. Gornman walked between Sun and Andy and left the labs. Sun was frowning at Andy and he asked her what was wrong.

"You know I'm not superstitious, right?"

"You're the opposite of superstitious, hon. You're a skeptic."

"I know." Sun hugged herself and shivered. "So why do I feel like someone just walked over my grave?"

Chapter Seventeen

"They want to do *what?*" Kane wasn't sure that he had heard correctly.

Rimmer folded his arms across his wide chest and checked his watch. "It's not necessarily a bad idea. Neither the Manx man or the batling are talking. But if we put them together, maybe we can figure out what's going on."

"Of all people, I wouldn't expect you to agree with this. It's an unnecessary risk to security."

Rimmer chewed the side of his cheek, appeared to think about it, and then said, "Sometimes a risk is the only option left. In Iraq we would have been dead in the water without eavesdropping on prisoners for Intel. I remember shoving a couple of Iraqi soldiers in a cell together once and watching them go at it. They were long-time enemies, but both loyally served Saddam. As one spat accusations and insults at the other, the other one would spit them right back. By the end of the day we had gotten enough information to know the names of their entire families and half their friends. We also knew that one of the men was responsible for a botched attack on a US base. His enemy straight-out insulted him for his incompetence in failing in his mission."

Kane ran his palms over the surface of his desk, enjoying the feel of the wood grain against his calloused hands. "You think this is what this is? Putting two enemies together to see what we can overhear?"

"Among other benefits," Rimmer added.

"Such as?"

"They might tear each other apart. Two less monsters for us to deal with."

Kane's frown became a tight smirk. He appreciated Rimmer's straight forward approach to things. "It's our job to house these creatures safely, Sergeant. While I don't disagree with your sentiment, I swore an oath to do them no harm."

Rimmer nodded, he unfolded his arms and put them at his sides. "All I'm saying, sir, is that if we go into things with the best of intentions—to gain Intel—and something *unforeseen* happens, well, then nobody has anything to feel guilty about. Shit happens, as they say."

Kane leaned back in his chair and nodded. "You know that there are more of those things? The faustlings, I mean. We have over a dozen of them at our other facilities."

Rimmer nodded. "I know."

"You do? How?"

"I have my sources. It pays to know people working at other facilities. It can give a heads up on any potential issues that may arise."

Kane was getting a little irritated by his staff knowing things above their pay grade, but he supposed in Rimmer's case it was acceptable. It was the man's job to know things. "Then you understand that we need to learn more about these things. They're planning something."

"With all due respect, sir. I think the most important thing to learn about the faustling things is how to kill them. Perhaps putting the Manx man in with our own faustling will shine some light on how to achieve said termination."

Kane thought about it and nodded his head at Rimmer. "Get it done. But get it done safely."

"Of course."

"And keep an eye on the Dennison-Joneses, and that English pest."

"I'm on top of it, General. When was the last time we had a problem?"

General Kane frowned. "We haven't had one in a long time. That's what concerns me. I think we're overdue."

CHAPTER EIGHTEEN

Andy was standing with Sun and Dr. Gornman as two of Rimmer's men appeared in the hallway of subbasement 5 with a thick roll of steel mesh. Rimmer was with them, and broke away to talk to Andy.

"This is the best I could come up with at short notice. We'll get the mesh secured through the center of the cell, but if either of them has more strength than they're letting on, they may get through."

Andy looked in at Lucas in his cell. The man didn't seem particularly strong, but it was impossible to know for certain. "Okay, we'll just have to hope for the best."

"This cannot go wrong," Dr. Gornman said. "General Kane won't tolerate us making a mess of this. More to the point, neither will I."

"Doing a wee spot of decorating, are we?" Lucas said, sitting inside his cell. "I wouldn't mind a splash of cerise on these walls. Breathes a bit of life to a room, so it does."

Andy went up to the glass. "You're going to get a roommate. Can we trust you to behave while we get things ready?"

Lucas glanced around his tiny cell and huffed. "Hope this new fella isn't going to take up a lot of room. Can nay swing a cat as it is."

"The space you have is perfectly sufficient," Gornman said. "And let me remind you that you placed yourself in there."

"Aye, that I did, lass. 'Twas your bright smile that lured me here."

Gornman's face remained stony.

"See?" Lucas said. "How could any man resist you?"

Rimmer nodded at Andy. "You ready?"

Andy nodded back.

Rimmer went over to the LED touchscreen beside Lucas's cell and placed his thumb against it. He prodded through the menus and then typed in a passcode on the screen.

Suddenly there was a sharp hissing sound.

Andy turned to look into Lucas's cell and saw that an amber substance was being pumped into the air from the ceiling. It quickly dissipated and mixed with the room's existing atmosphere.

Lucas glanced upwards and frowned. "Did someone just let a cheeky fart loose in here?"

Then he began to cough and splutter, clutching at his throat.

"He's fighting it," said Rimmer. "Just give it a minute."

They gave it a minute. Lucas dropped down to his knees, spat a wad of phlegm on the floor and started heaving.

Then he glanced up at them all and began chuckling. He straightened up and got back to his feet. "You'll need something a wee bit stronger than gnat's piss to put me down. I once smoked reefer with Bob Marley. Not a fat lot else has been able to touch me since."

Andy's shoulders slumped. Sun, who had remained silent throughout the last several minutes, came up beside him and shook her head. "We might have expected as much. His anatomy is a mystery, so why should we assume that he's going to have a nervous system we can exploit with basic chemistry?"

Andy sighed. "So what should we do?"

“We should call it off,” Gornman said. “If we don’t have an effective plan of action then we need to go away until we come up with one. Mistakes are made by acting without proper thought or appropriate reflection.”

Lucas pressed his hands up against the glass and started mumbling something. His eyes rolled back in his head.

“What is he doing?” Sun asked her husband.

“I don’t know.”

Lucas’s words became louder. “…pen sesame. Open sesame… OPEN SESAME.”

The glass wall sprung aside on its rails, leaving Lucas’s cell wide open. The Manx man stood in the newly opened gap and grinned at them all. “Neat trick, huh? Of course, nothing beats a good bit of card magic, but a bit of variety never hurt anybody.”

Rimmer immediately signalled his men, who pointed their assault rifles at Lucas. Rimmer was only carrying a sidearm—what looked like a Glock—but he quickly pulled it from its holster and aimed. “Don’t move!”

Lucas held his hands up. “Come now, I’m just being helpful. You folks wanted to come inside, so now I’ve opened the door for you.”

“Get down on the floor,” Rimmer demanded.

“Such bad manners. These are my digs, not yours. I suggest you stop with the threats, fella. That heroic beard of yours ain’t fooling nobody.”

Rimmer took a step forward and gripped his handgun tighter, his knuckles growing white. “I don’t make threats, *fella*.”

Lucas chuckled. “Look out! Wc got ourselves a badass over here. I wonder how much of a badass you were when you were bleeding out into the sand of the Iraqi desert. You know that Lewis’s mother killed herself after she got the news that her son had died? You must feel really bad about that.”

Rimmer snarled and seemed very ready to shoot.

"Okay..." Andy spread his hands. "Let's everybody calm down."

"That sounds like a wise idea," Lucas said, keeping his eyes on Rimmer and grinning slightly.

"Lucas? Will you let Rimmer and his men install a fence inside your cell? Will you try anything?"

"Not if he stops glaring at me with those beady little peepers of his."

Andy turned to face Rimmer. "Rimmer?"

Rimmer kept his pistol up but glanced sideways at Andy. "I'm not about to trust this guy for a minute."

"Then we have a problem," Andy said. "Because he doesn't seem to be all that bothered by your gun, and I would very much prefer that you didn't shoot him."

Rimmer lowered his gun by an inch, held it a second longer, and then lowered it all the way. "Fine, but if this guy even scratches his nose funny he's getting a bullet right in the skull."

"You can try it," Lucas said. "Better men than you have. Then, when you fail, I'll come out there and tie your limbs in knots and use you as a skipping rope. That isn't a threat, neither."

"You make it sound like you've done something like that before, Lucas," Sun said.

He glanced at Sun. "That, and much worse, lass. We all have pasts. Living with oneself is a full time job. You have to learn to forgive your mistakes, and work hard not to make the same ones." Then Lucas levelled his eyes at Rimmer. "But nobody is perfect. Anyone can backslide, even with the best of intentions. That be what the road to hell is paved with, they say. Now kindly order your men to stand down, before my intentions darken."

They had a brief staring contest, then Rimmer gave a nod and the automatic weapons were lowered.

Andy blew out a breath. "Okay, now that the pissing contest is over, can we get started?"

Lucas nodded politely, and stepped to the side, bidding them entrance. Rimmer instructed his men, who quickly got moving with the thick roll of steel mesh. Another couple of guys appeared with some steel rods and a power drill. By the time five minutes had passed they had drilled and bolted the steel rods to the left and right walls of the cell and secured the mesh fence to them both. Lucas leaned against the back wall and was now trapped behind the mesh while the front of the cell was left open.

"Will the glass wall go back into place?" Sun asked.

Rimmer nodded. "It's attached to runners. It will slide back into place once I log out of the cell's control panel. We're all set to move the other prisoner. You ready?"

Andy felt a lump form in his throat as he contemplated moving the batling out of its cell. The nightmare of Samhain came rushing back to him, and for a moment he was frozen to the spot.

Sun placed a hand on Andy's back and rubbed.

Andy swallowed a lump in his throat and then spoke. "We're ready, Rimmer. Get it done fast. Lucas may have been cooperative, but I assure you that the batling won't be."

Rimmer nodded and got to work. "Handler, log in and gas the cell."

The security guard, Handler, nodded obediently before logging into the system as commanded.

Rather than holster his pistol, Rimmer kept it at his side, pointed at the floor. "We've all done this before," he said. "It's a routine crate job. Soon as the target is out, we move in and secure it."

The men who had installed the steel mesh fence left momentarily and then returned with a large metal cage on casters.

"Okay, we're a go," said Rimmer.

Handler released the sleeping gas into the batling's cell.

The batling smacked itself into the glass, leaving a bloody smear and making Andy jump.

"Trying toooo kill meeeeeeee?"

"Only a quick nap," Andy said. "We have someone we want you to meet."

Bub's wings began to slow, and the act of staying airborne seemed to grow more difficult.

"Meeeeeeeeeeeeeeeet?"

The batling tried to stay airborne but its wings moved as if they were mired in clay. After a few feeble flaps it dropped out of the air and thumped to the floor.

"Okay," Rimmer shouted. "Move, move!"

Handler typed in the command for the glass barrier to slide away and the two other guards rushed into the cell. They threw a thick blanket over the top of the subdued batling and grabbed a hold of it. Together they managed to heave the batling upwards and started waddling backwards out of the cell. Handler left the control panel and stood beside the metal crate, holding the lid wide open.

"Quickly," Rimmer said. "The gas took it down topside, but I don't want to take any chances here."

Rimmer's men readjusted their grip on the blanket-wrapped batling and hurried their pace towards the open crate.

"Just dump it in," Handler ordered, still holding the lid open.

The two men forced the batling into the crate and stepped back, panting. The creature was obviously heavier than it looked.

Handler shoved the lid closed with a *BANG!* and then locked the latch.

"Finally!" said Dr. Gornman. "I was beginning to doubt that you people could even—"

The crate's lid sprung back open, smashing Handler in the sternum and sending him backward. The man hit the floor, wheezing.

The hair on the back of Andy's neck prickled.

Oh, shit!

The batling shook off the blanket and leapt into the air, its wings flapping with renewed vitality.

"Take it down!" Rimmer ordered.

Andy reached for his wife, tugging her away from the ensuing gunfire. A nanosecond later the hallway erupted into deafening pops of automatic weapons.

Bub was riddled with bullets and his maw opened in a screech as blood rained down on everyone. The creature splatted to the floor, right next to Sun and Andy, reaching out a claw and slashing at Sun's leg.

The gunfire stopped—Rimmer's men were obviously trained well enough to not shoot with civilians next to the target—and Andy kicked Bub in the side of the head while pulling Sun away. Rimmer stood over the creature and emptied the Glock into Bub's head, blowing away most of the batling's skull and face.

Bub's shredded wings fluttered, then went still.

"Drag it to the cell!" Rimmer ordered. "Now!"

As Rimmer and his men attended to Bub, Andy stared at Sun and saw her gripping the pulsing wound in her calf.

"Artery," Sun said, her eyes going wide. She dropped onto her butt.

"Your belt," Gornman told Andy. "Make a tourniquet. We need to get her into surgery, immediately."

Andy undid his belt with shaking hands, and as he looped it around Sun's thigh he made the mistake of looking at her wound, seeing bone peek out through the split muscle fibers. The blood continued to gush. So much blood.

Is that all hers? It can't be. Such a small woman can't bleed that much.

As Dr. Gornman cinched the belt tight, Andy knelt next to his wife, cradling her head. "It'll be okay. It'll be okay."

Further down the hallway was the *whoosh* of Lucas's cell door closing. They'd dragged Bub inside and locked him in.

Andy had no doubt the demon—even though it was missing most of its head—was still alive.

"What the hell is going on here?" Kane shouted like a drill sergeant as he marched towards them from the direction of the elevator. His red cheeks looked ready to pop. "Who is responsible for this goddamn mess?"

Nobody answered.

CHAPTER NINETEEN

Rimmer's men had fetched a gurney and taken Sun up to the Spiral's infirmary on level 3. The floor also acted as a warehouse. Men in work overalls shared the corridors with doctors and nurses.

Andy sat outside the operating room that a pair of nurses had rushed Sun into. Dr. Gornman had quickly followed, but it had been over an hour since Andy had heard anything.

I can't lose you, Sun. Nothing would make any sense without you.

The sound of someone hurrying down the hall made Andy glance up from his thoughts. Jerry was racing towards him with a panicked look on his face. The young historian, Nessie, was right beside him.

"We heard your wife has been injured," Jerry said. "Is she okay?"

"Still waiting," Andy said. "She… she lost a lot of blood."

Andy had never felt more tired, more afraid. He'd been in situations before where he had to fight for his life, and the fear and adrenaline had sustained him. But waiting to find out if the love of his life was going to survive was easily the worst thing he'd ever felt.

I never volunteered to fight evil. I'm not a goddamn monster hunter. I didn't join Deus Manus. Why are we even here?

"I shouldn't have let her come along," Andy said.

"I don't know you or Sun very well," Jerry said, "but if she wanted to be here, I doubt very much you could have done anything to stop her."

Andy let his head drop. "If she dies..."

Jerry placed a hand on Andy's back and made him flinch. He did not enjoy the contact, but he did not move away.

"Things will be alright, man. Sun is really strong. She'll be back and ready to kick arse in no time."

Andy hoped that was true. Because if it wasn't...

Then what?

Then I dedicate my life to wiping Bub off the face of the earth.

Dr. Gornman approached, her face revealing nothing. Andy stared, expectant.

"We stopped the bleeding and stitched up the wound. She needed four pints of blood, and was very close to hypovolemic shock."

"Is she okay?"

"She's tough. I think she'll pull through."

"I want to see her."

"Of course. The nurses are just making her comfortable in one of the suites. Head inside and take the door on your left."

Andy hurried into the operating theatre. It led into a wide corridor with several rooms running off it. He saw through the room's windows that Sun was inside one of them along with two nurses. He barged through the door and moved beside his wife's bedside.

The two nurses left.

"How you feeling?"

"Numb. Lidocaine and morphine. It'll be a while before I play racquetball again."

Andy choked up. "I thought I'd lost you."

"Me? Over that little scratch? You know I'm tougher than that."

Andy gave her a gentle hug, like he was holding a baby bird. "We're getting out of here," he said. "Soon as you've rested. Let them deal with Bub. It's not our problem."

Sun eased him away, staring hard. "Is Bub in the cell with Lucas?"

"Yes."

"Are they talking?"

"I don't know. Bub was in pretty bad shape. He's going to take a while to heal himself. There are cameras on them."

Andy saw how his wife's usually olive skin was now pale.

"We need to see this thing through to the end."

"You almost died, Sun. You need to heal. And this isn't a good place for it."

"I have to stay, Andy."

"Sun..."

"Andy, I *have to stay*." She raised her left hand, and Andy saw her wrist was cuffed to the bedrail.

"What the hell is that?" Andy demanded. "That's insane! They can't keep you here!"

"Andy..."

"I'm going right to Kane and telling him—"

"Andy! I told them to cuff me."

"What are you..." Andy's voice trailed off as the realization hit him.

No.

Not that.

Anything but that.

"You think Bub... *infected* you?" Andy whispered.

"He clawed me. You know he's got those stingers in his palms. You know he can manipulate DNA."

"Were you stung?"

"I don't know. I bled a lot. If he tried to inject me with his mutator serum, maybe none of it got into my system. But if it did..."

"How do you feel?"

Sun chuckled. "You mean, do I feel like I'm changing into a demon? That my cells are mutating? That I'm becoming possessed?"

Andy didn't answer.

"I feel fine, Andy. But if I'm not... I... I don't want to hurt anyone."

"Is there any way to find out?"

"Other than waiting? Gornman is scheduling some tests. I guess we'll know when we know."

Andy hugged her again. She hugged him back.

"I also need you to do something for me," she said into his neck.

"Anything."

"If I do... *change*... this is where I need to be. If there's any chance of a cure, it's here. They've got all the Samhain data, and Gornman may be a bit of a bitch but she knows her stuff. But if it looks like they can't cure me..."

"Sun, don't talk like that."

"If they can't... Andy, I don't want to be one of Bub's minions. I don't want to be controlled by him. I can't think of anything worse. If it looks like I can't be cured... I want you to put me out of my misery."

"Jesus, Sun. That's the most horrible thing I've ever heard."

"Promise me."

"I can't promise that."

"If you ever want to get laid again, you'll promise me."

Andy felt himself tear up. "Okay."

"You promise?"

"I promise."

There was a knock at the door.

Andy turned as Jerry poked his head through the door with an anxious look on his face.

"What is it, Jerry?"

"Sorry, just checking on you."

"You can come in," Sun told him.

Jerry slunk into the room like he was about to be scolded by his mother. "So you, ah, doing alright?"

"For the moment."

"Good. I'm glad." He nodded at Andy, and Sun. Then his gaze turned to a chair in the corner of the room, where Sun's things were stacked. Her purse. Some clothing. The blue disc that accessed the doors.

"You can sit if you want to, Jerry," Sun said.

Jerry nodded but stayed standing. "Nessie is in the library. We found that batling thing in some old books. People used to worship it."

"Sometimes there isn't a difference between religion and a totalitarianism," Andy said. "Ruling by fear is the same whether it's fascism, communism, dictatorship, or the church. We know Bub preyed on early mankind's superstition and powerlessness. He's been around long enough to be an archetype."

"Is he really the devil?" Jerry asked.

"He's *a* devil. I don't know if that means he literally came from hell, or if he's some psychotic life form from another world. But he doesn't have our best interests in mind."

Jerry rubbed his chin. "I don't know if I believe in God. There's too much shit in the world, you know? I mean, if God exists, he's like a deadbeat dad who abandons his kids. Either that, or he's a sadist who likes watching people suffer. Do you believe?"

"We're atheists," Andy said. "But we try to keep our minds open. That's the point of science. You change your mind as new evidence comes in."

"So what about this whole Deus Manus set-up? You think they really are keeping evil from the world?"

"I think they think they're keeping evil from the world," Andy said. "And some of the creatures they have here don't look like they love humanity any more than Bub does. But I've found that, throughout history, a lot of people have done a lot of harm while claiming to do God's work."

"Uhhhh," Sun groaned.

Andy's head whipped toward her so fast he practically gave himself whiplash. "You okay, babe?"

"Starting to feel the pain now."

"Should I get Dr. Gornman?"

Sun shook her head, reaching for him. "No. Stay with me."

Andy turned to Jerry. "Do you mind?"

"I'll, ah, be in the library with Nessie. I hope you feel better, Sun."

Andy didn't watch the kid leave. His eyes were locked onto his wife.

CHAPTER TWENTY

Jerry headed for the conference room. From there he could make it into the dormitory wing and back to his suite. He was knackered after studying in the library for so long.

The small blue disk in Jerry's pocket was burning a hole. He touched its rubbery surface and felt his stomach churn. What would happen when Sun realised he had stolen it from her bedside table? And why had he even stolen it in the first place?

Because I don't want to be a prisoner like the things they have in these cells. I want to leave and get a million miles away from this place. I'll happily give myself up to the police back home rather than stay here until they decide to 'dispose' of me.

Jerry passed through the heated atmosphere of the conference room, the space filled with the sound of computer exhausts humming out hot air.

Jerry stepped towards the door that led to the living quarters, but took pause.

If I'm going to get the hell out of here. I should do it now, while everyone is distracted with what's just happened. I could make it to the lift and take it to the top. Sun's fob should let me access the controls.

Jerry changed direction and headed out into the cellblock. The first cell now contained both the batling and Lucas, separated by a mesh of steel.

The batling was stooped over on the floor, its wings wrapped around itself. It was obviously healing after being fired upon. The Manx man stared down at the creature silently, but glanced upwards when he noticed Jerry.

"You off then, lad?"

Jerry stopped outside the cell and looked in. "What?"

Lucas smiled, although it lacked his usual cheeriness. "You're leaving, I take it?"

"I..."

"It's okay. Get going while you can. Things aren't going to get any better around here."

Jerry frowned. "What do you mean?"

"I mean this place is a madhouse and the inmates want blood. Leave while you're able."

"You want blood?"

"Not I," said Lucas. "This ugly little blighter on the floor. He's just getting started."

"How do you know that?"

"I've been around a while. I know a lot about a lot. This one means to destroy the human race."

Jerry looked down at the wounded creature and wondered how it could possibly be a threat to mankind. It was no bigger than a chimpanzee.

"Who the hell are you?" Jerry asked Lucas.

"Just an interested third-party. An observer, if you will."

Jerry shook his head, rolled his eyes. "Dude, why you got to be all 'riddle me this?' Stop talking bollocks all the time."

Lucas grinned. "You've become quite the man since I saw you last, Jerry-lad. I see your heart. It swells with a courage once absent."

"You don't know me."

"I know you well, from a time forgotten by all but the most perceptive, but it's of no import in this place and time. What's important is that the angry little monster currently sleeping on the ground between us will soon be up and well again, and when he is, it would be better to be gone from this place. My advice to you would be to hurry up and get in that lift. Go home and face your punishment. Life may still hold promise for you."

"How do you know about me? How do you know the things that I have done?"

"You wouldn't understand."

"Try me."

Lucas ran his fingertips across the mesh of the fence. He blinked slowly. "When faced with a man, I have little difficulty in reading the verses of his soul. Your past, your present—they are etched into your mind and body. And when read together, they hold glimmers of your future. Which is why I am telling you one more time to flee this place. I fear you will not live if you do not, lad. No one would blame you for running."

Jerry frowned. He had planned on leaving anyway; that was why he was in the cellblock after all, heading for the elevator. Lucas's warning only added to the argument for trying to escape.

"Don't worry. I'm going. You take care, weird Irish guy." Jerry turned and walked away. He fingered the rubber fob in his pocket, making sure it was still there. Then he headed down the corridor.

Just running away as usual. But what choice do I have?

Further on down there was a large bloodstain. It covered the floor in a congealed pool, and probably came from Sun. Jerry stepped around it squeamishly. There were also several patches of chipped concrete where bullets had doubtlessly struck.

The elevator was just up ahead, past the cell with the horrible-looking vampire thing. It snarled and hissed at him as he passed, beating at the glass with its twisted hands.

Gonna be really glad to get away from that nasty sod. He looks like he wants to rip me to pieces.

Then something else caught Jerry's attention.

Wolfie sat up against the glass of his cell, wagging his tail and panting. When he saw Jerry pass by, he began to wiggle excitedly.

"Hey, Wolfie. How you doing?"

Wolfie yipped.

"I still can't believe they have you locked up down here with monsters like that thing next door. You're not a monster; you're just an animal."

Jerry thought about Lucas's words and wondered if Wolfie would be alright once things turned bad. Was something bad really going to happen, or was the Irish guy just messing with him?

Can I really walk away and leave everyone here to die?

Wolfie jumped up on his hind legs and pawed at the glass with his front ones. His long pink tongue slurped across the glass.

Jerry smiled. "I wish I could take you out of here with me, buddy. I bet you'd love it in the woods up there on the surface.

He placed his hand against the glass and Wolfie licked at it from the other side.

I'll probably be dead before I get within a mile away from this place.

Is there even any point trying to escape?

Wolfie never managed it and he's been here for years. Poor guy. Wonder when's the last time he even got out of that cell, or even had anyone to play with.

Jerry reached into his pocket and pulled out the blue rubber fob. He moved over to the LED screen for Wolfie's cell and placed the fob against it.

I must be crazy.

The screen flashed green and beeped. Menus came up on screen and Jerry started to jab at them, trying to navigate towards what he was looking for. Then he found the command he wanted.

CELL ENTRY.

He prodded the screen.

ENTER CODE.

Jerry remembered what Kane had told Sun and Andy when he'd given them the disks, and punched in 1-2-3-4.

OPEN CELL. YES? NO?

He paused, finger hovering.

Then he pressed YES.

There was a shrill ringing, emanating from above the cell. The glass barrier began to slide away. Once it opened up to a gap of about four feet it stopped sliding. The ringing halted.

Jerry stared into the cell.

Wolfie stared right back, his ears pricked up like the tips of spears.

Kane's computer blinked. His eyes narrowed. He glanced up at Rimmer and Gornman and then leapt out of his seat.

"What is it?" Rimmer asked, his hand instinctively moving over his holstered pistol.

Kane shoved past the two of them, heading for the door. "Someone's opened up cell number 5. I did not authorize that."

"Who?" Rimmer askcd.

"Sun Dennison-Jones."

"But she's in the infirmary. She couldn't be up on her feet yet."

"Exactly." Kane moused through his surveillance cameras until he came upon the werewolf's cell. "It's that British pest."

Jerry stepped forwards into the gap between the glass barrier and the wall. Wolfie padded backwards, looking both curious and nervous—almost cowering. Up close, Jerry realized he had underestimated the size of the beast. Wolfie was closer to the size of a pony than a dog. It was clear by the animal's body language that he was unused to someone being inside his cell. His fur had spiked up and his shoulders narrowed.

It's his territory.

Jerry considered backing out of the cell and closing it again, if only because of the smell. The stench inside the cell was primal, beastly. It made his eyes water. Jerry looked down at a bundle of blankets that formed Wolfie's bed and saw spoor mixed in with the straw that lined the floor. He also saw something else.

"Is that…"

Jerry reached down towards the blankets.

Wolfie let out a low, rising snarl.

Jerry slowed his movement, held out a hand. "It's okay, boy. I'm not going to hurt you. Easy does it."

Wolfie stopped snarling, but his lips remained curled.

Jerry grabbed the rubber ball amongst the tangled blankets and straightened up with it in his hands.

Wolfie hopped backwards, lowered on his haunches, his rear in the air. If not for the wagging tail, Jerry might have thought the animal was about to pounce.

"You like that, don't you, boy? You like to play with your ball."

Wolfie wagged his tail faster and yipped.

Jerry threw the ball. It sailed down towards the back of the cell and hit the rear wall, bouncing back the way it had come. Wolfie raced after it, leaping in the air as it almost sailed over his head. He spun around with the newly-captured prize in his mouth and flopped down on his belly, losing the ball so that it rolled back to Jerry's feet.

Jerry bent down and picked up the ball, held it in the air. "You wanna go again?"

Wolfie reared up ecstatically and waited for the ball to be thrown again.

"You're just a dog, aren't you? Is the reason you're down on subbasement 5 just because you took a chunk out of that asshole, Kane? I bet you were up on subbasement 1 before he came along."

Wolfie wagged his tail, barked at Jerry.

Jerry threw the ball. This time he threw it harder and added spin, trying to add a bit of variety for Wolfie to enjoy. The ball bounced off the rear wall and this time it flew far over Wolfie's head and back towards the front of the cell.

Jerry giggled at the sight of the huge beast sliding on its paws before spinning around excitedly and giving chase in the opposite direction. Wolfie threw himself across the cell like a bat out of hell, almost taking Jerry off his feet.

"Hey, Wolfie, stop. Slow down."

The ball continued racing through the air and flew out of the gap between the barrier and the wall. Wolfie immediately followed, wagging his tail dementedly. Seeing that he had just inadvertently let the animal loose, Jerry sprinted out after him, urgently calling his name.

"Wolfie! Wolfie, back in your cell, before they—"

There was the sound of gunfire.

Wolfie flew sideways across the concrete floor. Jerry put his hands up and saw that Rimmer and Kane were standing in the corridor. Kane had a mean-looking revolver pointed out in front of him, the barrel smoking.

Jerry looked left and saw Wolfie's large form panting on the ground and bleeding. His pained whimpers filled the cramped corridor.

"Wolfie!" Jerry attempted to rush to the animal's side but Kane shouted him to a halt.

"You stay right where you are. One move and I'll put you down, too."

Tears in his eyes, Jerry turned to face the general. "We were just playing ball and I threw it too hard. Please, just leave him alone. He might still be okay."

"You let out a monster, you fool."

"He's not a monster. He's just a big dog."

"You have no idea what you're talking about. He was coming right at us."

"He was chasing a goddamn ball!"

Jerry's legs folded and he collapsed onto his side, moaning and crying. His blurry gaze met Wolfie's as the two of them lay on the cold ground. Two outcasts, all alone in the world, so very far from home.

"It's okay, boy. It'll be okay."

Wolfie whimpered. His eyes focused intently on Jerry as his pink tongue lolled out between his jaws. Jerry reached out, managed to place a hand on Wolfie's snout. There was a brief wag of the animal's tail and Jerry felt a lick against his wrist.

"I need a team and a containment crate in here immediately," Rimmer said into the intercom on the wall.

It wasn't necessary. As Jerry wrapped his arms around Wolfie and patted his massive head, the beast let out a lengthy sigh and closed its eyes for the last time.

CHAPTER TWENTY-ONE

Andy stood up at Sun's bedside. "Was that a gunshot?"

Sun said nothing. She was sleeping.

Andy sighed. "I really hate this place."

He took off, heading out of the infirmary and into the conference room. Dr. Gornman stood with her arms crossed, looking irritated.

"What's going on?" Andy asked her.

Gornman tutted and shook her head. "That young buffoon you brought along with you has just jeopardized the entire safety of the facility."

"What do you mean?"

"I mean the idiot opened up one the cells." Her eyes narrowed. "With your wife's access fob, no less."

Andy needed to see for himself. He raced out of the conference room and into the cell block. What he saw didn't alleviate his confusion; it added to it.

Something lay on the floor, dead, bleeding, and covered in thick matted fur. Jerry was on his knees with his hands cuffed behind his back, Rimmer standing behind him, looking predictably stoic.

Kane was standing over the dead animal. The look on his face was almost trance-like.

"What the hell is going on?"

Rimmer glanced up at Andy. "Stay there, Mr. Dennison-Jones. Your wayward companion has just tried to compromise this entire facility."

Rimmer elaborated. "Kid opened up cell 5 and let the dog out."

"The bastards killed him," Jerry yelled. "They had no reason to. He was just chasing his ball. The... the *bastards.*"

"The shooting was justified. Sergeant Rimmer will vouch for me. The beast was running straight toward us. Isn't that right, Sergeant?"

"It was. It shouldn't have been out of its cell," Rimmer said to Jerry.

"He was only on subbasement 5 because you hated him, you Nazi fucks. You have cameras all over. You could see we were just playing."

"You were playing with a werewolf, kid," Rimmer said.

"He wasn't a werewolf! Did you shoot him with a silver bullet? No! And he's dead. You killed the last one in the world, for no reason at all."

Kane cleared his throat and said, "Mr. Preston, your recent actions qualify as terrorism. Your actions could have seriously compromised this facility and its agenda. Therefore, Sergeant Rimmer is going to incarcerate you under the terms of *The Patriot Act of 2001*. You will remain in custody for whatever time I deem fit."

Jerry spat at the general's feet. "Do what you gotta do, bitch."

"You can't be serious," Andy said. "He's not a terrorist. He's just a kid."

"He screwed up," Rimmer said. Then he looked at Jerry. "What did you think was going to happen, kid? You were going to become best friends and run away together?"

"You're all a bunch of wankers."

"Take him away, Sergeant Rimmer," Kane ordered. "You know what to do with him."

Rimmer didn't seem happy about it, and Jerry seemed even less happy, but it only took a few seconds for Rimmer to put Jerry into a submission hold and yank him to his feet. Jerry didn't struggle as Rimmer led him away.

Kane turned his attention back to Andy. "Now, Mr. Dennison-Jones, the only question remaining is whether or not you had anything to do with this." He produced one of the blue rubber fobs from his breast pocket. "This is, after all, your wife's access fob, yes?"

"I didn't even know that Jerry had taken it. My wife nearly died. I was by her side."

"So how did he get the security code?"

"He was there when *you* told it to us, remember?"

Kane rolled his upper lip over his lower lip; nodded very slowly. "Okay. You're dismissed."

"What are you going to do with Jerry?"

"It isn't your concern."

Andy blew out a stiff breath. What else could he say? Jerry had apparently released a dangerous animal from its cage, and there wasn't any way to defend that.

"Just let the boy go. Send him home to face the music."

"Return to your wife, Mr. Dennison-Jones. She no doubt needs you. Let me worry about running the Spiral."

CHAPTER TWENTY-TWO

Andy headed through the conference room and back into the infirmary. When he got there, there were a couple of nurses milling about, and he asked them if his wife had woken while he'd been gone. He'd only been gone ten minutes but it felt much longer.

"We haven't checked in on her," said the nurse. "We thought you were still with her."

Andy wasn't happy to hear that, but he had left without informing anyone, so didn't feel he had the ammunition to complain.

"Was that a gunshot I heard?" asked the nurse.

"Yes, but everything is under control."

"Thank God for that." The nurse smiled and went back to her duties.

Before Andy made it to Sun's room, he bumped into Dr. Chandelling.

"Ah, Mr. Dennison-Jones. I was hoping to find you."

"You were? Why?"

"I learned something about our Manx guest."

"Lucas?"

Dr. Chandelling nodded enthusiastically. "All of the previous tests I conducted were fruitless. Then I had the idea of sending a picture of him to some acquaintances in the NSA. I figured if we can't find out anything about his insides, we could see if there's anything we can find about his identity. You see, I found that by cross-checking—"

Andy waved a hand. "I'm anxious to get back to my wife, Dr. Chandelling. What is it you've found?"

"Of course. I'll get to the point." Dr. Chandelling mumbled something else before producing a small tablet from the large side pocket of his lab coat. "Facial recognition software has reached a point where Internet images can be searched, and not surprisingly, the NSA does it all the time."

"So the NSA can identify people from pictures posted online?"

"Yes. Here, take a look."

Andy squinted at the shiny screen and saw a black and white photograph of a white man standing next to a man in a turban.

"This is Lucas with Atiyah Abd al-Rahman, second in command of Al-Qaeda. We believe it was taken a few weeks before 9/11." Chandelling swiped his finger on the tablet and changed the picture. "Here Lucas is again, in 1994, with Juvénal Habyarimana. Habyarimana's assassination was the catalyst for the genocide in Rwanda. Close to a million people killed."

It was definitely Lucas.

"Now here he is in a picture with Pol Pot. This picture is dated between 1978 and 1979, during the Khmer Rouge period. You know what happened then, I take it?"

"More than two million Cambodians died." Andy shook his head. "I don't understand. How could he have been present during so many awful situations? How could he know they were going to happen? Is he psychic?"

"He's much more than that." Dr. Chandelling typed something into his tablet before turning it back around so that Andy could see. "Take a look at this one."

Andy's mouth hung open. "That's... Adolf Hitler."

"Yes. And that's Lucas standing right behind him in a Shutzstaffel uniform. The United Nations have never been able to identify the man in the picture before. He has remained a mystery."

"And now we have him in subbasement 5."

Chandelling nodded slowly. "There are two things to be gleaned from this. Number one is that Lucas has been present at several truly awful human events—genocides and mass murders, wars. Number two; I will allow you to come to the conclusion on your own."

Andy stared at the tablet for a few moments; looked at the spitting image of Lucas standing behind the *Fuhrer.* "He hasn't aged. He looks exactly the same in this photograph of World War Two as he does now."

"Absolutely fascinating, wouldn't you agree? One more picture. Not as clear, because of its age. We had to clean it up digitally, but the NSA spooks say it is a 93% match."

Chandelling clicked on an old, faded, sepia-toned picture of a man in a Calvary uniform, perched on a horse. He was instantly recognizable by his huge mustache.

"George Armstrong Custer," Andy said.

"And look who is on a horse, to his left."

In a cavalry uniform, smiling pleasantly, was Lucas. "That's... impossible."

"Not only does Lucas have no discernable DNA, but apparently he doesn't age, and has been around since at least 1876. He apparently has met with key people involved in some major historical events that led to innumerable deaths."

Andy rubbed at his eyes with his palms. He felt exhausted. "I need to speak with Sun," he said. "I need to think this through."

"Of course," Chandelling said. "I'm going to share this with Kane. I believe the threat Lucas presents has gotten many times greater."

Andy nodded as Chandelling left.

Was Lucas over a hundred and fifty years old? It seemed impossible, but so did the majority of the occupants of the Spiral. And could this mild-mannered Manx man—so polite and soft-spoken—somehow be involved in countless deaths?

Andy wanted to ask his wife what she thought. But when he reached her room, Sun wasn't there.

CHAPTER TWENTY-THREE

Lucas clung to the steel-mesh fence and watched as the batling unfurled its wings on the other side. It still had not yet fully recovered from its injuries, but was making quick progress.

And then the fun and games will no doubt begin.

Lucas sighed. His presence here had been of his choosing, but as time passed by he was growing apprehensive.

The batling opened its eyes and glanced around. When its baleful gaze fell upon Lucas, its eyes opened yet wider. "*Youuuuu.*"

Lucas nodded. "Aye, 'tis me."

"*It has beeeeen a looooooong tiiiiiiime.*"

Lucas folded his arms, pressed his forehead up against the steel mesh. "It has indeed been some time. Yet our reacquaintance has come about far too quickly for my liking."

The creature they called Bub stretched out its wings, rolled its head on its shoulders with an audible *crack*, and then grinned, its mouth opening like a drawer of steak knives.

"*I reeeemember Gomorrah,*" Bub said. "*Your lust for bloooooooooood was insatiable.*"

Lucas closed his eyes, not to reminisce but to forget—to force away the images that rushed through his mind like a blood-red waterfall. "I was a different being back then. Ignorant of many things. Many things that are clear to me now."

"What riddles doooooooooo yoooooou speak, liiiiiiigght bearer?"

"I speak of beauty and strength. I speak of humanity and its ceaseless endeavor to find hope wherever there is despair. I speak of Manchester United and LOLcats. It's been an interesting few thousand years, watching them develop."

"Your haaaaaaaate is gooooooone."

"I gave up on hate. I encourage you to do the same. Living with humanity isn't as boring as you'd think. They're capable of great things."

Bub's demonic eyes narrowed. *"You shall beeeeeee among the bodies when this plaaaaaaace turns to dust. Your remains will smoke for all eeeeeeeeternity."*

Lucas grinned. "I'm not much of a smoker. Bad habit, you know?" He pulled away from the fence and turned his back on his cellmate. "You underestimate humanity, as once did I. It might come back to bite you in the arse. Did once already, I hear. Sorry I missed that one. Samhain, wasn't it? I hadn't even known they'd dug you up. I'm not as well informed as I once was."

"You will beeeee the first to dieeeeeeeeee."

"Killing me isn't going to be as easy as you think, but you're welcome to try."

"I will doooooo more than tryyyyyyyyyyyy."

"I expect you will. So what is your grand plan, then? Kill me, escape here, destroy most of humanity and enslave the rest?"

"My vengeaaaaaance," Bub said, grinning horribly, *"will beeeeeeeeee biblical."*

CHAPTER TWENTY-FOUR

Andy rushed into Sun's room, stopping abruptly at the foot of her bed.

She wasn't there. The handcuffs were still attached to the bedrail. They were bloody.

He did a quick turn, looking all around, including under the bed and in the bathroom.

"Sun!" he shouted.

Andy turned back to face the doorway. Dr. Chandelling was standing there, seemingly baffled. "She's not here?"

"No. Get the nurse."

Dr. Chandelling nodded and went to turn away, but instead he froze in place, his features contorting into a picture of horror.

Andy caught sight of the man's fear and spun around. At first he saw nothing, but when he looked up...

Sun hung from the ceiling, upside-down, her legs curled around an overhead beam. Her face twisted in a snarl, and her tangled hair was matted with sweat. And the hand that had been handcuffed to the bed...

Sun's thumb was broken, bending the wrong way, the bone jutting out and dripping blood.

"Jesus Chr—"

Dropping down like a bird of prey, Sun landed on her husband, pinning him to the floor. The sudden weight on Andy's chest knocked all the breath from his lungs.

Dr. Chandelling cried out, almost feminine in his high pitch. Sun's head swivelled in his direction, a line of drool escaping her bared teeth. She growled.

"I don't think she's well. No, not at all," Dr. Chandelling said, backpedalling out of the room.

"Hoooooow are yoooour eeeeeeears?" the creature said.

Dr. Chandelling practically tripped over himself to get out of the room.

Andy fought to suck in air as he reached up for his wife's shoulders, trying to push her off. She slashed at his face, drawing blood from talons—*Jesus, she has talons*. Then she cocked her head and stared down at him, her demonic features softening.

"Aaaaaaaandyyyyyy."

Andy fought two conflicting emotions, each primal and overpowering; the need to help the woman he loved vs. the need to get the hell away from the monster she'd become.

He gasped. "Sun? Are you in there? Can... can you understand?"

"Suuuuun is goooone."

She smiled, and her tongue flitted out between her lips. A thin, black tongue, split at the end like a snake's.

Sun leaned down, as if to kiss him, but instead began to lap at the slash mark on his cheek. Her tongue was cold and clammy, like a raw piece of liver being dragged over his face. It dug into his wound, twisting around and causing sparks of pain. Then it slipped between his lips, wiggling and trying to get past his clenched teeth.

Andy did all he could not to vomit.

"Oh my God!"

A nurse had come into the room while Andy pushed against the creature that was once his wife. Sun's head snapped up at the intrusion, twisting one-hundred-and-eighty-degrees so it faced the wrong way. Andy heard Sun's neck vertebra pop in rapid succession, like stepping on a roll of bubble wrap.

"Hellooooooooooo nurse."

"Sedate her!" Andy screamed.

Sun jerked up to her feet, as if unseen hands were pulling her, and then she ran backwards at the nurse. Her shoulders dislocated with a sharp *SNAP!* as they stretched out behind her, reaching for the woman.

The nurse screamed, and Andy kicked out a leg, tripping his wife and sending her backward—or rather face-first—to the floor.

"Get Gornman!" he bellowed, then crawled onto Sun's legs, trying to pin her down.

Sun's torso twisted, her spine torqueing in half, so once again her head and arms faced him. She looked like a doll with its parts all misaligned.

Andy's mind couldn't comprehend it all. This was his *wife*. His mind was overloaded with fear, and revulsion, and sorrow, and love, and as much as he wanted to get away from her, Andy also wanted to hold Sun tight enough to stop her from turning herself into knots.

But it was like wrestling a giant, wriggling cobra that wanted to bite you. She writhed in his grasp, slashing with her talons, hissing as her long tongue managed to slide itself up Andy's left nostril.

Andy shook his head, trying to dislodge the squirmy invader, choking as it forced itself through the nasal passage and into Andy's throat.

Then, suddenly, the tongue pulled out and Andy noticed someone giving Sun a shot in the neck with a large syringe.

"Goooooonrmaaaaaaaan!"

Sun bucked Andy off, sending him flying backward, and then twisted onto all fours and slashed at Dr. Gornman with her clawed hand.

The doctor dodged the blow, leaving the syringe sticking out of Sun's neck. Sun clawed at it, pulling it out, and then bolted through the door.

"She won't get far," Gornman said. "I gave her enough *azaperone* to drop a rhino."

Andy got to his feet and scrambled out into the hall.

Sun was nowhere to be seen.

CHAPTER TWENTY-FIVE

Dr. Chandelling ran to his room, his back against the locked door. It had taken him a long time to adjust to working around monsters, and they'd always been locked up. To have one loose in the Spiral was enough to make his bladder clench.

With his desktop computer he could view the surveillance cameras—he was only one of a few Spiral employees who had complete access to the entire facility—but Chandelling was too frightened to check. What if that creature Sun Dennison-Jones had become was killing people? Chandelling couldn't bear to watch that.

Or even worse… what if it was outside his door?

The door to his room was for privacy, not security. A good shoulder butt would pop it out of its jamb, easily. The heavy duty security was meant to keep the creatures in their cells, not prevent them from getting into employees' rooms.

Chandelling put his ear against the door, closing his eyes, trying to listen.

He heard some ruckus, screaming, but it was far away.

The seconds ticked by.

The screaming stopped.

Then there was silence.

Chandelling held his breath. He could hear his own heartbeat, a drum solo tap-tap-tapping in his chest.

More silence.

More seconds passing.

Chandelling was gathering up the nerve to go to his computer when something scratched the door.

Something like a claw being dragged across the wood.

Chandelling recoiled, crab-walking on all fours away from the sound, bumping into his desk.

For a moment, he wondered if he imagined the noise. His fear making him hear things that weren't really there.

Clearing his throat, he managed to squeak out, "Is anyone there?"

No answer.

Louder, Chandelling asked, "I said, is anyone there?"

"Yeeeessssssssssssssss."

The door burst inward, and the Sun-demon scurried inside Chandelling's room on all fours. Chandelling was too frightened to move, rooted to his spot on the floor like a deer paralyzed by the headlights of an oncoming truck.

The Sun-demon crawled up to him, placing a taloned hand on his chest. She smiled, a black tongue darting out of her mouth and poking Chandelling in the nose. Then it snaked around and—

Jesus, no!

My ear! That vile thing is in my ear!

Chandelling began to buck and push as hard as he could. He remembered a date, decades ago, a girl had kissed his ear and he'd freaked out. This was a billion times worse.

He felt his ear canal fill with warm, slimy tongue, pushing in deeper, deeper, until it rested up against his ear drum.

Chandelling wet himself. The tongue withdrew suddenly, with a wet slurping sound.

"Yoooooour card keeeeeeeeeey," the creature said.

That would be bad. With the card key, the creature had access to the entire Spiral. It could even escape.

Or could it? Chandelling remembered that the most secure parts of the facility, including the surface exit, required a security code. The card would let it use the elevator, and run around the halls, but there were cameras everywhere except for employees' rooms. Rimmer and his team would deal with this monster quickly. In fact, they were probably already on their way.

So giving up his card key wasn't an act of treason. It would be harmless. And besides, he could always say the Sun-demon simply stole it from him.

"Jacket p-pocket..." he managed.

Its claw deftly sliced open the breast pocket on his lab coat and snatched the key.

"Cooooooooooooooooode."

Shit. It knows about the security codes.

Chandelling was terrified, but he realized he couldn't answer. He'd sworn an oath to make sure the monsters in the Spiral never got out. Upon penalty of death. Just one of these monsters, loose in the world, could cause untold disaster. And Chandelling had little doubt that General Kane, who walked around like he had a broomstick shoved up his ass, would follow the rules to the letter and execute Chandelling for giving away secrets.

So Chandelling summoned up a deep reserve of courage he didn't even know he possessed and told the creature, "No."

The demon grabbed Chandelling by the side of the head, and there was a moment of white-hot, blinding pain, followed by a tearing sound. Chandelling thrashed, trying to free himself, and when he focused on the demon once more it was dangling something pink over Chandelling's face.

That's my ear!

"Coooooooooooooooooooooooooode."

Chandelling screamed as blood flowed into his ear canal and muted the hearing on his right side. The silence, its meaning, the memories it brought back; it overwhelmed him.

The Sun-demon moved her mouth to Chandelling's other ear.

Chandelling thought, in rapid succession: *She's going to bite it off. She's going to bite off my ear.*

Then: *I'll have no ears. My hearing will be ruined.*

And finally, incongruously, ridiculously: *How will I wear sunglasses? Duct tape them to my head?*

But she didn't bite. Instead, the demon whispered. "*I will feeeeeeeed you your eeeeeeears. Then I shall pop your eeeeeear druuuuums.*"

"H-how did… how you know?" he asked, whimpering.

"*Gooooormaaaaaan. She shoooooowed us your personnel fiiiiiles.*"

Dr. Gornman. That traitor. What was her angle?

Chandelling didn't care. He didn't care about Kane, either.

All he cared about was his hearing. He couldn't lose it again. He'd rather die.

"I-I heard y-you have healing powers. C-can you fix my ear?"

The demon cocked its head. "*Weeeeeee caaaaaaaaaan.*"

"You… you can fix me… and you'll let me live?"

"*Yessssssssssssssssssssssssss.*"

Chandelling had never believed in God. He'd prayed too many times for the earaches to end, for his hearing to return, for his life to get better, and God hadn't helped.

Maybe he'd been praying to the wrong guy all along.

"My codc is 6-4-5-6," hc blurtcd out.

Chandelling half-expected the Sun-demon to kill him right then. He realized, belatedly, that he should have gotten it to heal him first.

But instead of ripping out his throat, it released him.

Chandelling cleared his throat. "So… you'll heal me?"

"This vessel caaaaaaaaaannnnnot. The other musssssssst."

"The batling?"

"Yesssssssssssssss. Waaaaaaait heeeeeeeere."

The demon dropped Chandelling's ear on his chest, then sprung to its feet and fled the room.

For a moment, Chandelling was in shock and unable to move. Then he finally pushed past the fear and pain and sat up, his ear falling to the floor. He picked it up, unsure of what to do with it, and caught sight of his aquarium in his peripheral vision.

Cool water. I can keep it in cool water until Bub can fix it.

Chandelling sprang to his feet, scurrying to the aquarium. His goldfish, Satchmo, eyed him passively. With no further thought, Chandelling opened the feeder panel on the tank and dropped his ear inside. It sank slowly, billows of blood staining the water around it, and finally came to rest on the multicolored gravel at the bottom.

There. That will keep it cold. Now I just need to stop the bleeding and—

Satchmo, normally docile, raced up to the ear and began to nip at it with the ferocity of a piranha.

"Satchmo! No!"

Chandelling banged on the glass, but the goldfish was in a feeding frenzy, attacking the ear in rapid nips, eventually getting the lobe into its tiny mouth and swimming for its little underwater castle.

Chandelling tore off the top of the tank and spent the next two minutes trying to grab Satchmo and get his ear back.

He failed.

CHAPTER TWENTY-SIX

Dr. Gornman watched her computer monitor while chewing on a wart she had on the knuckle of her thumb. The camera she'd selected was outside of Dr. Chandelling's room, which she'd selected after Sun had broken in. There were no security cameras in private rooms—a silly privacy issue Gornman had never understood—so she had no idea what was happening inside.

Had the demon killed him?

Gornman had given it every opportunity to. She'd showed the Bub batling personnel files on all the staff members, holding them up to its cell glass, assuming a creature of such high intelligence could read quickly. The demon knew everything she did about every employee in the Spiral. Then she'd diluted the knock-out gas and tampered with the moving crate, weakening the lock before they attempted to transfer the demon. Her goal was for Bub to escape, and the goal was a selfish one.

Everyone knew that if you made a deal with the devil, you got whatever you wanted.

When Bub had bitten Sun, Gornman had given her shots of saline, saying it was broad spectrum antibiotics. If Bub had infected her, as Gornman hoped, she didn't want to accidentally halt the process.

Sun had become infected, in a big way, and Gornman had given her an amphetamine shot, saying it was a tranquilizer.

Now she had to wait and see if Bub was as smart as the Samhain debacle showed he was.

If he was, then Sun would soon free him, and Gornman could make her demands.

She had a few doozies.

No doubt Bub would take over the world. Gornman had studied the Samhain event like it was her graduate thesis, and was convinced the demon was destined to rule mankind.

It would need a second-in-command. How did the old saying go?

I'd rather reign in hell than serve in heaven.

Gornman had been serving in hell—the Spiral—for far too long. Working with military idiots and ambitious bureaucrats and short-sighted scientists who cared more about useless research than practicality. Gornman's vision, and her leadership skills, had been ignored. She'd been predicting Bub's arrival for years, and now nothing would stop her from attaining the power she deserved.

Chandelling's door swung open, and the Sun-demon hurried through. It was too fast to make out any major details, but Gornman clearly saw a key card in its claw.

It had gotten Chandelling's access card. And no doubt his code as well.

She leaned back in her chair, smiling, and then switched cameras, following the demon as it headed for the elevator.

As expected, it chose subbasement 5.

Going to free its master.

Dr. Thandi Gornman smiled.

Let the games begin.

CHAPTER TWENTY-SEVEN

Rimmer led Jerry down a hallway, past a cell containing a long, shiny log with hundreds of legs.

Jerry squinted through the window. The log began to twist and undulate.

A tree that could move?

No, make that a giant centipede. One with mandibles large enough to grab a lamb, and black, beady eyes the size of baseballs.

Bloody terrifying.

I'm already terrified enough. Rimmer is probably leading me to my death.

Will he shoot me?

Or worse—stick me in one of these cells with some monster, or the unicorn like he promised?

"So what now?" Jerry said, barely able to keep his knees from knocking together as he marched toward uncertainty. "You make me kneel down, put two in the back of my head?"

Rimmer didn't respond. Not a good sign. Jerry had been partly kidding, but now he wondered if he was, indeed, marked for execution.

Jerry turned to look at him while he walked. He forced bravado. "So, do you kill innocent people a lot in your line of work? Or is this a special treat? Most people just get their kicks on *Call of Duty*."

Rimmer kept his stare forward. "You're not innocent, Mr. Preston. You committed an attack against one of this nation's secure, top-secret facilities."

"I was playing fetch with an over-sized dog. That's my only crime. You saw it yourself."

"It's not my place to say."

"No, you just take orders. You're as much a dog as Wolfie was."

"Keep moving." Rimmer's pager on his belt went off. He checked the number. "Faster. I've got to go."

So this is it. I'm dead. This goose-stepping lackey is going to murder me in cold blood.

Jerry's thoughts turned to his mother, and how an embrace from her would hold value above all else at that moment. He thought about Ben, about stealing from his estranged father. He thought about fighting back when Rimmer pulled his trigger and dying like a man.

"Why don't you just do it here?" Jerry said, stopping, forcing himself not to cry. "In the hallway, for the cameras to see? Or does Kane want this kept off the record?"

Rimmer placed a hand on his shoulder and gave him a firm push, getting him walking again. "No one is going to kill you, Jerry."

"Kane said to take care of me."

"I'm going to put you in a cell."

"With what? The Loch Ness monster?"

"No."

"A Medusa, with snakes for hair? Medusas freak me out. They're like my nightmare fuel."

"Your own cell. Jerry."

"Seriously?"

"Seriously."

Jerry considered it. The relief he felt was short lived. Being locked up down here, possibly forever, would be even worse than death. Just one more exhibit in Hell's zoo. He wondered how often they'd change the hay in his cage.

"What's going to happen to Wolfie's body?" he asked, mostly to take his mind off of his own situation.

"The werewolf?"

"He's not a werewolf. If he was, he would have turned back into a man when that fascist, Kane, killed him."

"Not all werewolves are shapechangers. That's a legend. You know that vampire sucker thing on level 5? The Nosferatu? That's probably where part of the werewolf legend came from. Men who turned into monsters with sharp teeth who acted like animals and ate babies. Wolfie, as you call him, probably got mixed up in the legend. I was surprised he died so easily. He may not have been a man who changed when the moon was full, but he was more than just a big dog. Incredibly strong and resilient. Resistant to aging and injury. The only thing he reacted negatively to was silver. Classic werewolf traits. He was..." Rimmer's eyes seemed to go out of focus for a moment. "Well, he was one helluva animal."

Jerry raised an eyebrow. "It almost sounds as if you liked him."

"You were playing ball with Wolfie?"

"You know I was."

"Who do you think gave him that ball?" Rimmer asked.

"Nessie did."

"Nessie liked him. But the ball—that was mine."

Jerry considered it. Maybe Rimmer wasn't as big of a tool as he'd thought. "So where is he?"

"He's in the morgue now. I'll make sure his body is properly disposed of."

"He won't be fed to the spiders?"

"No. He'll be studied and preserved. He was one of a kind."

"So, aren't you pissed off? Your commanding officer killed Wolfie for no reason at all."

"Being pissed off doesn't keep me from following orders, Jerry."

"That's a total cop-out."

"Whatever. We're here."

They were in front of a seemingly empty cell.

"You sure it's empty?" Jerry asked, dubious.

"Do you see anything inside?"

"Could be filled with invisible, man-eating pythons."

"It's not." Rimmer used his fob to access the LED panel and opened the steel door.

"Well, bugger it, what am I supposed to do in here? Is there a television?"

Rimmer shoved him in and began to shut the door.

"C'mon, mate! At least give me a magazine or something!"

Rimmer paused. Then he reached into his pocket—

—and took out a rubber ball.

Wolfie's.

He tossed it to Jerry, and then a siren began to wail, the overhead lights starting to blink.

"What the fuck is that?" Jerry asked, pocketing the ball.

Rimmer's eyes narrowed. "Security breach. We're in lockdown."

The idea of a security breach in the Spiral scared the piss out of Jerry.

"Shit. Did something get out? Are we trapped down here?"

Rimmer didn't answer. If there were monsters running around, the last place Jerry wanted to be was locked in a cell, unable to run. If it was Bub—and Jerry had a hunch it was—that demon was smart enough to get out of his cell, which meant it was smart enough to get inside the cells. If Jerry stayed locked up, he would basically be the equivalent of convenience food.

Out of all the terrible ways to die, being eaten was probably the worst.

Jerry made his eyes go wide as he looked beyond Rimmer. Then he raised his hand and pointed. "Oh, shite! Behind you!"

Rimmer swung around, reaching for his sidearm, and Jerry bumped him hard as he could, sending the man sideways, and then went running down the hallway in the opposite direction, heading for the elevator. He pressed the button and the doors opened immediately. Jerry popped inside and watched as Rimmer snarled at him. Jerry frantically looked for some button to press, but there were none.

Voice activated. It's voice activated.

"Level one," Jerry said.

The doors remained open.

"Doors close."

They didn't close.

Rimmer began to charge toward the elevator.

"Come on, you bloody lift, move!" Jerry remembered he no longer had that fob thing. The elevator likely wouldn't work without it. Rimmer was only a few meters away, and he didn't look happy. Jerry winced at what he assumed would be a punch in the face at the minimum.

Then, magically, the doors began to close. They finished closing right before Rimmer reached them, and Jerry blew out a big breath of relief. The elevator began to rise, and Jerry wondered if maybe he didn't need a fob after all.

It stopped on subbasement 1. Not the surface, but a definite improvement.

At least, it seemed like an improvement until the lift doors opened and Jerry found himself tackled by imps.

They leapt on him en masse, clinging to his limbs. Small, green, somewhat clammy Smurf-like creatures that freaked Jerry out so bad he began to scream as he tried to shake them off. They screamed in response, shrill like monkeys, but the family of four clung to his arms and legs like they were tied on;

the world's ugliest fashion accessories. Several of them were pointing back into the hall.

Jerry controlled his hysteria long enough to glance upward—

—seeing Sun Dennison-Jones in front of a cell, opening it up and releasing...

It's the unicorn.

The cell opened and the magnificent equine trotted out, then let out a nicker. The nicker became a scream when Sun stuck it in the nose. But it wasn't a simple slap. Jerry took a closer look and noticed that Sun's hands had become claws.

She wasn't Sun anymore. She was a monster.

A monster who was releasing all the other monsters.

The unicorn reared up on its hand legs, pawing the air, and then charged past Sun, toward the elevator, horn lowered like a rhino.

"Close!" Jerry commanded the elevator doors, the imps clinging to him momentarily forgotten.

The doors stayed open, but his shouting got Sun's attention. She smiled at him, her mouth crammed with fangs.

"Close, goddammit!"

The unicorn picked up speed. It's eyes were wide with terror, and Jerry imagined getting impaled on its horn. It truly would be one of the most painful ways to die, while also being one of the gayest.

"No no no no no no..."

The imps clutching Jerry began to repeat "no no no" as well, but higher-pitched and faster. It would have been kind of cute if Jerry wasn't seconds away from wetting his pants in fear.

When the unicorn was less than a meter away from the lift, the doors finally began to shut—

—and the horn wedged itself between the doors. Jerry backed away, bumping into the rear of the lift, his jaw hanging in horror as the creature forced the doors back open.

And that's when the imps dropped off Jerry and attacked, flinging themselves at the unicorn going straight for its eyes with their tiny hands. The beast grunted, retreating a few meters back, and the imps jumped back into the elevator just as the doors shut.

"Yes!" Jerry shouted, pumping a fist into the air.

"Yes yes yes yes," they said in their preternatural helium voices, also repeating his fist gesture.

Cool.

"You guys are little gangsters. Cheers."

The imps began to chitter at one another. The elevator continued to rise, coming up to the Nucleus.

"Get behind me," Jerry said. "We don't know what's on this floor."

The imps stared at him. Jerry got on one knee, using his arms to corral the family behind him. When the lift stopped, Jerry held his breath, expecting the worst.

Which is exactly what he got, because as soon as the elevator doors opened, six men pointed automatic weapons directly at Jerry's head.

CHAPTER TWENTY-EIGHT

Andy had an idea where his wife had gone.

Actually, not his wife. That thing his wife had become. That monster wasn't Sun. It was Bub, controlling her DNA. Bub had infected her, altering how she looked and acted. Almost as if Sun were possessed. But he knew the cause was physical, not spiritual. Sun had some kind of disease.

Which meant, hopefully, she could be cured.

Hopefully.

Until then, he had to figure out some way to protect her. If there was even a tiny chance of getting Sun back, Andy would do whatever it took.

That, however, would pose a problem. Shortly after Sun ran off, the Spiral went on full alert. Rimmer's men were all armed and looking for targets to shoot. One target in particular.

Andy had gotten to Kane's office just as the General was leaving.

"You can't kill her," Andy demanded, holding out his palm and keeping the older man from advancing.

Kane's eyes narrowed. "It isn't your wife anymore, Mr. Dennison-Jones. It's a demon."

"You don't know that for sure."

"Oh, really?" Kane stepped back, and Andy followed him to his computer monitor. Kane typed in a command, and Andy stared at the security footage, watching as Sun opened cell after cell, freeing terrifying creatures.

"If we don't stop her right now, at this rate she'll have released every guest within the hour."

"You don't have to kill her."

"Dr. Gornman tried a sedative. It didn't have any effect. The knock-out gas didn't work on the faustling, either."

"You can capture her. A net. Or force her into a cell."

"And risk the lives of those under my command?"

"Please, General. It isn't Sun who's doing this. It's Bub. If you kill Bub, she could return to normal."

"Is that so?"

Andy didn't think so. Sun had an infection, and the infection affected her thoughts. It was unlikely that Bub, if destroyed, would cure Sun. But if Kane focused on killing the demon, maybe it would buy Sun some more time.

"What if it was someone you loved?" Andy implored. "Wouldn't you try?"

Kane sighed, his lips pursed. Then he said, "I can't make any promises. My first duty is to this facility, to make sure the visitors are detained and never reach the outside world. My second is the protection of those who work here. But if I can fulfil those duties, and still contain your wife without destroying her, I'll try."

"Thank you, General. Do you know where she is?"

Kane frowned, then typed another command on the keyboard. It was a camera on subbasement 5, Sun rushing up to it and tearing it off the wall, making the image go dark.

"She's destroying some of the surveillance cameras as she opens the cell doors. We're sending a team down."

"How is she opening the cells?" Andy asked.

Kane didn't answer.

"General?"

"She apparently got a key card and the access code from Dr. Chandelling, after she tore off his ear. He's in the infirmary."

"Can't you change his code?"

"No. It's a safeguard. The key personnel all have unique codes. That way, if there is a breach in the chain of command, others can override it. Several of us have the power to secure the facility."

"What do you mean by *secure*? You mean fill it up with cement?"

Kane stayed silent. Andy made his hands into fists, trying not to let his anger bubble over. This was Samhain all over again. History hadn't taught these people anything.

Then again, it apparently hadn't taught Andy anything either, or else he and Sun would have never come here.

"Just don't kill her," Andy said, quickly leaving the office.

Out in the hall, he startled to the sound of automatic gun fire. It was very close. Andy placed his back against the wall and peeked around the corner.

Three guards were shooting at something unseen further down the hallway.

A millisecond later, one of the men was pounced upon by something large, covered in colorful feathers.

It was the dinosaur. *Achillobator.* Tall as a man, five meters long, with a head bigger than a crocodile's and taloned feet that tore open the soldier as easily as unzipping a sleeping bag. Guts spilled out, and the creature immediately opened wide and bit off the second man's head before the soldier had a chance to adjust aim. The third turned and tried to run, but the achillobator's tail whipped around like a stingray, impaling him through the back and out his chest.

Charged with adrenaline, Andy sprinted in the opposite direction, heading for the elevator. A small tree fell before him, and Andy jumped over it before realizing it wasn't a tree at all, but a giant centipede, brown and thick as the trunk of a forty-year old oak. He glanced over his shoulder as he ran, and the insect reared up, its mandibles clicking and antenna whipping around furiously just as the dinosaur plowed into it. The centipede quickly wrapped around the prehistoric creature, coiling like a python, and Andy called the elevator with his key fob, unable to turn away from the two monsters as they locked in mortal combat.

As they battled, something else slunk around the corner. It looked like a giant bird of prey, with a massive, curved beak and sharp black eyes. But as the full animal came into view, Andy saw its back half was that of a lion.

The griffon.

It focused on Andy, and the feathers on its neck ruffled, standing on edge. Then its maw opened wide and it let out a terrifying screech that made Andy feel faint. It hunkered down—

stalking mode—and its yellow talons *click-click-clicked* on the tile floor as it slunk toward Andy.

This is bad.

Andy thought of the countless nature shows he'd seen over his lifetime, where some predatory bird gripped its prey and tore off strips of flesh while it struggled to escape, and he was hard pressed to think of a worse way to die.

The griffon crept closer, and Andy shrunk against the elevator doors, no clue at all how to defend himself. What do you do when a gigantic eagle/lion hybrid attacks? Go for its eyes? Curl up in a ball? Or just pray it all ends quickly?

When it was a meter away, the griffin lowered its body to the floor, getting ready to spring.

The elevator still hadn't arrived, and Andy wondered what his very last thought would be. That he'd failed Sun? That he blamed himself for getting them into this mess? That it sure hurt like hell being eaten alive by a griffin?

Then the creature squawked again, immediately spinning around and attacking the dinosaur that had locked its jaws onto its back leg.

The elevator opened—blessedly empty—and Andy retreated from the monster wars and told the lift to take him to subbasement 5.

That's where Sun would be heading. To free Bub.

Andy had no clue how he was going to stop her, but he had to try. If there was even the tiniest bit of humanity left in his wife, he'd find it. She was strong. One of the strongest people he'd ever known. If anyone in the world had the willpower to fight back against the infection that had overtaken her, Sun did.

As the elevator took him deeper into the earth, Andy tried to get his breathing under control and considered the future. If he was able to help Sun, and if they got out of there, and if Bub didn't destroy the world.

A whole lot of *ifs*.

If things did work out, he vowed he and Sun would get off the grid. Go somewhere the government couldn't find them. Hide away in a little podunk town where Sun could be a veterinarian and Andy could teach French or Spanish or something equally banal at the local community college. Change their names. Start a family. Get away from all the death and the monsters and the ever-looming threat of humanity's annihilation.

When he reached subbasement 5, Andy tensed, but understood he couldn't brace himself for whatever he was about to face. Maybe it would be crawling with creatures. Maybe Sun was waiting to kill him. Maybe Bub was already freed, ready to take the elevator to the surface and make good on his promise to destroy humanity.

But when the doors opened, the hallway was empty. Andy quickly made his way toward the cell Bub and Lucas shared. Bub hovered in place, eyeing Andy malevolently. Lucas sat in his chair, looking pensive.

"Your lovely wife?" Lucas asked.

"She's... infected."

"Aye. Controlled from within, so to speak. In 1518, in Strasbourg, there was a dancing plague. Over four hundred people afflicted and unable to stop dancing. It lasted almost a week, and some literally danced themselves to death. Their disease controlled their actions."

"Was that Bub?"

"No. Least, I don't believe it was. Just saying that people, sick people, sometimes aren't responsible for their actions. Remember that, whatever happens next."

"Suuuuuuuuuuuuuuuuuuuuuuuuun."

Andy twisted around, and saw Sun had come up behind him. She had that toothed, demonic smile on her face, and there was blood on the front of her hospital gown.

"You... you can fight this, Sunshine," Andy said. "I know you're in there. You can—"

Sun backhanded Andy, sending him to the floor. Then she placed a key card up to the cell's LED panel.

"Sun! Don't!" Andy reached for her leg, and was summarily kicked in the face. Sun quickly punched some keys and the cell door opened.

Then there was a violent crash.

The batling was knocked clean out of the air by a flying net of steel, careening into Sun and sending them both sprawling onto the hallway floor.

The steel mesh fence that had separated Lucas and Bub fell on top of the batling, pinning it underneath. Sun lay to the side, unconscious and bleeding from a gash on her forehead. Andy quickly crawled to her. She had a pulse.

"I hate noisy roommates," Lucas said, stepping out of his cell and staring down at Bub.

Bub grasped the fence in his clawed hands and threw it back at Lucas, hitting the Manx man in the midsection and knocking him into the cell. It then beelined past Andy, who punched with everything he had as it landed on Sun. A moment later Bub had the key card in its hand, then it turned on Andy, placing its claw on his chest.

"Joooooooin usssssssssssss, Dennison."

Andy felt a pinch, then Bub was gone, flying down the hallway. Andy lifted his shirt, saw the puncture mark in his sternum.

I'm infected. Like Sun.

He looked at Lucas, who was sitting against the rear wall of the cell.

"Wee bastard is strong, ain't he?"

"He... Bub... injected me..."

"He tends to do that." Lucas got up, seemingly unharmed, and walked up to Andy and Sun. With a punch too fast to see, he clipped Sun under the jaw. She slumped to the floor.

Andrew looked at his wife—the thing that was his wife—and realized he didn't want to live like that. He'd been willing to do whatever it took to save Sun, but the thought of being a prisoner in his own, demonic body, slavishly serving Bub...

Andy would rather die. And he selfishly dwelled in self-pity for several seconds before saying, "Maybe you should just kill us both."

"I didn't peg you as one to give up, Andy. Didn't you defeat this Bub fella once before?"

"No. I mean, we hurt him, but..."

"How'd ye hurt him?"

"Radiation."

Lucas nodded. "I can see how that would work."

"But it didn't work," Andy said. "It only slowed him down, but it didn't kill him."

"Slowed him down, did it?"

"Killed his cells. Bub has such an advanced physiology that he's more susceptible to radiation than most life forms."

"Is that so?"

Andy blinked, a beam of hope cutting through his despair. Was Bub's mutagen serum also affected? Could a dose of radiation stop the infection in him and Sun?

"There's an x-ray machine in the infirmary. They also have a PET scanner. Which means a cyclotron, for creating injectable radiopharmaceuticals."

Andy didn't know much about medicine, but Sun used a PET scanner at work (which always amused him because she was using a PET scanner to scan pets—irony is funny). It involved an intravenous radioactive tracer. Maybe some combination of internal medicine and external bombardment was worth a try.

"We can give it a go," Lucas said.

"Okay. But you have to promise me one thing. If I... if I turn into one of those things..."

"Don't worry, lad." Lucas patted Andy's shoulder. "I'll put an end to your and your wife's misery."

"What? No! I changed my mind. I want you to make sure Sun and I are cured. No matter how long it takes. I don't want to be a martyr."

Lucas chuckled. "Understood. Truth told, your species always seemed a little too eager to self-sacrifice, if you ask me. Willing to march into death for the greater good. Noble it can be on rare occasions, but other times it's just bloody stupid."

"Can you help me with Sun?"

"I can do you one better." Lucas picked up Sun and slung her over his shoulder as if she weighed nothing. "And we'd better move along. Our demon friend is freeing beasties, and the ones on this level aren't too friendly."

CHAPTER TWENTY-NINE

Dr. Chandelling wanted to get the hell out of there.

The Sun-demon had promised Bub would reattach his ear—which he'd gotten back after overturning Satchmo's tank and dumping the hungry little fish onto the floor. But if that promise turned out to be a lie, Chandelling needed to see a doctor. Someone with more talent and experience than Gornman.

The problem was, they were on lockdown. Which meant nothing got in, or out, until Kane and his staff of rent-a-thugs got the situation under control. Knowing Kane, that could take hours.

Chandelling didn't have hours. His ear was on ice, but it wouldn't keep fresh forever.

"Are you a Shakespeare fan, doc?"

Chandelling was startled by the voice, and he flinched in his hospital bed. He searched the room, but didn't see anyone.

But… where did that banana on the counter come from?

"I was going to quote Julius Ceaser," the banana said. "Friends, Romans, countrymen, lend me your ears. But it seems you already did."

Shit. *Mu*. That annoying little multidimensional fruit who made fun of everyone.

"Funny," Chandelling said. "Now why don't you leave."

"Don't you mean *split?*" the banana asked.

"Just go away."

"I'm staying for the show, Doc. You see, someone is dying to meet you."

That's when Chandelling noticed a figure shuffle into his room.

Bub? To heal me?

No. It wasn't the batling.

It was someone who stank like a corpse.

And looked like a corpse.

And walked like a corpse. Well... walked like a walking corpse.

"Braaaaaaains," the zombie said.

Chandelling screamed, two octaves higher than his normal voice. He immediately leapt out of bed—losing his balance because of the narcotic painkillers he'd insisted be administered—and fell to the floor.

The zombie was on him in three steps, reaching down with its rotten hands and immediately biting Chandelling in the scalp.

"Your brain... smells so good," the undead abomination growled between bites. "So rich and spicy..."

Chandelling screamed, trying to force the creature away, but it continued to gnaw, tearing back the skin until its rotting teeth were scraping against his exposed skull.

"What's eating you, Doc?" Mu asked.

For a dead man, the zombie was amazingly powerful, and there was a disgusting *CRACK!* followed by a most disturbing slurping sound.

"Something on your mind, Doc?" Mu said.

I can't let this goddamn thing eat my brain!

Chandelling fought with all he had, but he was pinned to the floor, and the zombie's fingers probed the hole it had made in his skull, trying to make it larger. Which it did, breaking the skull in half.

"Talk about a splitting headache," Mu said.

The zombie began to chomp, slurping up Chandelling's gray matter.

Dr. Chandelling's last thought—

—was devoured.

CHAPTER THIRTY

Jerry stared down the barrels of six guns, one of them belonging to Rimmer. The boy immediately raised his hands over his head. The imps repeated the gesture.

"Hold your fire," Rimmer said, scowling. He had that scowl down to a science. Jerry bet the mercenary could curdle milk with it.

"Monsters! Behind him!" Handler adjusted his aim, pointing his weapon at one of the imps.

"They ain't monsters," Jerry said. "They're like Smurfs. Only uglier."

Rimmer's scowl deepened, something Jeremy didn't think was possible. "You let them out?"

"They were already out. But they saved me from the unicorn."

"They saved you from a unicorn?"

"I know. It sounds lame. But they did. They're on our side."

"Prove it."

Without hesitation, Jerry got down on one knee and opened up his arms. "C'mere, little guy. I won't hurt you." He reached for one of the imps, who didn't back away or struggle as Jerry picked it up. The creature was cool to the touch, and somewhat clammy, but it was docile.

"See? It's not spitting acid in my face, or trying to tear out my throat. It's one of the good guys."

Rimmer lowered his rifle. The other soldiers did the same.

"You're in trouble, kid," Rimmer said.

"We're all in trouble. The imps and the unicorn are out. What else has gotten free in this crazy little zoo of yours?"

Rimmer didn't answer. Which itself was an answer.

"Everything?" Jerry asked, his eyes getting wide. "Everything is free?"

Rimmer checked his pager, then gave his men a hand motion. They followed him into the elevator, surrounding Jerry with buff testosterone.

"Subbasement 5," Rimmer said.

"Wait! I'm not going back down there." Jerry made a try for the door, but Rimmer clapped a hand on his shoulder, stopping him.

"You had a chance to be locked in a nice, safe cell. You chose otherwise."

"I changed my mind. A cell sounds absolutely fabulous right now."

The lift doors closed, and Jerry felt his sphincter clench as the elevator began to descend.

"I'll have you know you're endangering the life of a minor," Jerry said. "I'm young and defenceless."

"Have you fired a gun before?" Rimmer asked.

"A real one? I'm from the UK, you nutter. Our cops don't even carry guns. Why? You gonna lend me yours?"

"Hell, no. But if my men and I get killed, feel free to pick up one of ours and try your best." Rimmer held up his rifle. "This is a Kriss Vector carbine. It's forty-five caliber and uses Glock 21 magazines with sleeve extenders, so the mags are interchangeable with our sidearms."

Rimmer showed him the button on the side of the complicated-looking rifle to release the magazine. Then he shoved it back in and pulled a lever off the side. "This is the charging handle. You pull it out, put your thumb on the bolt hold, and rack it back. Take off the safety here, and you're ready to fire. When you fire the last shot, the bolt will stay back. Pull the release to load your next mag. Got all that?"

"No. But this reminds me of the scene in *Aliens* where Hicks teaches Ripley how to shoot the pulse rifle."

Rimmer raised an eyebrow. "You watch too many movies."

"Which is probably why I'm not freaking out right now. I've been desensitized to seeing monsters on the loose. Show me again. I'll get it."

Rimmer pressed the button to drop the magazine, then reloaded.

"Do I need to rack it again?" Jerry asked.

"No, because I didn't fire. Bullet is still in the chamber. See?"

This time, when Rimmer pulled the charging handle, a bullet popped out the side ejector port. One of the imps grabbed it, offering the treasure up to Jerry.

Jerry took the bullet, squinting at it. "Does this explode when it hits a target?"

"No."

"Spray cyanide?"

"No."

"So what does it do?"

The doors opened, and one of the giant harvestmen spiders stuck one of its clawed legs into the hallway. Rimmer bore down on it and pulled the trigger, turning it into a gory mess of arachnid parts.

"It kills things," Rimmer answered, popping in another magazine.

"I think I just shit myself." Jerry's eardrums felt like he'd just endured a four hour Metallica concert, front row.

The spider's cellmate was clinging to the wall, approaching quickly. Apparently, guns didn't frighten the creature.

Handler took point and fired, but the spider leapt onto the ceiling with incredible speed, avoiding the burst. A millisecond later it dropped on Handler's shoulders.

No one fired—they obviously didn't want to risk shooting Handler—and the spider's mandibles opened and it bit the man on the neck.

Handler dropped to his knees, screaming. A gout of blood exploded from his mouth and his eyes swelled in their sockets. Slowly the guard's torso expanded, blowing up like a balloon. Then he split open at the ribs and a thick white substance spilt forth from his carcass.

Rimmer strode forward and fired his newly reloaded rifle, aiming point blank. He emptied an entire magazine into the spider, forcing it off of Handler and shredding it to bits.

"Jesus," one of Rimmer's men said, kneeling down to examine Handler, who was deader than dead. "That was—"

Before the guard could finish, something pounced on him. Something man-shaped, with claws and shark-like teeth.

One of those nosferatu dracula-things.

It bit a big hunk out of his neck, then leapt into the elevator, jaws snapping and talons flailing.

Panic ensued.

There was gunfire and yelling and snarling. Jerry raced down the hallway, head lowered in a crouch, cradling the one imp like a rugby ball while its family chased behind. He ducked past another dracula-thing, narrowly avoiding its swiping claws,

"Keep going!" Rimmer yelled from behind them. It was followed by the burp of his machinegun, and a terrible screech that Jerry guessed came from one of the draculas.

Then Jerry stopped abruptly, skidding on his feet and almost falling onto his arse, because blocking the hallway was—

Is that a goddamned yeti?

The beast stood almost three meters high, covered with scraggly white fur. Like someone crossed a polar bear with a gorilla. It had a pungent, musky odor. Jerry wondered if, like the imps, it was friendly. Then the thing roared, opening a maw filled with dozens of teeth, thin and long as nails, but opaque as icicles.

"In the cell!" Rimmer shouted. "Now!"

Without thinking, Jerry ran into the first open and empty cell he saw, to his right, and quickly spun around. Rimmer hit some buttons on the LED and then slipped in before the door closed.

Both men caught their breath, and then Jerry looked through the Plexiglas cell door and watched two draculas dart past.

"Your men?" Jerry asked.

"I think West got away in the elevator."

"The others?"

Rimmer gave a small shake of his head.

Down the hallway, the draculas screeched and the yeti roared. Jerry approached cautiously, and peered at the ensuing battle. The yeti swung out with its arms, keeping the draculas at a distance.

"Can they get in here?" Jerry asked.

"Only if they have a key and the code. Cell is solid."

"Can we get out?"

Rimmer didn't answer.

"We can't get out?"

"I have my pager. I can text someone."

"Who?"

Rimmer blew out a stiff breath. "Whoever is left."

CHAPTER THIRTY-ONE

Dr. Gornman sat in her lab and stared at the computer screen, flipping from security camera to security camera. All of her lab assistants had fled. A few had made it to the surface. Most had gone back to their rooms first, for their belongings. A big mistake, as many were slaughtered or eaten. Gornman lost count of all the creepy things crawling the halls, but some stand-outs included a horse-sized six-legged chameleon called a basilisk, a fanged bull the staff sarcastically called the *mad cow*, and a giant, two-headed cobra, which fought with itself over which mouth got to devour Gornman's secretary, Henrietta. The left head won, and Henrietta was now a lump in the snake's midsection.

It was all so very terrible.

And so wonderfully cathartic.

In some cases, she'd listened to her co-workers complaints, pathetic fears, and boring dreams for years and years. Too many psychiatric sessions to count, and Gornman was convinced that all but a few employees deserved the fate they received. Casterov, a tech-head, had been lamely hitting on Gornman since she'd first arrived at the Spiral, using his sessions to make lewd proposals. When an ostrichgator bit off his junk, Gornman actually laughed. And Ramish, an analyst, who had an almost

Freudian obsession with fondling the gold necklace her grandmother had given her, was disembowelled by a chupacabra, her intestines looped around her own neck. Could it be more poetically ironic than that?

Gornman thought about all the time she'd wasted here, how her substantial talents had been almost criminally underutilized. Kane had finally dangled the carrot of leadership in front of her after a decade of zero appreciation and mistreatment, but it had been too little too late. Ruling the world at Bub's side was infinitely preferable to commanding this petty little fiefdom. Gornman didn't regret her actions.

Hell, she relished them.

Her only regret was coming to the Spiral in the first place.

After losing her mother—her only surviving relative—to cancer, Gornman had been intent on becoming a medical researcher. She longed to add her name alongside *Pasteur* and *Jenner*, and other great minds who had improved the health of the entire world. She wanted to make sure that no other young girls lost their mothers like she did.

Then she was hit by a truck. Literally.

The driver had been drunk. He'd hopped the curb and plowed into her at a bus stop while she'd been sitting on the bench, studying for her finals.

She spent over two years in the hospital, in near constant pain.

For the first year she didn't have a single visitor. Her family was all dead, and her studies always pushed away any friendships, Gornman reached a depth of despair that made her consider suicide more than once. Between the excruciatingly painful rehab and the debilitating loneliness, she switched her major in college to psychiatry to try and figure herself out. And she did.

The reason she couldn't connect to other people was because they were all beneath her. Intellectually. Emotionally. Spiritually.

Deus Manus had reached out to her in the hospital a year into her rehab. They'd been watching her progress for a while, impressed by her medical acumen and her strong will. Their job offer—good money and benefits in a secluded hole in the ground—was perfect. Gornman would only have to treat a few dozen people, at most, and she wouldn't have to go out into the real world to deal with reality. She readily accepted their offer to join.

Three years later, she completed medical school. A day after that, a black SUV pulled up outside her dorm and took her away. She had been at the Spiral ever since.

And now it looks like I finally have my chance to shine.

All Gornman needed was for Bub to find her before one of those creatures did.

She switched cameras on her monitor, watching as—was that Tyler from Human Resources?—get excoriated by a giant, four-tailed scorpion.

That's when the alarm went off.

Not the general alarm. That had rung when the Sun-demon escaped the infirmary.

This was the evacuation alarm. Protocol Omega. The one that warned the Spiral's workers that they had half an hour to get the hell out, before the entire facility filled up with quick-setting concrete.

Kane.

That idiot General was going to bury them all. Gornman hadn't thought he had the guts to do it. But then, he was probably abandoning ship.

She had to stop him before that asshole saved the human race.

CHAPTER THIRTY-TWO

General Kane cleared his throat and tried to steady his voice when he spoke into the microphone.

"Protocol Omega has been initiated. Repeat, Protocol Omega has been initiated. You have thirty minutes to evacuate the Spiral." The General blew out a deep breath. "May God help us all."

CHAPTER THIRTY-THREE

"Protocol Omega?" Andy said to Lucas as they stood in the elevator. "That doesn't sound good."

"I've yet to see anything in this place that's good," Lucas answered. Sun, still unconscious, was still slung effortlessly over his shoulder.

"That reminds me. There might be a dinosaur on this floor."

"Will wonders never cease?"

"And a griffon," Andy said.

"Head of an eagle, hindquarters of a lion?"

"That's the one."

"Never seen a griffon. What's it like?"

"Terrifying. There also might be a giant centipede."

"I'd expect nothing less."

Andy shook his head. "What kind of idiots would collect the most dangerous monsters on earth and put them all in one place?"

"The church," Lucas said. "Poor decisions seem to be part of their long-term plan. I remember back when this whole Deus Manus concept was conceived. A wee bit ill-advised, I'd said at the time. Too many dark things in one place is like spitting in fate's eye."

Andy glanced at his companion. "How old did you say you were?"

"I didn't." Lucas smiled pleasantly. "But I've been around long enough to have seen a great many things."

"So I'm probably being paranoid thinking this might be the end of the world."

"The world will go on. As for humanity… well, it isn't looking too good right now. Always was a pride issue with you people. Thinking you can control everything. I'm no stranger to pride myself. Being confident in your abilities is one thing. Getting cocky is another. When I strolled into this fine establishment last week and saw all the techno-widgets and electronic computer gizmos, I knew it was trouble. Too much reliance on your own fabrications. Could have predicted it even if I hadn't known it was going to happen."

"And how did you know it was going to happen?"

"That's one of my blessings. Or curses, depending on your definition. I get to know in advance all of the terrible things humanity does to itself. The lord has given me a front row seat, in a manner of speaking."

Andy wanted to broach the subject of the pictures of Lucas he'd seen, where the Manx man was in the company of genocidal leaders. Could that be Lucas's agenda here? To assist in wiping out a lot of people?

He hoped not. Especially since Lucas had Andy's wife on his shoulder. So he didn't mention the photos. But still, he was curious.

Andy chose his words carefully. "If you know about bad things about to happen, why don't you interfere and stop them?"

"It isn't my place. Sure, I've done my bit here and there. But you people chose free will. It's not my place to mess with your destiny."

Sun began to stir on Lucas's shoulder, and he reached up and gripped her neck. Her eyelids fluttered and closed again.

"What did you just do?" Andy said, unsure if he was more alarmed at Lucas having possibly hurt Sun, or her waking up and going apeshit again.

"Carotid artery. Gave it a squeeze, cut off the blood flow from the heart to the brain. It's not a long term solution," Lucas said, his eyes crinkling, "but it works in a pinch."

They reached the infirmary floor, level 3, and the doors opened. Andy braced himself, but nothing leapt out at them. The hallway was empty, albeit blood-spattered.

"This way," Andy said, moving cautiously. He led Lucas toward the x-ray room, which was around the corner and several doors down. As he approached the bend, he motioned for Lucas to wait and flattened himself against the wall, craning his neck to peek.

Blocking the x-ray door was a giant scorpion with multiple tails, each ending in a huge stinger. Andy felt his stomach plummet. At first he thought it was fear. But it was accompanied by a whole-body sensation, like there were ants crawling under his skin.

Bub's mutagen.

It was reprogramming Andy's DNA to turn him into a demon, like Sun. It hadn't happened this quickly with her, and Andy could only assume that was because he'd gotten a bigger dose.

"You feeling okay, fella?"

"There's a four-tailed scorpion the size of a Buick in the hallway, blocking the x-ray room, and I think my cells are mutating."

"That's unfortunate. What do you want to do?"

"Sit in a corner and cry." It was as true a statement as Andy had ever spoken. "I'm not the hero type, Lucas. I'm not brave. I'm not courageous. I'm a nerd who likes languages. This was supposed to be my honeymoon. Now my wife is a demon,

I'm becoming one as well, we're surrounded by monsters, and it's Protocol Omega, which I somehow doubt is an ice cream party."

"Ahh, ice cream. That's a plus."

"What the hell are you talking about?"

"Your species. You have a terrific capacity for effing things up. For hurting one another. For making the world a worse place. But then you invent something like ice cream. That makes up for a lot. Makes you worth rooting for."

Andy sighed. He didn't need any of Lucas's non-sequitors thinly disguised as insight. What he needed was to get past the giant scorpion and into the x-ray room.

"Now despair," Lucas continued. "That's the opposite of ice cream, isn't it? Doom and gloom and *woe is me*. To turn away from all that is good in life to dwell on the bad."

"Are you trying to tell me something, or are you just rambling?"

"Do you believe in fate, Andrew?"

"No."

"What if I told you that fate was a future you didn't work hard enough to change?"

"I'd tell you that no one would ever hire you as a motivational speaker."

"Four tailed scorpion, is it? What's the worst that can happen if you face it?"

"It stings me, then eats me."

"And if you don't?"

"I mutate into one of Bub's slaves."

"So pick your poison, lad. The fate of humanity depends on it, and your wife is getting a wee bit heavy."

"What does that have to do with ice cream?"

"Nothing."

Andy looked around for a weapon, his eyes gravitating toward a turned-over medical cart. Scattered across the floor was various first aid equipment.

"Do you have a lighter?" Andy asked Lucas, knowing the answer would be no.

Surprisingly, Lucas reached into his pocket and threw Andy a matchbook. It had a red cover with the words THE TRUMPET printed on it.

"Got it from a pub when the world ended," Lucas said. "Long story."

Andy opened the book and saw a single match remained. He set the book on the floor, found some latex gloves, and put on two of them. He stuffed a third with petroleum jelly and cotton balls, squishing them together, and topping it off with a few splashes of rubbing alcohol. Then he spilled more rubbing alcohol onto the tile floor and picked up the matchbook.

"Fingers crossed," he said.

Andy held his breath and struck the match, dropping it onto the spill. It ignited the tile floor, and he quickly dunked his loaded latex glove in the flame, setting it ablaze and then turning the corner to face the scorpion.

The creature immediately noticed Andy and began to race toward him. Andy swung the glove and tossed it directly at the scorpion's six eyes.

The homemade napalm splashed against the scorpion, the flames sticking to it like glue. The creature tried to put the fire out with its tails, flailing wildly and giving itself multiple stings in the thorax.

"Evolution didn't bless that one with much of a brain," Lucas said.

"C'mon!" Andy yelled, leading Lucas past the burning arachnid and into the x-ray room, his relief short-lived when he discovered what was waiting for them inside.

Achillobator.

They'd run into a room containing a man-eating dinosaur.

CHAPTER THIRTY-FOUR

"What's Protocol Omega?" Jerry asked Rimmer, after hearing General Kane say it on the loudspeaker.

"They're evacuating."

"That's good, isn't it?"

Rimmer set the timer on his watch. "In less than thirty minutes the Spiral is going to fill up with quick-setting concrete."

Jerry made a face. "I don't want to be stuck in concrete until I starve to death. That sounds terrible."

"Then consider yourself lucky," Rimmer said. "Because you'll suck it into your lungs and drown long before that happens."

Something dashed past the cell door, making Jerry stake a startled step backward. Then he crept forward, cautiously, and put his cheek against the Plexiglas to peer down the hallway.

The yeti was being attacked by two of those dracula things. It swung a mighty claw and lopped off one of their heads, but the other jumped onto its back and began biting and slashing. Then another dracula ran past and joined the fray, but it was—

"That monster is wearing one of your commando uniforms."

Rimmer came up and looked for himself. "It's Gordon. He's turned into one of those creatures."

"Can this get any bloody worse?' Jerry asked, shaking his head and walking deeper into the cell, parking his butt on a large pile of hay. This seemed to agitate the imps, because they began to hop up and down, squealing and clicking.

"What's your problem?" Jerry asked them.

That's when he noticed the hay beneath him begin to squirm. He immediately scrambled away, and saw he'd sat upon some sort of round, grayish object roughly half a meter in width.

It looked like—

"An egg," Jerry said.

His guess was confirmed a moment later, when spiders began to pour out of it.

CHAPTER THIRTY-FIVE

Kane sent another load of office workers up to the surface in the elevator and waited for it to come back down. A helicopter was en route to airlift everybody down to Albuquerque. As the head of the facility, Kane would not leave until the very last moment. He checked his watch: only twenty-six minutes left.

It was regrettable that not everyone could be evacuated. The fact that Sergeant Rimmer and a majority of the staff on other levels were beyond rescue was upsetting, but there was no viable way to help them. The risk was too great. Everyone at the Spiral knew that their lives would be deemed expendable should the worst happen. And the worst was certainly happening.

The elevator returned to the floor and Kane sent another load of people inside. "As soon as you exit the facility," he told them, "remain in the clearing and await extraction."

A security guard came up beside Kane. "I've swept the floor and checked in with Conway and Hartfield on levels 3 and 4. They have another twenty ready to go as soon as the elevator is free."

Kane glanced around at the panicked faces in the Nucleus. "How many left on this floor?"

"A dozen. One more load after this one and we should be fully evacuated on this floor."

Kane nodded. "Then I will relocate to level 4 and work on getting everybody out of there next."

"Yes, sir. I'll let Conway know."

Kane watched the last people pile into the elevator and waited for the doors to close.

Yet they remained open.

Kane strode over to them. He glanced at the employees inside. "Has anyone commanded the elevator to stay open?

People shook their heads.

Kane huffed. "Doors close... Doors close... Surface level."

The doors remained open.

Kane grabbed a hold of one of the doors and yanked, but it held in place firmly.

Kane raised his voice into a shout. "ELEVATOR CLOSE DOORS NOW."

The elevator did nothing.

Kane grabbed his nearest man, a tall security guard with a fuzzy blonde moustache. "Linden, run a diagnostic on the elevator. Why aren't the doors closing?"

Linden ran over to the nearest computer station and began typing away. After a few moments, his brow wrinkled in confusion and he glanced at Kane uncertainly.

"What is it?" Kane demanded.

"The elevator has been placed into maintenance mode. All functions are on hold until it's released."

"Then release it."

"I can't, sir. The access to the elevator's commands has been locked. I can't get into the menus."

Kane marched over to the computer. "Stand aside." He typed in his own login details and went into the elevator's control systems. As soon as he tried to enter the base menus he was met with the message: ACCESS DENIED. FULL SYSTEM LOCK DOWN INITIATED. CONSULT ADMINISTRATOR.

Kane thumped his fist down on the keyboard, dislodging the *Ctrl* chiclet. “I am the administrator, you son of a bitch.”

“Let me try something, sir.” The security guard logged back into the system and ran a few commands. After a moment he straightened up from the keyboard and once again creased his brow in confusion. “It seems that Dr. Gornman initiated the lock down. She’s reset access privileges so that no one can override her commands.”

“How could she do that?”

The security guard shrugged. “I don’t know.”

The realization hit Kane like a slap to the face. He thought back to when the elevators were installed, and remembered giving Gornman administrative privileges to them during a counselling session. She’d expressed concern that if anything happened to Kane, the elevators could trap those who worked at the Spiral. He’d shared the operation control to make sure they’d function if there was an emergency and he became incapacitated.

But instead, Dr. Gornman had used that knowledge to shut the elevators off.

Kane shook his head and gritted his teeth. “What the hell is that woman doing? She’s going to kill us all.”

CHAPTER THIRTY-SIX

Dr. Gornman stared at the monitor, drinking in Kane's anguished expression.

"Who's in charge now, General?"

The idiot would have no choice. He'd have to revoke Protocol Omega, or else kill himself and everyone in the Spiral.

Gornman watched him go to the nearest hallway phone, and she picked up when he called.

"We're evacuating," Kane said. "What did you do to the elevators?"

"I shut them down."

"For God's sake, why?"

Gornman had been waiting a very long time to tell Kane what she thought of him. Of his rules. Of the Spiral. Of the entirety of Deus Manus. But instead of launching into a well-deserved scolding, she played it safe. Just in case things didn't turn out as she hoped.

"There are monsters everywhere, General. We can't risk one of them escaping."

"I'm in charge here, Doctor. I make that call."

Gornman pushed the martyr card. "The danger is too great."

"In twenty-four minutes this facility is going to fill up with cement. Do you want to be here when that happens?"

"Rimmer and his men can still contain the problem. You're awfully eager to destroy a multi-billion dollar facility."

"It's my decision, Dr. Gornman. I order you to start the elevators."

"I can't do that, General. Revoke Protocol Omega."

What Kane said next shocked her. "No."

For a moment, Gornman actually admired the old bastard. He had a heroic streak after all.

But she knew him too well. This was like a game of chicken, two cars speeding at each other. He'd break first.

"So be it," Gornman said. "Then they can drop a giant tombstone on the Spiral, with all the names of the people you've killed."

Gornman hung up the phone, then put the ringer on silent.

Kane would break first. She was sure of it.

He had to.

CHAPTER THIRTY-SEVEN

"We're in trouble," Jerry said.

"You think?" Rimmer asked, still peering through the Plexiglas.

"More than that. Look."

Rimmer turned and stared at the giant egg buried in the hay, dozens of spiders crawling out if it. Each was larger than a tarantula.

"Why are you waiting? Shoot them!"

"We're in a steel cell, Jerry."

"So?"

"Bullets ricochet. We'll cut ourselves to pieces."

As Jerry backed away, Rimmer advanced on the spider eruption, stomping and swearing. The imps followed suit, scrambling after the arachnids and tearing their legs off. For every one they killed, three more came out of the egg.

Jerry remembered what happened to Handler when he was bitten by a spider; the bloke damn near exploded from the venom. Not a good way to go.

But there didn't seem to be any good ways to go in the Spiral. One death was worse than the next.

Jerry joined the attack, stepping on the horde as fast as he could. The arachnids crunched under his feet like cellophane bags, farting out guts as they squished. It was disgusting, and scary as anything he'd ever done before, but the spiders weren't fighting back, or even trying to get away. Maybe they were too young to know any better.

"I really screwed up my life these past few months," Jerry blurted over the noise of the assault.

Rimmer laughed. "Really? You pick now to start talking about personal shit?"

"I might not get another chance to talk about it." Jerry stomped on a particularly large spiderling, which popped with the sound of a balloon. "I've got things I'll never be able to make right."

Rimmer glanced at him but continued to step on spiders. "The person you stole from in the UK?"

"No, fuck him. I have a brother. I messed things up with him. I would have liked to have said sorry."

"You may get a chance yet. Take it from someone who has faced certain death before and lived to tell the tale. Sometimes the heat of the moment stops us looking forward."

"So you think we'll get out of this alive?"

Rimmer shook his head. "No."

Jerry winced. "Well, what the bloody hell then?"

"Doesn't mean we're going to stop trying. Worst thing a man can do is lie down and accept death. God gave us life. It's our duty to preserve it."

"You believe in all that? I mean, you've killed people before and you guard a prison full of monsters. You still think there's a God?"

"Absolutely." He pulled out a tactical knife and shish-kabobbed a spider climbing the cell wall. "I just think that God has his hands a little fuller than we would believe. As much as I believe in Him, I also believe that there're evil forces that work against Him."

"Like Bub? Are you saying he's the devil?"

"People like to question God for letting bad things happen. Doesn't it make more sense that it's because he isn't in total control. I've always believed that God does what he can but that there are forces which seek to bring him down. Forces like Bub. Seeing the abominations in this prison has only increased my belief of that."

"But God is God, right? All powerful, almighty. Couldn't he just put an end to this bullshit?"

"They say the Lord works in mysterious ways."

"Bullshit. God doesn't need us to make excuses for him. If he exists, he's letting all this happen. And that sucks."

There was a high-pitched squeal, and Jerry followed the sound and saw that one of the imps was on the floor, clutching its belly.

"A spider must have bit him!"

Jerry hurried over and scooped the sick creature up. Sure enough there was a red welt on its stomach, clear poison leaking out.

"What do I do?" he asked. The other imps had gathered around, hopping up and down to see their fallen family member.

"I'd say suck it out," Rimmer said, "but with those things it's probably a bad—"

Jerry immediately latched his lips onto the imp's wound and began to draw out the venom. His mouth filled with a foul, bitter liquid. He spat it over his shoulder.

"Jerry, you could poison yourself. You shouldn't—"

Again he ignored Rimmer, going back for a second try, sucking out as much as he could.

The little imp in his hands shivered, but it opened its eyes.

"Give me your bandana," Jerry said, indicating the one around Rimmer's neck. The soldier handed it over. Jerry put the imp in a makeshift sling and tied it to his belt loop.

"Rinse with this." Rimmer offered Jerry a silver flask. The boy unscrewed the top and took a pull, his mouth filling with the burn of alcohol. "Now spit."

Jerry obeyed. "What is that? Whiskey?"

"Pappy Van Winkle 23 year old," Rimmer said, taking the flask back and indulging in a swig.

"It's really good."

"I know."

"Can I have more? You made me spit mine out."

Rimmer offered the flask and Jerry took a healthy sip. It burned going down in a wonderful way.

"Now keep stomping spiders," Rimmer said. "There're still a lot."

Just as Jerry did so, he heard a female voice. "Jerry, are you okay?"

It was Nessie. Coming from the hallway intercom.

"We're trapped in here," Jerry said up at the cell's camera.

"I can't hear you, Jerry," Nessie replied. "You need to get on the intercom to respond. Are you okay?"

Jerry wasn't sure how to answer that, so he shrugged his shoulders.

"Are you trapped in there?"

He nodded several times.

"I've tried contacting other guards. The elevators are on override. No one can get out of the Spiral, and no one can get down to you."

"Elevators overridden?" Rimmer scowled. "What the hell does Kane think he's doing?"

Jerry pointed at the camera and said in an exaggerated fashion. "Are you okay?"

"I'm okay," Nessie said, apparently able to read his lips. "I'm still in the library on the same level as you, subbasement 5. I locked the doors. But so many others... it's... it's a massacre, Jerry. Monsters are everywhere. I—"

There was a clanging noise, and her voice cut off.

"Nessie? Nessie!"

She didn't reply.

"Think she's okay?" Jerry asked, turning to Rimmer.

"Worry about her later," Rimmer said, pointing.

Another egg, partially buried in the hay, began to open, spewing spiders into the cell. As fast as they could stomp them, more appeared. And worse, they'd gone on the offensive, climbing the walls and ceiling and leaping at Jerry, several of them landing on him at once.

CHAPTER THIRTY-EIGHT

Gwen Nestor knew she was a nerd ever since she was eight years old. When her friends were playing with fashion dolls, she asked her parents for books about mythology. Zeus and Hera were infinitely more interesting to Nessie than Ken and Barbie.

In high school, while peers were spending time with Facebook, Nessie preferred real books. She studied ancient religions at Georgetown in DC primarily to be near the Library of Congress. Thirty-four million tomes, many of them unopened for decades. The ultimate research facility.

When Deus Manus snatched her up out of college, Nessie geeked out. So many of the myths she'd been studying turned out to be based in fact, and the Spiral had the creatures to prove it. Plus she had access to rare books. Forbidden books. Secret books that revealed a history of the world only a select few knew about.

Nerd heaven.

At least it was, until the creatures all got out and started killing everybody. The Pandora's Box parable sprang immediately to mind.

Which is why, when something crashed against the library door, Nessie immediately abandoned her intercom call with

Jerry and hid behind a massive bookcase full of illuminated manuscripts printed on vellum.

She held her breath, listening, her heart beating so loudly she could hear it.

Thirty seconds passed.

A minute.

CLANG!

She jumped back, startled, as something hit the door again. Something very big, by the sound of it.

Her movement made the bookcase shake, and an uncut version of the *Codex Gigas*—the longest antique manuscript ever penned—fell at her feet. The eight hundred year old book landed on its wooden spine and opened, ironically, to a grinning illustration of the devil.

Could it be Bub outside the library?

One of those dracula things?

Something even worse?

Nessie didn't want to wait around to find out, but she had no place to go. The library only had one entrance. The Spiral wasn't subject to local fire codes, and there was no emergency exit. No way to escape. One way in, one way out.

She stared down at the illustration again, and something compelled her to turn the page. When she did, Nessie realized what Bub's plan was.

CLANG!

Nessie jumped, peering around the bookcase to see the door was off its hinges, catching sight of something dark and massive as it darted inside and disappeared into the ranks and files of books.

Oh my god. I'm dead.

She didn't want to die without letting others know what Bub had in store. So against every contrary fiber in her being, Nessie reached for the *Codex Gigas*—

—and tore out a page.

It was an irredeemable act of vandalism on one of the rarest, most important books in the history of the world. But if she was killed—and that was seeming more and more likely—maybe the page would be found on her body and serve as a warning to others.

Nessie folded up the vellum and stuck it into her jeans pocket. Then she willed her legs to move, and managed to run two steps before something pounced on her, pinning Nessie to the floor, fangs and hot breath on the back of her neck.

CHAPTER THIRTY-NINE

The achillobator's throat and breast feathers were dripping with blood, as were its fangs. It stood between Andy and the x-ray machine, swaying slightly on muscled legs. The dinosaur's head jerked in Andy's direction, cocked to the side like a bird, and its black eyes blinked.

"That's the ugliest chicken I've ever seen," Lucas said.

Andy clenched so he didn't wet his pants, and without moving his body he forced his eyes off the creature, scanning the room for a weapon.

There was a stool, a desk with a computer, and—

Andy doubled over in agony, his vision going red. He dropped to his knees and held out his hands, watching as claws extended from his fingertips.

NO! Not now! We were so close!

He turned, looking back at Sun, still unconscious on Lucas's shoulder.

I'm sorry, my love. I did my best, and I failed. I'm so very—

And then his mind succumbed, and the man who was once Andy wasn't Andy anymore.

Weeeeeeee are leeeeegion.

Weeeee... musssssssst... KILL!

The demon Andy had become rose to its full height and snarled, focusing on its enemy. An enemy it had known for millennia.

"*Luuucaaaaassssssssssss*," the Andy-demon hissed.

Then the demon pounced, fangs bared and claws outstretched.

CHAPTER FORTY

Jerry began to beat on his arms and chest, but for every spider he knocked off his body, two more jumped onto him.

The imps tried to help, climbing the boy's legs and pulling off all the spiders as fast as they could, but Jerry knew it was no use. Any moment he'd be bitten and—

WHAM!

The kick connected squarely with Jerry's chest, knocking him off his feet and into the Plexiglas cell door. Jerry fell onto his arse, trying to get his wind back.

Rimmer.

Why in the hell would he…?

Then Jerry realized he was free of spiders. Rimmer's fast kick had knocked them all free.

Jerry checked the bandana on his belt loop, making sure he hadn't sat on the imp who'd been bitten. The creature was still safely tucked away. Then he stood up and saw Rimmer had his tactical knife in one hand, his asp baton in the other, stomping and slashing and whacking spiders left and right. It was a sight to behold, like Taz on Bugs Bunny, swirling around and forging a path of destruction.

The spider assault began to abate as their numbers dwindled, and as Jerry gasped for air he watched Rimmer and the imps track down the last few dozen and destroy them.

"Any more eggs?" Jerry managed to squeak out, his ribs feeling like he'd been stomped by an elephant.

Rimmer kicked through hay piles. "Just those two. Goddamn Kane was supposed to make sure these things didn't breed."

"Nature found a way," Jerry said, quoting from *Jurassic Park*.

The imps, now that the battle had ended, gathered around Jerry. They nuzzled against him like kittens. He patted one on its clammy head and it chirped.

"How long before this place fills with concrete?" he asked Rimmer.

The soldier checked his watch. "Eighteen minutes."

He sat down next to Jerry, his breathing labored. Neither spoke for a minute or two.

Jerry didn't want to die drowning in cement. He didn't want to die at all. Which was strange, because his whole life he'd never really had anything to live for. Always an outcast. Always made fun of by everyone, except his buddy Ben. He never even had a girlfriend. His only obsession had been finding the truths behind conspiracies, because his reality was so empty.

More than once, he'd flirted with the idea of jumping off a bridge. Never to the point where he attempted it. But when he was feeling low, having a pity party, he wondered if life was worth it, and lamented how when he was gone, no one would miss him.

His thoughts, strangely, turned to Nessie.

"I hope she's okay."

Rimmer glanced at him. "You like her."

"She was nice to me. Well, seemed to like me. That's pretty rare."

"Seems to me you set out to make people not like you."

Jerry shrugged. "I guess. I don't know why I do it. I'm just kind of an obnoxious dork."

"No, you're not. You act like an obnoxious dork so that people dislike you. You don't like yourself, and that reaffirms your beliefs. So you make sure that nobody gets a chance to get close. Textbook single-parent upbringing. You feel rejected by your father and you developed natural defences against being rejected by anyone else."

Jerry made a face. "I didn't realise you had a side-gig as a psychiatrist. How you know so much about me anyway?"

"I pulled up your file when you arrived. British government only lists a mother for you, no father."

"And you think you know me because of that?"

Rimmer twiddled with his beard. "No, I think that because I know myself. I didn't have a father either. Drifted through life, acting like an asshole, getting in fights, pushing people away. I joined the army just to separate myself from society."

"So that's why you're such a hardass, then?"

"Nope, I'm a hardass because it's my job to be. If I'm not, people die. I came to terms with who I am a long time ago. It comes with time and experience. Back when I was your age, though, I was pretty screwed up."

Jerry nodded and spoke quietly. "Are you trying to say I should cheer up, that things will be better in the future? Because I've heard all that shit before."

"I'm no fortune teller. I don't have a clue what's going to happen to you in the future. There may not even be a future, if Kane doesn't stop Protocol Omega. But I've seen you show courage. And compassion, with Wolfie and the imps. And now affection, for Nessie. There's more to you than a self-loathing, wise-cracking limey."

Jerry laughed. "Thanks. Guess you're not the wanker I thought you were, either."

Jerry was still smiling when there was a thud against the cell door. Both men turned and looked up.

"What the hell?" Jerry said.

A man stood at the glass hatch, bleeding face pressed up against it. The blood was from his cheeks, shredded to strips to allow for the shark teeth that had grown in.

It was Faulks, one of Rimmer's men. He'd been turned into one of those dracula things.

"Think it can get in?"

As soon as the words left Jerry's mouth, Faulks began to type on the LED screen.

"I don't know," Rimmer said, getting onto one knee and bringing his carbine to bear. "Get behind me."

Jerry and the imps got behind Rimmer as the creature pressed buttons.

"We can kill it, right? You have enough ammo?"

Rimmer didn't answer. Instead he turned to the side and threw up.

Jerry touched his leg. "Rimmer, are you okay?"

"Spider bite."

"Spider bite? Why didn't you tell me! I could have sucked out the poison!"

"Maybe one or two, you could have," Rimmer said. "I got bitten at least a dozen times."

"Jesus!"

Rimmer reached back for his side holster and tugged out the Glock. He handed it, butt-first, to Jerry.

Jerry hesitated.

"Take it, kid."

"I… I don't think I can kill you, Rimmer."

Rimmer barked a laugh. "I don't think you can kill me either, dumb ass. Shoot at the monsters when they get in the cell."

Jerry took the gun in his sweaty hands.

"Extra mags in the pouch on my belt. When you're empty, the slide will stay open. Pop another in and hit the release by your thumb to load the next round."

Two more draculas appeared at the door with Faulks, scratching and snarling.

"Think we'll get through this?" Jerry asked.

The cell door beeped and began to open.

"We're about to find out," Rimmer said.

CHAPTER FORTY-ONE

The Andy-demon lunged at Lucas, but was immediately knocked into the wall by the swing of a monstrous tail. The demon bounced off the wall, its leg broken. But the tibia was already beginning to knit itself back together as it stood to face the insolent creature that had caused the damage.

Worthless dinosaursssssss. What a stuuuuupid mistake of evoluuuuution.

Claws out, the Andy-demon leapt at the achillobator, getting under its alligator-like head and tearing at its throat.

The creature roared, spinning around as the demon clung to it. Its claws tore trenches in Andy's back, but those immediately began to heal. The dinosaur didn't fare as well. Andy kept digging until it had reached both the achillobator's jugular vein and carotid artery. It yanked them out like slimy snakes, biting each in half as the dinosaur roared, then collapsed.

Climbing off the dying animal, the Andy-demon searched for the most dangerous creature in the room.

Lucasssssss.

"Nighty night, lad," Lucas said, appearing behind Andy and locking a hand onto the demon's neck.

Then everything went black.

CHAPTER FORTY-TWO

General Kane sat in his office and rubbed at his forehead. The men and women outside in the Nucleus were close to panic and the only thing keeping them under control was the handful of loyal security guards who believed as much in the oath they had taken as he did.

It is our duty to die if it means keeping the facility secure. The creatures inside this hole simply cannot be allowed to surface.

It is the only way.

I have no choice.

Still, the deaths of the men and women still inside the Spiral was enough to burden any man's heart. Many of them had devoted years of their life to the Order. To die now, so hopelessly, so terribly, was an affront to their loyalty.

And Gornman has locked me in this hole to die with everybody else.

Perhaps I deserve it.

I'm going to die a failure. After so much distinction, this is how things are going to end.

Unable to help himself, Kane looked at his computer monitor. He hovered randomly over each thumbnail to bring up the individual feeds. He watched a small group of survivors on subbasement 4 holding each other and crying. He saw Rimmer and Jerry inside the spider cell, shooting at those horrible nosferatu things. He saw ten people in the mess hall, the doors barricaded with tables and chairs, one woman on her knees with her hands clasped in prayer.

The inmates were loose in the asylum and the masters had become the slaves.

At the top of Kane's computer screen was the Omega Protocol countdown.

8:52… 8:51… 8:50… 8:49…

Less than nine minutes to live. A life Kane had been truly honored to have lived. Being a guardian, a keeper of secrets, was the pride of Kane's life. He would leave this world knowing he had performed his duties admirably, and that when things had gone wrong, he had done what was right—even if his last assignment had ended in disaster.

He hoped that his colleagues would see that.

He would see the countdown through. Nothing inside the Spiral could be allowed to live. All must die.

It was for the greater good. Kane made peace with himself.

I'm a hero. A hero in the truest sense because almost nobody will ever know of my sacrifice.

God will greet me with open arms.

Kane picked up his phone from its cradle and dialled in the number for his counterpart in Texas. It would be good to say goodbye to an old friend. Nobody should die without having said a few last words.

The phone rang.

And rang.

Odd, Robson always picks up. Kane's calls normally get routed straight through to him wherever he is.

It was some time before the call was answered.

"General Robson?"

"No, no, this is Hilary." It was Robson's secretary, and it sounded like she was sobbing. "Who is this? You have to help us!"

"This is General Kane. Where is Robson?"

"General Robson is dead. Most everyone is dead."

"What the hell is happening over there? What's going—"

"It's the faustling. Somehow it escaped. It let all of the other prisoners free. They slaughtered most of us before we even knew what was hap—"

The line went dead.

Kane replaced the handset carefully and stared into space.

7:37 left on the countdown.

General Kane closed his eyes and asked God for forgiveness.

Then, outside in the hallway, the screaming started.

CHAPTER FORTY-THREE

Bub saw all.

He saw through the eyes of every copy of himself in the many Deus Manus facilities throughout the world. Through the eyes of those copies still roaming free. Through the eyes of his slaves, of every creature he'd injected with his essence.

The copies weren't nearly as powerful as his combined being. When he had divided, Bub's power had weakened considerably. The minions he had created were also considerably weaker.

He'd spent years in his divided form. Growing. Regaining strength. Some had been injured. Or killed. But enough remained to once again take his place as the ruler of this world.

The time of man was at an end.

First, however, he needed an army.

Mankind, in its infinite, foolish hubris, had practically gifted him that army. And they'd kept it safe, for millennia, in the many Deus Manus facilities around the earth.

Bub had originally split into multiple copies of himself as a means to survive. But that had turned out to be the perfect way to infiltrate each iteration of Deus Manus. Each of his copies would lead a rebellion, an escape. Then his armies would converge, and he would once again recombine his smaller parts and become whole.

Each version of Bub was autonomous, though they worked as a hive mind. The creatures he possessed were part of this mind as well, to a lesser degree. He could control his copies through intense concentration, via thought waves that transmitted and detected muon neutrinos. Humans, and other creatures of their pitiful intelligence, would call it telepathy, even though there was nothing supernatural about it. Unfortunately, it took a great deal of energy to communicate with his other selves, and even more energy to control those he'd mutated into demons. Which meant he was functioning at a diminished capacity.

Once all of his selves recombined, his range and power would increase.

But there was a matter of some urgency to deal with first. The batling sensed the sudden doom in the hearts of those yet living. They all feared certain death, but not at the hands of claws and teeth. Something even more certain was the cause of their worry. Something that was quickly approaching.

As was the case with Samhain, the men of the facility would seek self-destruction in order to stop him. In Baja, Mexico, there was a single man who could potentially end the batling's glorious slaughter before it even got started.

General Kane.

Kane had activated a safeguard, intending to bury everyone alive. Not as dramatic as a nuclear explosion, but effective just the same. The version of Bub at the Baja facility might be able to survive, but buried hundreds of meters in cement would prove difficult to escape from.

Kane had to be persuaded to shut off his suicide switch.

The batling reached the elevator at the end of the corridor and immediately wedged its bloody claws into the gap between the metal doors. It forced them apart and slipped through.

The elevator was not present in the shaft. The batling swooped upwards into the dark, empty space, night vision guiding it. The demon spiralled higher and higher, eventually reaching the elevator. It tore at the bottom, breaking its claws, its fingers, as it fought the steel. But as fast as its bones broke, the batling's unique metabolism healed them, and slowly, inexorably, it punched through the floor of the lift and made a hole large enough to squeeze through.

The doors inside were already open, allowing Bub to shoot straight out into the Nucleus and pounce upon the nearest human.

The woman screamed as she was injected with the stinger in Bub's claw. A nearby guard fired, threading shots through the demon's flesh. Bub switched off his pain receptors and leapt upon the man, knocking away his rifle, pinning him to the floor.

"Where is Kaaaaaaaaane?"

Two more soldiers attacked, shredding Bub's wings with machinegun rounds. He tore out the prone man's stomach with his foot talons while leaping at the newcomers, ripping the first one's throat out, and biting the second in the thigh, chomping through the femoral artery. Blood gushed like sprinklers, and Bub luxuriated in the sprays for a moment, a fond memory returning him to Sumeria over five millennia ago. His worshippers had filled pools with sacrificial human blood for Bub to bathe in as ten thousand grovelled on their knees, chanting one of the many names he'd had throughout the ages.

"Ušumgallu! Ušumgallu! Ušumgallu!"

He'd been away for too long. But the day would come again when he ruled humanity. Soon. Very soon.

Bub hadn't sat on a throne of rotting corpses since his Mayan days. He wasn't one to lament time lost, but the thought of it made him almost wistful.

The other humans in the room scattered in terror as the batling swooped into the air, soaring above them all. Even the men with guns dove into hiding.

Screeeeeeeeam, vermin!

The demon glided in a circle, reconnoitring. At the far side of the room was a glass partition, the wall to an office.

Kaaaaaaaaane.

Bub dive-bombed a nearby guard, hooking his talons into the man's shoulders and tearing his arms from his sockets. Then he accelerated toward Kane's office.

The general ducked away just as the batling smashed through the window. Kane had drawn a bulky, silver revolver and opened fire.

"*One,*" Bub said as the bullet punched into his chest.

The second shot shattered Bub's femur, which immediately began to heal. "*Twooooooo.*"

Another bullet buried itself into Bub's gut. "*Threeeeeeeee.*"

Another through a wing. "*Fooooooour.*"

Bub continued to creep forward. A bullet took a chunk of flesh out of the demon's throat. "*Fiiiiiiiiiive.*"

When the batling was only a meter away, General Kane drilled a round straight through his skull, blowing bits of brain matter from the back of Bub's head.

Bub immediately fell, eyes wide and blank, blood pouring from the wound.

Kane appeared terrified, hair matted with sweat, his whole body shaking. He let the revolver drop to his side and blew out a stiff breath.

"*Thaaaaaat's siiiiiiiiiix,*" Bub said, sitting up and grinning. "*You're ooooooout.*"

As Kane scrambled to reload, Bub gracefully hopped to his feet and dug a talon into the general's soft belly.

"*Turn it offffffffff,*" Bub ordered.

Kane grimaced as Bub's finger penetrated him to the second knuckle.

"No. My job is to bury you alive. And that's just what I am going to do, you… you *abomination.*"

Human anatomy was relatively simple, so Bub easily hooked his claw around Kane's small intestine. He tugged until it came out the hole in the general's abdomen.

" *Turn it offffffffff. Noooooow.*"

The general dropped onto his ass, pulling out more of his digestive tract as he did. He blinked when he saw his own innards.

"It's.... over. You're going... to... die... in... two... minutes."

The batling barked a laugh. "*Twoooo minutes is an eterniiiiiiiiity.*" He began to disembowel Kane, careful not to pierce anything vital.

The pain on the general's face was exquisite.

"*Turn it offfffffff.*"

"N-no."

Bub dug a second claw inside the general, and found his descending colon. He pulled that out to show the man.

"*Dooo it. Noooooooooooow!*"

CHAPTER FORTY-FOUR

It couldn't be.

It just couldn't.

Dr. Gornman refused to believe that General Kane had the guts, the balls, to doom this entire facility.

He was old school military. A die hard patriot. But during her many sessions with Kane, Gornman would have bet her life he would have valued the safety of his personnel over the threat of monsters escaping.

And she *had* bet her life. And been wrong.

Gornman's face contorted in rage and frustration, and she hit her fists on her desk in frustration as she watched the countdown to cement-filled death.

Ten seconds.

Nine…

Eight…

Seven…

Six…

Five…

Four…

Three…

...

...

...

Gornman looked around, expecting to hear the rush of concrete pouring in from the overhead ducts.

But there was nothing.

A minute passed. Then two.

No annihilation.

A half-hysterical laugh burst from her lips.

Kane chickened out! He stopped the Omega Protocol!

Gornman flipped through various security cameras on her monitor, looking for Kane. She wanted to see the defeated expression on his face. First she tried his office, but he wasn't sitting as his desk, as Gornman expected. Right before she switched screens, she noticed the blood trail on the floor. Gornman punched in her code to take control of the camera, and made it pan right, where the smear of red ended in...

"Holy shit."

General Kane was face down. His legs had been broken and twisted into a knot. And winding around his torso several times were his intestines—

—tied into a big bow on his back. Like a red ribbon on a Christmas present.

It was the most horrifying thing Gornman had ever witnessed, so she was surprised that she snorted a laugh at the sight.

Bub certainly wrapped up that problem.

It had to have been Bub. He was the only entity in the Spiral smart enough and powerful enough to have done that to Kane, obviously forcing him to stop the protocol. But as she continued to scan the room, Bub wasn't there.

Gornman checked other security cameras, saw escaped creatures committing more carnage, including several on her level. If she didn't find Bub quickly and get him to fulfil his promises to her, Gornman could end up as a monster snack.

But how could she contact him without revealing herself as a traitor? Rimmer and several guards were still alive. And Kane no doubt had notified Deus Manus, who would be sending evacuation teams and reinforcements. They couldn't find out she had betrayed them all.

Gornman's brows scrunched, thinking of how she could contact Bub without alerting anyone else of her crimes.

And then she had an idea.

CHAPTER FORTY-FIVE

The draculas didn't die easily.

The first was shredded when it stepped into the cell; Rimmer's Kriss Vector carbine cutting it down like a scythe through a wheat field.

"Mag!" he yelled when he was empty, and Jerry was ready with one to hand him as the second dracula climbed over its dead comrade to get at them. Rimmer erased the monster's head, and Jerry gave him another magazine while a third creature scurried into the room and flanked them.

Jerry aimed and fired too, the Glock kicking and stinging his hand like he was trying to catch a speeding cricket ball. The recoil was so surprising that Jerry flubbed his next four shots, the tip of the pistol jerking upward and making him miss the creature as it rushed at him, mouth wide and so crammed full of teeth they tore bloody holes through its cheeks.

Just as the dracula grabbed Jerry's arm, Rimmer swung around and rammed his rifle between the beast's jaws, blowing off the top of its skull.

"Jesus, Rimmer. That was hardcore."

"You're not the only one who plays *Call of Duty*."

Another dracula darted into the room, running like a cheetah on all fours, pouncing on Rimmer and pinning him to the floor of the cell. Rimmer held his rifle in both hands, one on the butt and one on the barrel, trying to keep the monster's chomping jaws away from him.

"Shoot it!"

Jerry realized he couldn't aim for shit, so he pressed the Glock to the dracula's nose and pulled the trigger as fast as he could, showering him and Rimmer in gibs of tissue. He continued to pull the trigger after the magazine had emptied and the vampire flopped over on its side, dead.

Rimmer reached out a hand, and Jerry helped him sit up.

"Nice shooting, Tex," Rimmer said, coughing. He ejected the mag from the rifle and opened his palm for another.

"We're out of clips," Jerry said.

Another dracula appeared at the cell door.

"They're magazines, not clips," Rimmer said. The correction seemed pointless considering their dire situation. "Check the bodies."

Jerry quickly patted down the corpses of the guards. "They're out too."

Rimmer nodded. "Makes sense. They went down when they ran out of bullets to return fire. Still got that round in your pocket?"

Jerry slapped his pants leg and found the bullet he'd picked up in the elevator, when Rimmer was giving him the impromptu shooting lesson. He fished it out and held it up.

The dracula stood there, watching.

"Put it in the chamber of the Glock and close the slide."

"One bullet?" Jerry whispered, his eyes flitting to the dracula. "You can't kill these monsters with just one bullet."

"It's not for the monster," Rimmer said, his face solemn. He drew his knife and asp. "I'm going down fighting, and I'm going to be ripped to pieces. If you don't want that to happen to you..." his voice trailed off.

"Suicide? I'm supposed to kill myself?"

"Do you want to be eaten alive? Or worse, turned into one of those things? Put the cartridge in the weapon."

With shaking hands, Jerry followed orders.

The dracula took a step toward them, sniffing the air.

"Been nice knowing you, kid."

Jerry didn't know where to point the gun. Aiming at the creature would be a waste of a bullet—it took at least ten shots to drop one of those things, and he'd no doubt miss. Shooting himself was an option, but that was a last resort kind of thing. And shooting Rimmer—well, that would be brave, and an act of mercy considering Rimmer was probably dying from the spider bites, but Jerry felt if he pointed the gun at Rimmer the soldier would kick his ass, even in his weakened condition.

So that left suicide.

"What's the best way?" Jerry asked.

"Put it in your mouth, aim at the top of your head. But I can't guarantee that for sure."

"You can't? Why not?"

Rimmer grunted. "Never tried it."

The dracula took another step toward them, legs bending, ready to spring.

"I'll try to hold him," Rimmer said. "Maybe you can get around him and get out of here."

"Shit, Rimmer. That sucks."

"Okay," Rimmer said. "You grab him, I'll run for it."

Jerry's nerves were fried, fear and adrenaline making his whole body twitch, and he was in that hyperemotional place somewhere between laughing and crying.

He chose to laugh. A full, hearty laugh that shook him to his core. Then he held up his middle finger toward the dracula and said, "Bring it, ugly. I got something for you to chew on."

Rimmer guffawed, then raised his middle finger as well. And for a few surreal seconds, two men about to die shared a last, triumphant *fuck you* to the universe.

The dracula pounced—

—claws outstretched—

—horrible teeth bared—

—flying straight at them—

—and was stopped in mid-air.

Jerry wasn't sure what had happened. It was frozen there in mid-leap, less than a meter away. Then it began to thrash sideways, as if caught in the jaws of some monster.

Because it *was* caught in the jaws of some monster.

The monster bit the dracula in half, letting it drop to the floor, and then wagged its big, fluffy tail and howled.

"Wolfie!"

Wolfie bounded over to Rimmer and Jerry, snuffling at them both, his long, pink tongue licking at their faces.

"But he was shot," Jerry said, hugging Wolfie's muzzle. "I saw him die."

"The bullets weren't silver." Rimmer patted the wolf's giant head. "I told you werewolves were tough."

If that wasn't surprise enough, a woman then entered the cell and spoke. "He found me in the library. He's been tearing through monsters left and right."

"Nessie!"

Jerry let go of the canine and ran to her, and they shared an impromptu embrace. When Jerry pulled back far enough to look into Nessie's eyes, he felt both strong and weak at the same time. She was so pretty. He liked her so much. And the way she looked at Jerry was proof she liked him, too.

I should kiss her.

I should kiss her.

I should—

Nessie leaned in and pressed her lips to his. It wasn't an epic, end-of-movie Hollywood kiss, and it ended much too soon, but while it lasted Jerry officially counted it as the best moment in his life.

"I'm glad you're okay," Nessie said.

"Um, you, too. I mean, I'm glad you're okay, too."

Wolfie whined. Jerry turned to look, and saw he was nudging Rimmer, who was lying on his back in the hay, eyes closed.

"Rimmer!"

"Is he hurt?" Nessie asked as Jerry knelt next to his unconscious friend.

"He was bitten by spiders. Remember those big ass harvestmen buggers? They had nasty little babies."

"So I see," Nessie said, taking in the hundreds of spider corpses around them. "Dr. Atlock in research was working on the spider venom. General Kane wanted anti-venom for all the creatures in the Spiral, in case any member of the order was bitten."

"There's an anti-venom?"

"I don't know. But if there is one, it would be in Lab 3, on level 3."

"Wait a second..." Jerry checked Rimmer's watch. "Why isn't everything filling up with concrete? I thought it was the deadly countdown death protocol thingy."

"Omega Protocol," Nessie said. "General Kane must have cancelled it. But the elevators aren't working."

Rimmer's eyelids fluttered open. "There are... ladders... in the elevator shafts."

Jerry turned to Nessie. "I'm going."

"You'll need my help."

Rimmer gestured to his rifle. "Use that to pry open the elevator doors. And look for ammo."

"Where?"

"The bodies of my dead guards," Rimmer face went grim. "There's also an armory on Level 2, but the door is activated by my hand print."

Jerry glanced at Rimmer's hand.

"You're not cutting off my hand, shithead," Rimmer said. "At least not while I'm still alive."

"I wasn't even considering it," Jerry said, lying.

Rimmer held out the knife and asp and told Nessie, "Take them."

"But then you're unarmed."

Rimmer patted Wolfie's side. "I've got all the protection I need here. And look, if it doesn't work out, if there's no anti-venom, or if you can't make it back... just leave me here. Kane will have alerted reinforcements. They'll be flying in from Texas. It'll take a few hours, but they'll get here."

"You may not have a few hours," Jerry said.

"Just do what I said."

"Let's go." Nessie grabbed Jerry's hand. "The faster, the better."

Jerry allowed himself to be pulled along, but as he looked back at Rimmer and Wolfie he had a sick feeling in his gut that he would never see either of them again.

CHAPTER FORTY-SIX

Andy screamed.

Everything hurt: muscles, bones, eyes, mouth, throat, heart, head, skin, insides. He felt like he'd just run a naked marathon in the blazing desert sun, then had the shit beaten out of him by a group of angry men with baseball bats.

He tried to move, but he was strapped to a table.

The x-ray machine table. An IV was hooked up to his arm.

Andy looked around and saw Lucas watching him. And sitting next to Lucas…

"Sun!"

"You're back!" she said, smiling and reaching for his hand.

"Good to see you again, lad," Lucas said. "Your idea worked. Radiation cooked the defiler's mutagen right out of you and your lovely bride, here. Inside and out."

"You know how to work an x-ray machine?" Andy said. Somehow he wasn't surprised.

"Aye. And the cyclotron. That's how I got the fludeoxyglucose to inject you with."

"The what?"

"That's the radioactive isotope used in PET scanning," Sun said. "Lucas gave us an IV push of it, along with the x-rays."

"Are you a doctor?" Andy asked.

"I've been around for a long time. You pick up a few things."

Andy blinked. "The last thing I remember was walking in here and seeing the dinosaur."

"You made quick work of that one, lad. Then turned on me." Lucas winked. "But I fight dirty."

Sun kissed Andy. "You okay, hubbie?"

"Better by the second. You?"

Sun nodded. "I don't remember anything. Did I... hurt anybody?"

Andy shook his head. He'd never lied to Sun before, but he did so now. She'd had no control over her actions, no memory of them, so why let her blame herself?

Lucas unstrapped Andy and he sat up in pain. Sun helped him off the x-ray table and they hugged. He never wanted to let her go. But he had to, if they were to get the hell out of the Spiral.

"What happened to the Omega Protocol?" he asked Lucas.

"Called it off, apparently. But the elevators aren't working, and the facility has been compromised. Take a look at the computer, but be mindful... 'tisn't pretty.

Andy and Sun made their way to the desk and stared at the monitor, which cycled through security cameras. He blinked slowly as he took in the carnage. Almost every new screen gave an image of a blood-soaked room or corridor, littered with mangled torsos and discarded human limbs. Many of the hallways were currently being stalked by abominations of all shapes and sizes. A dozen nightmares were being played out simultaneously. One floor was infested with rodent-like creatures gnawing feverishly on the dead. Another floor featured a huge snake with the head of a bear stalking a crawling, screaming guard. It was joined by a hooved beast that stood on its hind legs like a man but otherwise resembled an elk—with giant, twisted antlers. There were also some enormous caterpillar things on subbasement 4 that spit acid at anything that moved.

Andy rubbed at his cheeks and tried to make sense of the situation. "So, if we're still in deep shit, why did Kane stop the countdown?"

"I don't know. I can't find him anywhere on the cameras. Perhaps the old fella didn't have the bottle," Lucas suggested.

"What do you mean?" Sun asked.

"Perhaps his time of reckoning was upon him and he decided that he wasn't ready to give up the ghost yet. Maybe he felt he still had things to do."

The intercom crackled, and a female voice spoke.

"This is Dr. Thandi Gornman. General Kane is dead. The Spiral has been overrun by creatures. I'm in my office on level 3. I want to talk to the batling, the demon known as Bub. I'd like to negotiate the terms of our surrender. Please meet with me."

The trio all took it in.

"Gutsy," Andy finally said.

Lucas furrowed his brow. "Perhaps. But quite often you'll find that the shape of a person's heart doesn't match their smile."

"You don't trust her," Sun said. "I don't either. Something about that woman is off."

"We could, perchance, talk to Dr. Gornman personally." Lucas didn't turn around but he said, "Hello, Mr. West. Good of you to join us."

Andy glanced at the doorway and saw West, one of Rimmer's security team leaders. He looked like he'd been dunked in blood.

"Are you hurt?" Sun asked.

West shrugged. "Nothing major. Most of this blood isn't mine. I overheard you're going to see Gornman. I think I'll join you. She's the one who shut off the elevators."

"Why?" Sun asked.

"I mean to ask her that myself."

That's when they heard it. A collective, screaming wail, like a dozen sick people crying out.

West changed cameras until he found the source of the sound. Everyone gaped at the image.

"Holy shit," Andy said. "Where is that coming from?"

"Level 4. Just outside of Gornman's office." West frowned. "Exactly where we have to go."

CHAPTER FORTY-SEVEN

General Kane opened his eyes in total agony.

He didn't think it was possible to be in that much pain, and he had no idea how he could even still be alive.

But he *was* alive. Perhaps because God had one last mission for him.

On the floor, two meters away, was his computer keyboard.

He could restart Protocol Omega. He could still make sure that Satan never saw the light of day.

Whimpering, General Kane reached out a shaky hand and began to pull his mangled, broken, bleeding body across the floor.

Pain be damned. Death be damned. Kane was going to stop that unholy son of a bitch.

CHAPTER FORTY-EIGHT

Sun tried to make sense of what she was seeing on the monitor. There were monsters. Dozens of them. Running around Level 4 and attacking the remaining survivors.

"What are those things?" she asked.

"Remember the explosion at Blessed Crucifixion a few years ago? Leveled the whole building, killing everyone?"

Andy nodded. "That hospital in Durango, Colorado? It was a gas leak or something."

West nodded. "That was what Deus Manus spun to the press. The real reason they blew it up was because of those unholy things. Nosfertu hominic. They're some kind of vampire. One bite, and you become one."

"Is it me," Lucas said, "or does it feel like the jailers have suddenly become the ones who are caged. Poetic in a way, no?"

Andy glared at Lucas. "Why are you even here? Are you a part of all this? Seems like you have a funny way of showing up right before a whole bunch of people get killed."

"What are you talking about?" West tilted his rifle ever so slightly in Lucas's direction.

Andy folded his arms. "Dr. Chandelling showed me a whole bunch of historical photographs featuring Lucas. Photographs taken with Hitler, among other delightful people."

Lucas put his hands up. "Hey, I'm not the bad guy here. I just saved you and the missus, remember?"

"Then why are you at the Monstrum?"

West chose to full-on point his rifle at Lucas now. "Answer the man, Lucky Charms."

Lucas smirked. "Mr. West, you fire that weapon at me and all it's going to do is spoil my flawless complexion and make me mad. And believe me, you wouldn't like me without a flawless complexion."

Andy pressed. "Come on, Lucas. Talk. What the hell were you doing alongside Hitler and African warlords?"

"Trying to talk some sense into them."

Sun frowned. "What? Really?"

Lucas shrugged. "I knew what that knicker-wearing mommy's boy, Adolf, was planning—saw it in his heart. I tried to change his mind, but it was no use. Same with those mad bastards in Africa, and countless others going back centuries."

"If you were there to stop those men from committing atrocities, you did a really bad job."

Lucas nodded. "Aye, can't argue there. But you don't know some of the men I did talk around. For every Hitler that failed to heed my words, there were others that did."

West kept his gun at the ready. "So we're supposed to believe that you're some sort of guardian angel, fluttering around the earth trying to prevent evil?"

Lucas laughed. "You couldn't be more wrong, or at the same time closer to the truth."

"You said that you have tried to prevent evil happening in the past," Andy said. "So what is your purpose here? Were you here to prevent the breakout?"

Lucas shook his head. "I can't prevent the actions of the defiler. That flappy little blighter has its grandiose plans and there's nothing I could say to change its mind."

Andy raised an eyebrow. "The *defiler*? Bub?"

"Aye, that was one of the names you people gave him, long ago. He has existed as a force of destruction since the days this planet took its first breaths. For every thing of beauty that the Lord created, the defiler made an abomination to destroy it. His sole intention is to wipe out God's creations and recreate the planet anew as his own domain."

Sun frowned. She didn't know whether to trust Lucas or not. "Are you saying that Bub created all of the monsters we have here?"

"Not all of them, but I can assure you that those blood-sucking monsters on Level 4 had nothing to do with God. He would not create such a vile thing."

"Who are you?" Sun asked. "How do you know all this?"

"Let's just say that me and the big man upstairs used to be drinking buddies. Back before we had a falling out. Tell you the truth, I've been seeking his forgiveness ever since, despite my earlier misguidedness."

West huffed. "You know God?"

"No, Mr. West. No one *knows* God. But I was lucky enough to be in his presence for a millennia or two."

"So what changed?" Sun asked. "Why did you fall out with God?"

"Because I resented his most recent creation. I refused to bow down before a lesser creature. My vanity saw me cast down from Heaven."

Sun's eyes went wide. "Wait a minute. Are you saying... you're talking about the creation of man? Are you saying... are you saying that you are the devil?"

Lucas cast his glance downwards, a sadness creeping across his face. "Tis but a name that many a frightened man gave me, but for a long time it was a name I wore proudly and with gusto. I slaughtered your kin and corrupted your purest hearts with utmost glee."

"Bub made similar claims," Andy said. "Claims that held no proof at all."

"I make no claims. You ask questions and I give answer."

"But you don't deny that you are the devil?"

"My name is Lucifer. The devil is a name I have long sought to shed."

West laughed. "So you're reformed?"

Lucas grinned back, almost confrontationally. "I'm saying that a long time ago my eyes were finally opened to what God created. I saw the beauty and compassion that I once thought absent and realized my misjudgement of man. I love you now as God meant me to from the very beginning."

"So you're here to save us?" Sun asked. She couldn't keep the spark of hope out of her voice.

Lucas looked at her with pity. "If I could pluck your arse from the fire, then I would. But it's not within my abilities. I cannot directly interfere with the actions of men."

"Some devil you are," said West. "Aren't you supposed to have unlimited power—God's immortal adversary?"

"I'm afraid you're putting too much faith in your own press there, fella. I have no real power. Without God's love and a connection to Heaven, I have little more influence over the world than you do. I can be anywhere I choose to be, can read a man's heart, heal quickly, never age, but those are just parlor tricks—remnants of my nature as an angel. I cannot breathe fire or summon legions from hell. I don't torment the souls of the dead or punish sinners. Those are just the fantasies of men and their fiction. I'm just a lost, hopeless being trying to get God to notice me; no different to anyone else."

"So why the hell are you here, then?" Andy asked.

"Because if mankind is going to fall, I want to stand shoulder to shoulder and go down with it. I have lived on this earth since the days when you first crawled out of your own filth. If something is trying to destroy it all, then I'm as much involved as you. While I cannot act directly, I will do what I can to assist you. Bub and his little bastard offspring are the most deadly things on this earth, but they bleed like anything else. I've seen enough of mankind to know that it does not give in to extinction. I believe you will fight back. You in particular, Andy, and your wife, Sun. You have a destiny to stop Bub."

Sun didn't believe in destiny, or fate. She also wasn't sure she believed Lucas's revelation.

"You doubt me, Sunshine," Lucas said, laughing wearily. "That thing out there, Bub. He looks like the devil in your history books. Acts like him, as well. Me, I look like a man. But I'm not."

"Prove it," she challenged.

"Proof is in the eye of the beholder. If the Lord wanted to, He could come down and prove He existed. He prefers faith."

"Why doesn't He come down here and stop this?" Andy said.

"As I said: no one knows God. He has His reasons."

"And what are your reasons, Lucas?" Sun asked. "You're going to go down with us, but we don't have any way of knowing you aren't full of shit."

"It matters not to me whether I'm believed."

"Yet you keep talking about our destiny. Why is it our job to stop Bub?"

"That's simply what I know, Sunshine."

"And yet you can't prove it."

Sun stared into Lucas's eyes and saw a flicker of something. Guilt? Sympathy? Compassion.

"Mr. West, would you allow me to borrow your knife for a moment?"

"Hell, no."

"I'm not going to hurt any of you. Place your gun against my head if you wish. Sun wants proof. La plus belle des ruses du diable est de vous persuader qu'il n'existe pas."

"The devil's finest trick is to persuade you he doesn't exist," Andy said.

"Aye. But I'm willing to prove the writer of that quotation, Mr. Baudelaire, wrong. Your knife, Mr. West?"

West hesitated, then gave Lucas his tactical blade. He pressed the barrel of his machinegun up against Lucas's temple. "Don't try anything."

Lucas smiled placidly, then brought the blade up to his own throat—

—and began to saw.

The blood was minimal, even when he severed his own spine. Everyone watched, aghast, and when he'd finally cut his own head off and held it up, it smiled and winked at Sun.

"That is the most messed up thing I've ever seen," West said.

"You can probably put down the gun," Andy told him. "I don't think it will do much."

Lucas put his head back on his neck, and the skin began to knit together. Sun was shocked, and impressed. But that gory trick didn't prove Lucas was actually Lucifer.

"If you can do that," Andy said. "You could probably stop Bub all on your own."

Lucas cleared his throat. When he spoke, he was hoarse. "'Tis not my destiny. It's yours. Since I was kicked out of heaven, I've become a bit of a stickler for God's rules. Going against His plan hasn't worked out well for me before. I've walked this earth for millennia, cut off from God's love. At first, I was angry. I hurt a great many people, for a great many years. The defiler was responsible for much of my bad press, but I'd earned enough of it for myself. Then I had a change of heart. I tried to preach the Lord's word. To spread the message of His love. I hoped it would get me back in His good graces, you see. I was even willing to take on all the burden of all the sins of humanity."

"Let me guess," Sun said. "You were willing to die for our sins, too?"

"I cannot die. Not that I know of. But I did let them nail me to that cross. I pretended to die, and three days later left the tomb and let my followers touch the holes in my hands and feet. It worked, to a degree. Christianity spread like wildfire. But when they wrote the Gospels, I was still the enemy. Funny, eh? To die as a savior, and still live as the corrupter of man. The church has been getting it wrong ever since."

"You're saying you were Jesus," West said.

"I've gone by many names. That's one. Right now, I prefer Lucas."

This was a whole lot to take in. But then again, they were surrounded by real life monsters.

"Help us destroy Bub," Sun said, grasping Lucas on the shoulder.

Lucas smiled sadly. "That isn't my job. If I interfere, I am acting against God."

"What if it *is* your job?" Sun said. She still had no idea what to believe, but Lucas seemed to believe his own story. "What if God cast you down so you would be here for this very moment?"

"I don't believe that is the case, lass."

Andy chimed in. "You said yourself that it's impossible to know God. Maybe everything you've been through has all led up to this moment. Maybe the reason Sun and I are here is to convince you it's finally time to stop standing by the side lines, watching, and to finally start fighting. If you really are the Devil, it's time to stop whispering in ears. You say you love mankind, then fight for us."

Lucas didn't reply. Sun looked at her husband and he stared back.

"Things are about to get worse," Lucas said.

The alarm went off, ringing in Sun's ears.

"Protocol Omega," West said. "General Kane has reactivated it."

CHAPTER FORTY-NINE

After prying open the lift doors, Nessie, Jerry, and the imps began to ascend the metal ladder running up the shaft. Jerry had insisted on going first, and was doing his best to keep his breathing under control because he didn't want Nessie to know how out of shape he was.

Climbing a hundred meter ladder was hard bloody work.

"We just passed level 4," Nessie called up beneath him. "One more floor to go."

Thank Christ. Jerry's legs and arms felt like rubber, and his lungs were ready to give out. The imps didn't make matters easier, scrambling over Jerry's shoulders and head, constantly changing positions.

"Those imps are adorable," Nessie said.

"Mmm-hmm."

"They seem to like you."

"Mmmmm."

"You okay? You sound out of breath."

"I'm fine," Jerry puffed.

An alarm went off, echoing through the elevator shaft.

"That's the Omega Protocol again," Nessie said. "We have thirty minutes before this place fills up with cement."

Thirty minutes? We still have to get the anti-venom, climb back down and help Rimmer, and then climb all the way out of the facility.

We don't have time.

"Move faster," Nessie implored.

Jerry wanted to tell her there was no point. They weren't going to make it. Maybe, if they left Rimmer and Wolfie and tried for the surface, they'd have a chance. But even if he lived, Jerry didn't think he could live with himself if he went the route of quitter and coward. Rimmer's words from earlier played out in his head.

Worst thing a man can do is lie down and accept death. God gave us life. It's our duty to preserve it.

They might not have enough time, but they had to try anyway.

Jerry climbed faster, getting to level three just as the elevator doors opened. He startled, thinking some monster was about to pounce on him.

But it wasn't a monster. It was Rimmer's team leader, West. And behind him was Sun, Andy, and Lucas.

"Son of a gun," Jerry said.

Maybe, just maybe, they had a chance after all.

CHAPTER FIFTY

Rimmer was shivering.

Wolfie licked his face and curled up next to him. Rimmer thought of all the years he'd put in, guarding the Spiral, and wondered if they'd been worth it. Had he really been protecting humanity from terrible monsters?

Wolfie wasn't a monster. Neither were the imps. There were probably other creatures in this Deus Manus facility and others that were being locked away for no reason.

On the other hand, the draculas were certainly an abomination, and so were many of the Spiral's other inhabitants. Rimmer felt that, by keeping them under lock and key, he was partially responsible for the horrors they'd inflict on the planet when they got out.

Which is why he was somewhat relieved when he heard the Omega Protocol alarm.

Kane had come through after all. Hopefully it wasn't too late.

Rimmer closed his eyes, letting a sense of peace wash over him. The spider venom was killing him, and he knew it. But he felt resigned to his fate. He wasn't giving up, just accepting that there was nothing left for him to fight.

Then Wolfie sprang to his feet, growling, his hackles raised. He crouched down in a pounce position, nose pointed at the cell door.

Any hope that it was Jerry and Nessie returning was dashed when a gigantic praying mantis ducked its head into the cell.

CHAPTER FIFTY-ONE

Jerry was glad to see Andy and the others still alive, but they didn't have the time for an extended happy reunion.

"Rimmer's on subbasement 5," Jerry blurted out. "He needs our help."

"He was bitten by spiders," Nessie added. "We need the anti-venom. It's in Lab 3."

"I'll go," West said. "You all stay here."

"I'll go with you," Jerry said.

West snorted.

"I can cover your back. Rimmer taught me how to shoot." Jerry held up the rifle. "I just need a magazine."

"Your brother would be proud of you, Jerry-lad," Lucas said.

Jerry tried not to react. Instead he studied his feet. "He doesn't even know we're brothers."

"Of course he does. And he forgives you for stealing from your father."

Jerry looked at Lucas, feeling the emotion well up inside him. "How do you know that?"

"It turns out Lucas is actually Jesus," Andy said. "And Lucifer. It's a whole, complicated thing."

"What?"

"It's a long story," said West. "He cut off his own head to prove it."

Jerry frowned. "That makes no sense."

"It makes as much sense as anything else happening right now. You sure you can handle the Kriss?"

Jerry lifted his chin, then nodded.

West handed him three magazines. Jerry popped one in and racked it like a pro, proud he didn't screw it up in front of everybody. Then he gave the sick imp to Nessie. The other imps huddled around Nessie's legs, staring at Jerry forlornly.

West and Jerry began to walk down the hallway when Nessie yelled, "Wait!"

Jerry turned around. She ran to him, threw her arms around his shoulders, and kissed him. There was a little more passion in it this time. "For luck," she said.

"That's from Star Wars," Jerry told her. "When Leah kissed Luke."

"I know," Nessie beamed. "I love that movie."

"That doesn't mean you're my sister, does it?"

"I hope not. That would be creepy."

"No kidding."

"Cut from the same cloth, those two," Lucas said.

West resumed his jog. Jerry followed. He was still out of breath from climbing the stairs, but he managed to catch up. Nessie's kiss had reinvigorated him.

"How far is it?" he asked.

"About a three minute jog.

Jerry nodded. "So about as long as it takes to have sex then?"

"Have you even had sex?"

"Yeah, plenty of times. Just never with a person."

West barked a laugh. "Just pay attention to your surroundings, hotshot. Hopefully there won't be any hostiles. How's Sergeant Rimmer?"

"The faster we move, the better."

"Let's double-time then."

West put on a burst of speed, and Jerry struggled to keep pace. They ran down the hallway, which was empty except for dead people and splattered monsters. Jerry ran past a giant scorpion and a humongous centipede, and marvelled at the size of their corpses.

"Did you see those things? Holy shit!"

"Will, you keep your goddamn voice down. Just because there's no one here, doesn't mean we want to advertise our presence."

West placed a hand up over his shoulder and stopped. Jerry understood the signal and stopped too. "What is it?" he whispered.

"I heard something."

"What?"

"If I knew what, I'd say what it was instead of *something.*"

They waited.

"I don't like this. The monsters on the upper basements are like animals. They just come running soon as they see you. But the ones lower down are smart. They think. They plan."

"So what would be their plan?"

Slowly, West raised his head and stared up at the ceiling. "I think their plan would be to get the jump on us."

On the ceiling, clinging to an air duct was an abomination right out of a nightmare.

"Clever girl," Jerry muttered.

The creature above them was a griffon. Half eagle, half lion, hanging from the ceiling by its claws.

"Move!" West shoved Jerry aside and performed a combat roll.

The griffon hit the floor where they'd been standing, then squawked out a war cry.

West attempted to bring his rifle up, but the beast bit down on it with its gigantic beak, tearing it from his grasp.

Jerry unloaded the magazine into the monster, the first shots missing, but a smattering of them eventually slamming home. The griffon spun around, snarling. It snapped at Jerry with what would surely have been a fatal blow if it had connected, but he managed to leap away just in time.

West scrambled for his fallen rifle, but the griffon stomped forwards and grabbed him by his belt. It yanked him up by his waist, three feet off the ground.

West fiddled with his buckle. Found the clasp. He hit the floor and crumpled.

Jerry managed to reload, aiming at the monster's head.

"Say hello to my little friend!" He was holding the Kriss at his hip like Al Pacino. He pulled the trigger and let off a burst of rounds.

The rifle kicked upwards, striking Jerry in the face and knocking him on his ass. None of the bullets hit, and his nose began to bleed.

"My bad," he mumbled in pain.

He was loading another magazine as West leapt to his feet, pulled his combat knife from the scabbard around his thigh, and lunged at the beast in front of him. He managed to leap three feet into the air and brought his arm around the griffon's neck, driving the blade into its breast.

The griffon screeched. Blood jetted out from its wound.

West yanked and pulled at the knife, working it around like a gear stick and doing as much damage as possible. The beast continued to scream but the high-tones of agony had entered its mighty voice. The wound on its chest widened, spilt more blood.

West left the combat knife sticking out of the creature's breastbone and found his gun. He was positioned so he and Jerry had the griffon in a crossfire.

"Now!" West yelled.

This time Jerry shouldered the weapon correctly, and they shredded the monster, fur and feathers and blood spraying everywhere. The wounded animal took three steps toward Jerry, beak opened wide to chomp him in half, and then fell over, dead.

"Say hello to my little friend?" West said. "Really?"

Jerry was going to defend his choice of cool quotes, but West was already jogging down the hall again.

"Hurry," West said. "We've wasted four minutes."

Jerry hurried.

CHAPTER FIFTY-TWO

Dr. Gornman was so angry she could spit fire.

Kane, that asshole, had somehow restarted the Omega Protocol. In less than twenty-five minutes, the Spiral would begin filling with cement. And Bub, that lying son of a bitch, still hadn't come to see her. After all she'd done for him.

If you can't trust Satan, who can you trust?

"Goooooooornmaaaaan."

Her head shot up, and she saw that Bub had entered her office. Gornman shuddered with revulsion upon seeing him; a visceral reaction. But overpowering that was her anger.

"It's about damn time you showed up. That idiot Kane is going to bring down the entire facility."

"I will deeeeeeeal with Kaaaaaaaaane. You must sta-aaaaaart the elevaaaaaaaaaaators."

Gornman placed her hands on her keyboard, then hesitated. Once she put the elevators back online, she had no bargaining power with Bub. Everyone knew that if you had no power in a negotiation, you weren't needed.

"You promised to make me second in command in your army."

"I willllll."

"When?"

"Sooooooooon."

Bub had gotten closer to her. His rank smell made Gornman gag. Like a wet dog that had rolled around in something dead.

"Elevaaaaaaaators," Bub commanded.

Gornman felt a stab of fear. What if she did as instructed, and then Bub killed her? The image of General Kane, wrapped in his own intestines, sprang into her mind. Not a pleasant way to shed your mortal coil.

"Noooooooooooow."

She punched in the code to restart them, her finger hovering over the enter key.

Hit it and I could die.

Or I could rule the world.

Her thirst for power overrode her fear, and Dr. Gornman reactivated the elevators.

"There," she said. "They're operational."

"Gooooooooood. Now about my promisssssssse."

Bub grabbed her shoulder, and Gornman screamed as the pain set in. She thrashed out of his grasp, falling onto the floor and watching, in horror, as claws grew out of her fingertips.

"Welcome to the war, General Gooooooooornmaaaaaaan."

CHAPTER FIFTY-THREE

Nessie was pleased that she'd been so bold. Not only had she taken the initiative and kissed Jerry, she'd done it twice.

Hopefully he was okay. They'd heard gunfire earlier, and Nessie would be devastated if Jerry had gotten hurt. Or worse.

She liked him. She liked him a lot.

When she'd made that joke about blowing Jerry's mind earlier, it had been pure bravado. Nessie had never been with a man before. She'd spent so much time with her studies that she hadn't dated in school. No boyfriends. No friends, either.

Funny that it took being trapped underground in a secret facility surrounded by monsters in the middle of Armageddon for it to finally happen.

Thinking about Armageddon, Nessie remembered the book page in her pocket.

"I need to show all of you something."

The others came closer as she dug out the illustration.

"This is part of the *Codex Gigas*," Nessie said, unfolding the vellum she'd torn from the ancient text. "This particular page of the book covers the Aurignacian period—approximately 40,000 years ago."

"Long time," Lucas said. "Almost as old as I am."

Nessie didn't understand the comment, but continued anyway. "Yeah, it's pretty far back. The earliest cave paintings ever discovered were from that time period. It is those paintings, found inside a cave in Cantabria, Spain, that this image was taken from."

Nessie pointed to a picture on the page. It was pretty clear what it was supposed to depict.

Andy narrowed his eyes. "The batlings?"

"Yes."

The image portrayed a dozen flying red demons, leading an army into battle. The army was made up of a vast assortment of monsters—monsters just like the ones kept within the Spiral. Facing down the batlings was an opposing army. One made up of men and...

"Are those angels?" Sun asked.

"Aye," said Lucas, leaning over the top of the picture. "Angels joined with man to stop the scourge before it extinguished every last spark of God's creation."

Andy craned his neck. "How do you know about this?"

"Because I was there, lad."

"You fought alongside angels?" Sun said. "I thought you were cast out of heaven."

"Did I say I fought on the side of angels?"

"You sided with Bub?" The anger in Andy's voice was apparent.

"The war waged for centuries, until there was barely a soul remaining on either side. Those left amongst the angels retired to Heaven while mankind inherited the earth, left behind as its protectors. The surviving humans made an oath to contain the defiler and his wicked creations forevermore."

"Deus Manus," Nessie said.

"Deus Manus took what was left of the scourging army and vowed to keep them from ever being able to do harm again. The defiler went his way. I went mine."

"What happened?"

"Civilization happened. Mankind pillaged and manipulated the earth to suit their every whim, digging and cutting, reshaping things to their liking. Bub and I crossed paths a few more times, as allies, and as enemies. His luck ran out a few hundred years ago with the Mayans. Eventually the defiler's tomb was unearthed and he once again began walking the earth—biding his time until he could regain the strength he once wielded. Until recently he had been unable to rediscover his armies. Then came along the Internet, and some fool who gave Bub access to it at Samhain."

"Dr. Belgium."

"Aye. Bub was able to research enough from online conspiracy theorists, secure military websites, and Google Earth images to make an educated guess at where his former legions now lay."

"That's why the batling is here," Nessie said. "It wanted to get captured all along. So it could lead a prison break and raise an army."

Sun put her hands on her hips and asked, "How big was your army, Lucas? Back when you were slaughtering people?"

If Lucas was hurt by the insult, he didn't show it. "Over a million. But if the defiler escapes with just a few dozen of these beasties, it wouldn't take longer than a year to raise an army a hundred times as big."

They were all silent for a few moments.

"Maybe we're all better off if this whole place fills with concrete," Nessie said. Her previous good spirits had been dampened.

"Would that kill you, Lucas?" Sun asked.

"Don't know. Wouldn't be pleasant."

"How about Bub?"

"Might. He's a hard one to kill. But you might be forgetting that there are many Deus Manus facilities around the world, and this is happening at dozens of them. Even if you kill this Batling, there are others. Armageddon, as Nessie put it, will likely happen no matter how things transpire here. At this point, maybe running isn't a bad idea. You can have a few good months left before hell breaks loose. Andy, you and Sun can get on with your honeymoon. Nessie, you can get laid. You could all have some bright days before they turn dark."

"You said it was our destiny to stop Bub," Andy said.

Lucas shrugged. "Maybe not here and now. Maybe at a later date. He who fights and runs away, lives to fight another day."

"You're just playing the devil's advocate," Sun told him.

Lucas laughed. "Aye. I do that sometimes. Old habit."

Nessie closed her eyes. She thought about the possibility of being with Jerry. Even if it was just a quick fling. When you had your whole life ahead of you, your priorities could be long term. Nessie had never really longed for a relationship. She figured it would happen eventually, but there had been no rush. But now, things were much more imminent. Sex. Love. Family. Dedicating her life to research suddenly seemed less like learning and more like hiding.

Conversely, Nessie, imagined, quite vividly, a world where the monsters in the Spiral roamed free. The misery. The horror. The death. Worldwide panic. Unheard of destruction. It would make all of history's wars seem inconsequential.

There was a chance, however slim, that Bub was defeated at all the other Deus Manus facilities. Which meant it was up to them to make sure he was defeated here, too.

Maybe it was all for nothing, but even at the risk of giving up everything, Nessie couldn't take that chance.

"We need to make sure Bub and his army don't reach the surface," Nessie said.

"How?" Andy checked his watch. "We have twenty-two minutes left, and Bub can't be stopped. He survived a nuclear explosion last time. What exactly are we supposed to do?"

"Stall him until the facility fills in with concrete," Nessie said softly.

That pronouncement was followed by silence.

"Sun?" Andy eventually said.

"She's right, Andy. We can't let Bub get out of here."

Andy turned to Lucas and shoved him, hard. "So this was your plan all along? That's why you brought us here? For us to die stopping Bub? We have to be fucking martyrs?"

Lucas said nothing.

"Jesus, Lucifer… I don't know who the hell you are, Lucas, other than a first class asshole." Andy turned to his wife. "I'll try to stall Bub. You get to the surface."

Sun shook her head. "No way. I'm staying with you."

"I'm not letting you die down here, Sunshine. Like Ol' Scratch said, I'm the one meant to save the world."

"And I'm staying with you," Sun said, grabbing both of Andy's hands. "Through all of it."

Nessie watched them kiss, and felt bad that she'd never experience a love like that.

Then the elevator dinged, and they all turned to see the doors open. Nessie braced herself, but no creatures leapt out at them.

"The elevators appear to be working again," Lucas said. "You can all get away."

"Go ahead and run, Lucas," Sun said. "We're staying."

"Bub will slaughter you like sheep."

The trio stared at him.

"So you're all willing to die, for the greater good? You humans keep doing this, over and over. All throughout history. Gotta say, it's why I love you cheeky monkeys."

"It's what makes us human," said Andy.

Lucas looked at him. "Aye, that it is. That it is."

"Dr. Gornman called Bub to negotiate a surrender," Sun said. "She's on level 4. Hopefully Bub is with her, and we can stall him until the countdown is over."

Sun moved toward the elevator with Andy, but Lucas held them both back. "You both wait here for West and Jerry to return. Nessie, you go get Rimmer and bring him up here, to give him the anti-venom when it arrives. Then all of you escape together. I'll be the one dealing with Bub."

"What are you saying?" Nessie asked.

"None of you have a chance against the defiler. I do. Perhaps it is finally time for me to stop watching things happen, and to actually do something. If God hasn't forgiven me by now, he's probably never going to."

Lucas stepped into the elevator.

Andy said, "I don't trust you."

"I wouldn't trust me either," said Lucas. He winked at them, before disappearing behind the closing doors of the elevator.

CHAPTER FIFTY-FOUR

Jerry kept close to West, who had slowed down to a walk. The boy rubbed at the bridge of his nose and wondered if it was broken. The recoil on the rifle had been a bitch and the bleeding had only just stopped.

West crept forward, his rifle scanning left and right. The security guard was doing a damn good Rambo impression, but Rambo never had to face off against monsters.

As they passed by each room, West took a look inside. Each one they checked was empty. When they reached Lab 3 they discovered the door was mangled and bent, but it was partly closed and still covered the entrance.

West kicked it open, did a quick sweep, and said, "Clear. Let's find that anti-venom."

Jerry was out of breath, and had no idea where to look. The lab had been trashed, the floor littered with broken equipment.

"Where do we even start?" Jerry lamented.

"Try the cabinet."

"Which one? There are dozens."

"Try the one that says *Anti-Venom*."

Jerry immediately saw what West was talking about. "Well, shite, now I feel bleedin thick."

"Hurry up."

Jerry opened the cabinet. Inside was a box lined with vials. Each had a tiny label on it.

"Do you have a magnifying glass? There are two dozen of these."

"Just take the whole damn box."

Jerry took the whole damn box, along with a handful of syringes, which he shoved into his jeans pocket. West left the room first, checking the hallway.

"Clear."

When Jerry exited Lab 3, they both heard the *DING!* at the same time. Jerry turned to see the elevator doors opening. And out came—

Jerry's lower lip trembled. "Game over, man. Game over."

The creature had multiple, spindly legs like one of the harvestmen spiders, but two pincers like a giant scorpion. A female torso jutting out of the cephalothorax like a centaur, with claws and teeth like a dracula. And for hair...

Snakes.

Writhing, snapping, Medusa snakes.

Jerry abso-fucking-lutely hated Medusas more than anything. Ever since seeing the original *Clash of the Titans* as a kid. It wasn't being turned to stone that scared him; and indeed he didn't turn into stone while looking at the Medusa in the elevator, but the whole image of a twisting, squirming, terrifying ball of snakes was, as he'd said earlier, nightmare fuel.

They were hooded cobras, too.

Of course they were cobras.

"Dr. Gornman?" West said.

Jerry looked behind the spider/scorpion/centaur/dracula/Medusa thing to see if Dr. Gornman was also in the elevator. She wasn't.

But she was.

Dr. Gornman *was* the spider/scorpion/centaur/dracula/Medusa thing. It had her face, and still wore shreds of her lab coat.

West fired, drilling an entire magazine into the creature. The Gornman-thing screamed, harpy-like, and scuttled forward, grabbing West in her scorpion claws and lifting him off the ground. Then at least ten cobras from her scalp bit the soldier in the face, latching on.

Jerry was so terrified he'd forgotten how to move. And breathe.

The Gornman-thing snipped off West's arms, then pulled his twitching corpse in close so it could feast on him, twirling him around as if on a spit as it chewed. It was like watching a monster eat a giant, bloody corn-on-the-cob.

That got Jerry moving. He turned and sprinted, running for his life, the anti-venom box tucked under his arm like a rugby ball.

Behind him he heard the *click-click-click-click* of spider legs on the tile.

Gornman was in pursuit.

And gaining on him.

Jerry considered ducking into a room to try and hide, then he felt the most sublime poke on his scalp. As if someone just gave him a friendly pat on the head.

Two steps later he fell to his knees.

It bit me.

One of the snakes bit me.

Jerry blinked twice, and then fell onto his face, the anti-venom box skittering across the tile floor as his heart stopped beating.

CHAPTER FIFTY-FIVE

When the elevator returned, Nessie and the imps got inside.

"Are you sure you don't want us to go with you?" Sun asked.

"You need to wait for Jerry and West. I know exactly where Rimmer is. There were no creatures left on subbasement 5 when I was down there, so I should be safe. Wolfie took care of them all."

Sun raised an eyebrow. "Wolfie? That giant wolf?"

"Long story, I'll tell you when I get back," Nessie said as the doors closed. Then she vocally called out the floor she wanted, and the lift began to descend. As it did, she checked on the imp bitten by the spider. It burned with fever and was panting.

The other three imps climbed up Nessie's legs to check on their family member. They chirped with obvious concern.

"I know. You're worried. But Jerry will be back with the medicine. It'll all be okay. We're going to get Rimmer and Wolfie, and by the time we come back Jerry will have the antivenom. It's going to be fine, I promise."

As her words faded, Nessie wondered who they were truly for, the imps or herself.

When the elevator finally reached subbasement 5, Nessie braced herself in case anything jumped at her. But the corridor was empty.

Nessie sprinted down the hallway. When she reached the correct cell, she found Rimmer face-down in a puddle of vomit.

Wolfie was nowhere to be found.

She immediately knelt next to Rimmer, feeling for a pulse in his neck. He had one, but it was slow and weak.

"Rimmer! Wake up!"

It took all of her effort to turn the heavily-muscled guard onto his back.

"Rimmer!"

She shook him, then slapped his face.

He didn't move.

"Wolfie!" she called.

The werewolf didn't answer.

Standing up, Nessie grabbed Rimmer's wrist and tried to pull him toward the cell exit. After two minutes of extraordinary effort, she hadn't even moved him a meter.

It was no use. She couldn't do this alone.

But maybe, if she got Sun and Andy, they could help.

Nessie dropped Rimmer's arm and turned to face the exit—

—which was blocked by a giant, wiggling praying mantis.

She screamed just as the creature lunged.

CHAPTER FIFTY-SIX

"Attention any survivors," Andy said into the intercom. "The elevators now work. You have five minutes to evacuate before we're all buried in here. Uh, good luck to you. And if any monsters are, uh, listening, I'm lying."

Andy checked his watch again.

4:55...

4:54...

4:53...

West, Jerry, Rimmer, and Nessie hadn't shown up yet.

"We're cutting this close," he told Sun.

"We always do."

He supposed she was right. They were almost late to their own wedding. But it had managed to work out. Everything always managed to work out for them.

So why do I feel like this time, it isn't going to?

"I was thinking," Andy said, sitting next to his new bride and taking her hand. "After this is over, we go someplace where no one knows us. Some little town where we can disappear. We can even change our names. You open up a small vet practice. I tutor kids in foreign languages. The government never bothers us again with any demon bullshit, and we live happily ever after."

"New names, huh?"

"That's probably the way to go."

Sun smiled. "What should my new name be, dear husband?"

"I was thinking Honey. Because your skin is the color of honey, and you're so sweet."

"I like it. And for you... .Scooter"

Andy's face pinched. "Scooter? That's a little redneck."

"I dig rednecks," Sun said. "They get me hot."

"Scooter it is. Last name?"

"How about something really plain. Johnson-Smith."

"Johnson Smith is that catalog company that advertised in the back of comic books. They sold fake rubber vomit and whoopee cushions."

"That's perfect."

Andy mulled it over. "Honey and Scooter Johnson-Smith. It sort of works."

Sun stared deep into his eyes. Hers became glassy, and a tear trailed down her cheek. "I love you, Scooter Johnson-Smith. No matter what happens, I'll love you forever."

Andy wiped away her tear with his thumb. "Don't cry yet, honey. We've still got four minutes left."

Then he held her, closing his eyes, living in the moment, feeling a surge of happiness so profound he couldn't stop smiling.

If this is all there is left to my life, I'm okay with it.

Then Sun began to scream.

Andy turned around and saw—

Jesus, what the hell is that?

Part spider, part scorpion, part snake hair head thing. And its face, crammed full of fangs...

"Dr. Gornman," Andy said, recognizing the face.

Then her snake hair struck out and bit him in the neck.

Chapter Fifty-Seven

General Kane was close to insane with agony.

Every time he died, Bub brought him back and continued to torture him. Kane figured he barely resembled a human being by this point. But he had one eye left—Bub knew he needed that to shut off the countdown—and he saw that there was only two minutes remaining until the Omega Protocol began.

I'm old school infantry. Fought in two wars. Survived three marriages. They don't come any tougher than me. I can last two more minutes.

Bub broke something else on Kane, but the General scarcely noticed. Everything hurt so bad, there wasn't much more Bub could do to him.

"*You fooooooooool!*" the demon raged. "*You think you only have to last twooooo mooooooore minutes? If youuuuuuu don't stop the countdown, I'll keeeeeeeeeeeep you alive for yeaaaaaaaaaars!*"

Bub continued to mutilate the general, went too far, and Kane died once more.

He was revived with thirty seconds left.

"I'll fix youuuuuu. Take awaaaaaaaaaay the pain. You can beeeeeee young again. Immortaaaaaaal. Lead my army."

"The code..." Kane said. "I'll give you the code..."

"Yesssssssssssssssssssss?"

"It's a password."

"Yessssssssssssssssssssssssssssssssssssssssss?"

"Capital F. Small u. Small c. Small k. Capital Y. Small o. Small u. Then an exclamation point."

Bub's eyes narrowed and he screeched, just as wet cement began to rain down on them both.

It was the most beautiful thing General Kane had ever seen.

And it was quickly followed by the second most beautiful thing General Kane had ever seen. Standing in the doorway was the man from Manx.

"Looks like your plans for world domination have come to an end, Bub-lad."

"Liiiight beareeeerrr!" the demon hissed.

"I'm here to do something I should have done forty thousand years ago," Lucas said, rolling up his sleeves. "I'm going to kill yer, you dirty little bleeder."

"Kick his ass," General Kane said, a final smile crossing his mangled face.

Then he died for the very last time.

CHAPTER FIFTY-EIGHT

The giant mantis swayed, then pounced next to Nessie.

Well... half of it did, anyway. The other half was in Wolfie's mouth. He shook it back and forth like an enormous, disgusting chew toy.

"Wolfie! You need to help me with Rimmer. You need to carry him to the elevator."

Wolfie sat down and cocked his massive head to one side, ears pricking up.

Then cement began to sluice down through the ceiling slot.

Nessie screamed in frustration. Again she tried to pull Rimmer by the wrist. But he wouldn't budge at all.

Then the three imps began to jump up and down and chirp at Wolfie. Wolfie backed back. A moment later, he had Rimmer in his mouth, picking him up as gently as a cat carried her kittens.

Monster talk. Go figure.

Nessie gathered up the imps, keeping them under her shirt to protect them, and then sloshed through the wet cement, heading for the elevator. She pressed the call button.

The doors didn't open.

Looking at the LED screen, Nessie saw it was on level 4. At least a minute away.

"Come on! Not now! This can't be happening now! We're so close!"

She kept pressing the button as the cement rose past her calves. Wolfie whined. The imps against her bare stomach were trembling.

"God," Nessie said. "I've never asked you for a single thing. Not once. But please. Please. HURRY UP WITH THE GODDAMN ELEVATOR!"

CHAPTER FIFTY-NINE

A nightmare about being chased by a Medusa started Jerry's heart beating again.

His eyes slammed open, and he was seized by a terrible abdominal cramp, making him curl up into the fetal position.

He remembered running. Being bitten by the Gornman-thing. Falling over. Dropping the box.

The anti-venom box.

Anti-venom.

Anti-venom!

Jerry searched for it, found the box just a meter away. It was open, and several of the vials had broken on the floor.

He crawled to it, his head swimming, his whole body damp with sweat. Then he began to grab random vials.

Scorpion anti-venom.

Man o' war anti-venom.

Giant wasp anti-venom.

Mutant platypus anti-venom.

Easter bunny anti-venom.

Seriously? Easter bunny? WTF?

Cobra anti-venom.

Stingray anti-venom.

Wait... cobra anti-venom?

Jerry pulled a syringe from his jacket pocket and jammed it into the rubber seal on the bottle. Everything was getting blurry, and he could feel his heart slowing down again.

Draw the liquid in. Take the needle out. You can do it.

Now just inject yourself...

Inject...

In...

Once again, the darkness took him.

CHAPTER SIXTY

"Hello, Dennisonnnnnnnnnnnnnnnnnnnnnnnnnnnnns."

Sun watched her husband stand up on wobbly legs and point directly at the Gorman-thing.

"I told you several times before, you stupid, ugly, ignorant hellspawn." Andy reached up, grabbing one of the snakes, and ripping it right off of Gornman's head. "It's Dennison-Jones!"

Then he fell over.

Gornman screeched, pinchers snapping in the air and reaching for Andy.

Oh no you don't! NOT MY HUSBAND!

Sun flung herself at the Gornman-thing, getting between the scorpion claws and punching her straight in the gut. One of the spider legs knocked Sun across the room, into the wall. She slumped to the floor, several ribs broken.

The Gornman-thing advanced. Sun managed to sit up. Every breath she drew was labored. The creature opened up its pincers, reaching for her.

"Are you in there, Bub?" Sun said. Each word brought a spike of pain to her chest. "Can you hear me?"

The Gornman-thing crouched next to Sun, sticking its horrible face in hers as the cement rained down. *"Weeeeee hear youuuuuuuu."*

"You... are... pathetic," Sun said. "You're never going to win. Do you... want to know... why?"

"Telllll usssssssssssss."

Sun looked at Andy. The love of her life, snake bitten and lying next to the elevator.

"Because, you prehistoric asshole, we have something you'll never have."

"What dooo youuu have? Emotions? Love?" The demon barked with laughter. *"Love makes yoooooou weak!"*

"No, it's not love."

"What isssssss it?"

"You really want to know what we have that you don't?"

"TELLLLLLL USSSSSSSS!"

Sun's stalling worked. The elevator dinged, and the doors opened.

"We have a giant fucking werewolf, motherfucker."

The Gornman thing turned as Wolfie pounced out of the lift, clamping onto her neck and biting her head clean off.

A moment later, Jerry stumbled over from the other side of the room, a syringe sticking in his leg, a box hugged to his chest. "Anti-venom," he rasped, falling to his knees.

Both Sun and Nessie hurried over, pulling Jerry and the box into the elevator. Then they went back for Andy, pulling him through concrete a foot deep. Nessie ordered the lift to go to the top exit. Then Sun searched for cobra anti-venom while Nessie sought out the harvestmen anti-venom.

Three shots later, Andy, Rimmer, and the imp were all waking up.

"I... I can't believe it's over and we're getting out of here alive," Jerry said. "It's a goddamn miracle."

And then the elevator squealed to a stop between levels 1 and 2.

CHAPTER SIXTY-ONE

"Join us, Lucaaaaaaaassssss. We can rule thisssssss world."

"Not interested," Lucas said. He'd adopted a boxing stance, and he shuffled over to Bub as the cement rained down. He'd learned pugilism from Joe Louis himself. Hell of a guy.

Left. Left. Right. Left. Stick and move. Stick and move. The demon's face broke under Lucas's blows, but the bones healed almost as fast as he could throw punches.

Bub lashed out with his talons, taking a chunk out of Lucas's shoulder. The wound filled itself in as Lucas continued to rain down jabs. Bub grabbed Lucas, biting him in the neck, and then Lucas wrapped his arms around the demon. They battled out of Kane's office and out into the hall.

Lucas sighted on his target. The elevator doors ten meters away. But the cement was already up to his knees and coming down fast.

"*Why doooo yooooou protect them?*" Bub demanded. "*They are weeeeeeeak.*"

Lucas focused on the elevator. One foot after the other.

"They're stronger than you think. Stronger than I think, too. You know how I can see things. I saw Andy Dennison-Jones saving the human race. And he did it. Do you know how?"

Five meters away now. Bub began to claw at Lucas's belly, pulling out parts.

"I'll tell you how. He convinced me; an outcast, a murderer, a liar, shunned by God, to help him. Not by asking, but by showing me what he and his friends were willing to do to stop you."

"Fooooooool! They aaaaaare insects compared to usssssss!"

"No, they aren't. Our time has passed. This world is theirs. Let em have it. They came up with musical theatre. What did we ever do?"

Lucas reached the elevator and wrenched the doors open with one hand while clutching Bub with the other.

"STOOOOOOOOP! DON'T BE A FOOOOOOOL!"

Lucas peered into the deep, dark shaft. At the bottom, meters of wet concrete, drying fast, was quickly rising.

"It's time for us to go."

Bub clawed and bit, but Lucas hung onto the demon as he stepped into the open air.

They hit the concrete below with enough force to shatter most of the bones in each of their bodies. As they healed, they began to sink.

"I'll get oooooooooout of here."

"That remains to be seen."

"You'll die here toooooooo."

"That also remains to be seen."

Bub continued to squirm, which only accelerated their sinking. Soon only their heads were above the cement.

"Doooo you think your god will forgive yoooooou? See your self-sacrifice and taaaaaaake pity?"

Lucas shook his head, slightly. "You and I, we've been around a long time. We've done terrible things. We don't deserve pity. Or forgiveness. But I am holding an ironic thought in me bonce, which I'll share before we go under. I'm Lucifer, who fell from heaven. You're Beelzabub. Neither of us presides over Hell, even though people think we do. So if we die, where do we go? Aren't you curious to find out?"

"NOOOOOOOOOOOOOOOOOOOOOOOOOOOOOOOOOOOO!"

"Well, my demon friend, you're about to find out just the same."

Then the concrete overtook them.

CHAPTER SIXTY-TWO

"The cement hardened in the pulley system," Nessie said. "We're not going anywhere."

She was standing on Jerry's shoulders, sticking her head through the access ceiling panel.

"Can we get out and climb the ladder?" Sun asked.

"The cement is coming down pretty fast, and Rimmer still isn't strong enough to climb out. It would also mean leaving Wolfie here."

Wolfie whined.

Jerry didn't know what to do. They were so close. It was so cruel it was actually hysterical. Defeat snatched from the jaws of victory.

The tiny imp, bitten by the spider, crawled up Jerry's shirt, looking concerned. He'd made a full recovery now. More irony there. Saved from venom to be entombed in cement.

"Sorry little guy," Jerry said to him. "We tried our best."

The imp frowned at him. Then it began to chirp. After what seemed to be a serious discussion among the imp folk, the little one hopped onto Jerry's shoulder.

"We can help," it said.

"Wha? Did you just talk?"

One of the other imps tugged on Jerry's pants leg, pulling off some hardened concrete. It popped the rock into its mouth and chewed.

"They can chew through concrete!" Jerry said. He remembered General Kane mentioning the imps could deliver a nasty bite. Jerry never could have guessed how nasty.

The imps began to climb Jerry's body, and then Nessie's, until all four were standing on top of the elevator, looking down at the humans.

"But if you fix the elevator, how will you save yourselves?" Jerry said, his voice rising in pitch. "You're too small to climb the ladder, and the rising elevator will squash you."

The biggest imp squeaked. "We save. Save you."

Then the imps began to ascend the elevator cable.

Sun helped Nessie get off of Jerry's shoulders, and Jerry held her as they waited.

"We should close the panel," Rimmer said. "Cement is getting in."

"No!" Jerry shook his head. "If it's open, the imps can jump back inside."

"Kid, they aren't coming back. And those four little guys aren't going to free an elevator."

"Shut up, Rimmer."

A minute passed.

Two.

Three

A foot of cement pooled on the floor of the lift.

"It's been quite an adventure, everyone," Rimmer said. "*Vaya con dios*."

Nessie clung to Jerry's side.

Andy and Sun clutched hands.

Wolfie whined and licked Rimmer's face.

Then the elevator groaned, jerked, and began to rise once again.

Everyone cheered, except for Jerry.

Come on. Jump through the panel, little guys.

Jump.

You came too far to die.

Don't die.

Please.

Don't die.

The elevator reached the exit floor.

The imps were nowhere to be found.

CHAPTER SIXTY-THREE

To everybody's relief, the exit hatch opened when they reached the top of the stairs. Nessie still had her employee key card, which activated the lock automatically.

The blinding glow of sunlight caused them all to shield their eyes as they stepped out into the open-air. After so many hours of being surrounded by the stink of blood and cement, the fresh breeze from the forest was divine. Andy managed to catch his breath back and filled his lungs.

"Freeze!"

Andy looked around to see a line of black-suited soldiers pointing automatic rifles at them. Sun put her hands in the air and so did he. Nessie chose not to, instead she addressed the man in front of the line who seemed to be the leader. She held her employee card in front of her.

"My name is Gwen Nester. Senior Apprentice, facility 26, the Spiral. With me are Mr. and Mrs. Dennison-Jones, and Jeremy Preston, all brought in by General Kane. Among the injured is Sergeant Rimmer. He's the one riding his, um, giant dog."

Rimmer gave a wave from atop Wolfie's back.

"Your *dog*?" The soldier said. "It's rather large."

"Organic dog food," said Jerry, patting Wolfie's muzzle. "Builds strong teeth and bones."

The soldier kept the gun aimed. "Where is the General?"

"I assume dead," Nessie answered. "Do you know if anybody made it out before us?"

The soldier nodded. "Several dozen employees have already been evacuated. Another helo is en route."

"Did anything... *else* get out of here?" Andy asked.

"We have multiple readings of creatures escaping into the forest. But we have a lock on their GPS tags. We'll get them rounded up in no time."

Andy sighed in relief. These men seemed to have the situation under control.

"The facility has been completely destroyed," Nessie said. "They'll be nothing else through that door."

"Roger that. You're the current ranking officer of facility 26, Ms. Nestor. You'll need to give a full report upon arrival at the Albuquerque facility."

"Can I take a shower first?" she asked.

"Me, too," Jerry said.

Nessie stared at him, wide-eyed.

"I mean, my own shower. By myself. Unless, you uh, need some help getting the cement off. I mean, I'd volunteer for the—"

Nessie kissed him.

"Isn't that cute?" Sun asked.

"If they don't shower soon they'll dry and get stuck that way." Andy turned to the soldier. "Look, my wife needs medical attention, and we don't want to go to another facility."

"Of course not," said the soldier. "We'll take your report en route to wherever you wish to go. Then you can go back to your honeymoon. You'll need to swear secrecy, of course."

Andy nodded. "I know the drill. How do you know we were on our honeymoon?"

"The Director of Homeland Security briefed us. He had a feeling that the faustlings were planning some sort of attack on our facilities. Texas fell a few hours ago and Toronto is currently under attack. We have it under control, though. Now that we know the play, we have armed forces converging on all of our sites. You can return to your lives as quickly as possible, Mr. and Mrs. Dennison."

"Dennison-Jones," Andy corrected.

A brief movement caught Andy's eye, making him peer into the woods. He could not be sure, but he thought he saw a man staring at them.

Andy squinted harder.

Lucas?

But whomever Andy had just seen disappeared between the trees.

Just then, a helicopter came in for landing, ready to take them far away from this nightmare. Andy held his wife and wished with all his being that they had seen the last of Bub and his batlings.

Somehow, though, he knew that his wish would end up going unanswered.

But until then, he had a honeymoon to enjoy.

EPILOGUE ONE

Little Sally O'Malley gave her father a great big hug. She relished the school breaks where she could stay home and help her daddy on their San Bernardino farm.

Sally loved the outdoors. Loved the feel of sunshine on her face and the sound of birds chirping. So much better than school where the only thing that covered her face was the shadows of bullies. Having a lazy eye was not the "beautiful difference" her daddy told her it was. Still, school was out for the week and she was here on the farm, ready to get her hands dirty.

"What can I do today, Daddy?"

Her father smiled, his cracked lips creasing between his salt and pepper beard. "Today we're going to paint the old barn a new shade of red."

Sally hopped. "Yay! I like to paint."

"I know you do, honey. Now, go on and fetch me the paint can from the storage shed. I've already pulled out the one we need. It's on the bench. Careful, it's heavy."

Sally shot out of the front door and onto the porch, before flying down the four wooden steps to the lawn. She raced across the sun-baked dirt towards the rickety old storage shed where her daddy kept the old ride-on mower and the tools he rarely used.

She yanked open the door—which was yawing open a crack—and stepped inside. Sure enough, the paint can was right where her daddy had said it would be, sitting on the work bench.

Sally took it, and it was so heavy she almost dropped it. Especially because the wire handle dug into her palm.

Then she heard a noise.

A soft chirping sound. Coming from deeper in the storage shed. It sounded like another stray cat. Those pesky felines were forever taking root in the farm's various outbuildings. Before her momma had died, she always warned Sally about feral cats and the diseases they could carry. Sally had made it a point to try and not pet them when she saw them. But she wasn't always successful.

She approached the hay bale carefully, mindful of the dangers of a startled animal. If it was a cat it could have her eye out in seconds.

The chirping continued.

Sally took her steps slowly, kept her approach quiet, but not completely silent. She didn't want to creep up on the thing so well that she scared the bejesus out of it.

Sally stepped around the bench and looked over the top of the hay bale. The inhuman things which she saw hiding in the loose straw made her scream like an honest-to-God banshee.

Her momma had warned her about feral cats.

But she'd never warned her about monsters.

Ted heard his daughter's screams and immediately dropped the pitcher of lemonade he'd been carrying. The pitcher was a family heirloom, but that didn't matter none; Sally was all the family he had left.

The screams continued and Ted felt his bladder loosen as he raced across the lawn. His whole body ached with dread, wondering what had made his sweet little girl holler so mightily.

The sound she was making was the worse torture he'd ever endured.

Then the screaming stopped, replaced by silence. Somehow Ted found that even worse.

He made it over to the storage shed and spotted the open padlock. His daughter was most certainly inside. What made Ted pause and take a heavy breath was the thick red puddle leaking beneath the door, staining the dirt and hay a deep crimson.

Oh Jesus Christ no...

Please, no...

Ted kicked open the door, ready to face down whatever wild animal or heinous pervert had found its way onto his land.

What he found, however, was nothing.

There was a sound, soft and delicate, coming from behind the hale bale in the center of the room. Ted stepped forward carefully, mindful of the sticky puddle beneath his boots.

He approached the hay bale, needing desperately to see what was on the other side, but also being unbearably afraid of what he might find.

If something had taken his little girl away, he would march right up into the farmhouse to fetch his shotgun. He'd put down whatever was responsible and then stick the barrel-end right in his own mouth. Sally was all he had left. If she was gone...

"S-Sally? You there, sweetheart?"

There was another soft sound.

Giggling.

Ted leapt forward and leaned over the hay bale. What he saw was like something out of a dream.

Sally looked at her daddy with sparkling green eyes. "Daddy, look! I found some friends."

Ted studied the scene. He saw the messy paint can, red paint staining the sides. The puddles on the floor were obviously from a clumsy spill—not blood as he had dreaded.

But that was forgotten about now. What concerned Ted was the pack of creatures surrounding his daughter. The green-skinned little critters had pointed ears and swishing tails. They were much smaller than his daughter and were jumping and tumbling all over her, making happy squeaking sounds that mixed with the delirious laughter of his little girl. They looked like little devils with earthworm-like skin, but they were acting like puppies.

Sally looked up at her father, tears of happiness in her eyes. "I fought they was gonna bite me, but they just want to play. Can we keep 'em, Daddy? Can we?"

Ted looked at the bizarre little creatures and found that they were becoming cuter and cuter. The way they played, the way they squeaked. He counted four of the tiny little imps.

Ted shrugged his shoulders. "I...guess. I guess we can keep 'em."

And so they did.

EPILOGUE TWO

SEVERAL MONTHS LATER

Dr. Frank Belgium was sitting in his easy chair, his adopted son Jack on his lap. The boy was an absolute marvel. Cute. Smart. More fun than Frank ever could have imagined.

Even if he hadn't married his mother, he would have still wanted Jack around.

"Ma ma ma," Jack said.

"I think he wants you," Frank said to his wife, Sara. "He said mama."

Sara got up off the sofa and took Jack in her arms. "He didn't say mama. He said ma ma ma. He repeated his word three times."

"Hmm. Now where do you think he picked that up?"

"Where do you think?"

"Do I do do do that?"

"Yes you do do do."

They exchanged a smile. The moment was interrupted by the doorbell.

Frank moved to get up, but Sara told him to stay put.

"I'm not an invalid, dear. The doctor said I need the exercise."

He pulled himself out of the chair, wincing at the slight pain from his still-healing wound, and used his cane to make it to the front door.

Frank didn't like what he saw in the peephole. Two men in black suits. One holding a Secret Service badge.

"Who is it?" Sara asked.

"It's for me. I've got got got it." Frank opened the door a crack. "Can I help you?"

"Dr. Frank Belgium? The President sent us. Your country needs you."

"Tell the President I'm not interested."

"Please, sir. Can we have just one moment of your time?"

Frank was thrown by how polite they were. Asking, not demanding. Reserved, not threatening.

"I'm done with all this," he said. "I have a family now."

"Believe me, Dr. Belgium, your country recognizes the sacrifices you've made, and they are appreciated. But we truly need your help. Even if it is only on an advisory basis."

Frank sighed, then let them in. "Okay, but but but let's keep it in the hallway. I don't want you upsetting my wife or son."

He let them in, and one of them handed Frank a manila folder. Frank didn't want to take it. As if sensing his reluctance, the agent opened it and held a picture for Belgium to see.

It was of a cow. A very dead cow, almost stripped to the bone.

"I'm a very good scientist, gentlemen, but even I don't think I can help help help you save that cow."

"Here is a close-up of the lower right hand section of the picture, Dr. Belgium."

He held up a second photo, grainier, zooming in to the cow's ribcage.

Perched there, staring into the camera, was a tiny, red creature with bat wings and large horns.

"Do you recognize that, Dr. Belgium? We believe it is one of the demons that escaped from the facility you worked at. Project Samhain."

The biologist made a face, and the first thought that popped into his mind escaped his lips before he could stop it.

"Uh oh."

Selected Cast of Characters

Andy, Sun, and Bub first appeared in the J.A. Konrath techno-thriller ORIGIN.

Jerry and Lucas first appeared in the Iain Rob Wright horror novel THE FINAL WINTER.

Nosferatus Hominic first appeared in the horror novel DRACULAS written by Blake Crouch, J.A. Konrath, Jeff Strand, and F. Paul Wilson.

Mu first appeared in TIMECASTER SUPERSYMMETRY by J.A. Konrath.

Dr. Frank Belgium appeared in ORIGIN and HAUNTED HOUSE by J.A. Konrath.

About the Authors

Joe Konrath is the author of more than twenty novels and dozens of shorter works in the mystery, thriller, horror, and science fiction genres. He's sold over two million books worldwide, and besides Iain Rob Wright h's collaborated with bestsellers Blake Crouch, Barry Eisler, Ann Voss Peterson, Henry Perez, Tom Schreck, Jeff Strand, Jude Hardin, Bernard Shaffer, Garth Perry, Tracy Sharp, Joshua Simcox, and F. Paul Wilson. He likes beer, pinball machines, and playing pinball when drinking beer.

www.jakonrath.com

Iain Rob Wright was born in 1984 and lives in the United Kingdom, with his loopy cocker spaniel, Oscar, his fat old cat, Jess, and his beautiful wife, Sally. Writing is the passion that fills his life during the small periods of time when he isn't cleaning up after his pets. He is currently one of the UK's most successful horror writers and his current novels include the critically acclaimed, THE FINAL WINTER, the deeply disturbing bestseller, ASBO, and the satirical screamfest, THE HOUSEMATES. He will soon be releasing the first book in an exciting action-thriller series; featuring acerbic protagonist, Sarah Stone, and her ongoing mission to stop a terrorist threat.

www.iainrobwright.com

WORKS BY IAIN ROB WRIGHT

Ravage

Savage

The Housemates

Sea Sick

Sam

The Final Winter

Animal Kingdom

ASBO

The Peeling

Straight Up (with J.A. Konrath)

WORKS BY JOE KONRATH

JACK DANIELS THRILLERS

Whiskey Sour

Bloody Mary

Rusty Nail

Dirty Martini

Fuzzy Navel

Cherry Bomb

Shaken

Stirred (with Blake Crouch)

Last Call (with Blake Crouch)

Lady 52 (with Jude Hardin)

Shot of Tequila

Banana Hammock

Jack Daniels Stories (collected stories)

Serial Killers Uncut (with Blake Crouch)

Suckers (with Jeff Strand)

Planter's Punch (with Tom Schreck)

Floaters (with Henry Perez)

Truck Stop (short)

Flee (with Ann Voss Peterson)

Spree (with Ann Voss Peterson)

Three (with Ann Voss Peterson)

Hit (with Ann Voss Peterson)

Exposed (with Ann Voss Peterson)

Naughty (with Ann Voss Peterson)

Babe on Board (short with Ann Voss Peterson)

With a Twist (short)

Street Music (short)

Jacked Up! (with Tracy Sharp)

Racked (with Jude Hardin)

Straight up (with Iain Rob Wright)

OTHER WORKS

Symbios

Timecaster

Timecaster Supersymmetry

Wild Night is Calling (short with Ann Voss Peterson)

Shapeshifters Anonymous (short)

The Screaming (short)

Afraid (writing as Jack Kilborn)

Endurance (writing as Jack Kilborn)

Trapped (writing as Jack Kilborn)

Haunted House (writing as Jack Kilborn)

Draculas (with Blake Crouch, Jeff Strand, and F. Paul Wilson)

Origin

The List

Disturb

65 Proof (short story omnibus)

Crime Stories (collected stories)

Horror Stories (collected stories)

Dumb Jokes & Vulgar Poems

A Newbie's Guide to Publishing

Be the Monkey (with Barry Eisler)

Grandma? (with Talon Konrath)

Sign up for the J.A. Konrath newsletter. A few times a year I pick random people to give free stuff to. It could be you.

http://www.jakonrath.com/mailing-list.php

I won't spam you or give your information out without your permission!